BLOOD OF THE DEAD & DIVINE
TRINITY MATTHEWS

Copyright © 2025 by Trinity Matthews

All rights reserved.

No portion of this book may be reproduced in any form without written permission from the publisher or author, except as permitted by U.S. copyright law.

Cover art done by artscandare.

CONTENTS

Dedications	1
Prologue	2
1. Chapter 1	9
2. Chapter 2	20
3. Chapter 3	28
4. Chapter 4	41
5. Chapter 5	54
6. Chapter 6	71
7. Chapter 7	86
8. Chapter 8	98
9. Chapter 9	115
10. Chapter 10	129
11. Chapter 11	142
12. Chapter 12	154
13. Chapter 13	167
14. Chapter 14	179

15.	Chapter 15	192
16.	Chapter 16	207
17.	Chapter 17	218
18.	Chapter 18	226
19.	Chapter 19	248
20.	Chapter 20	258
21.	Chapter 21	274
22.	Epilogue	282
23.	Note from Author	285

You were why I became a reader and you were why I became a writer.
To you, Nani.
Although you couldn't be here to witness it, I did it.
Also, a special thank you to all of my readers who have supported me along my journey. Without my readers, this last book wouldn't have been possible. So to every one of my readers, may your pillow always be cold, your coffee orders always be perfect, and your dreams always come true. Because if it's possible for me, it's possible for you.
To you.

F lora wasn't able to determine the last time she had felt such fear permeate her body. It was like it latched into her soul and was sucking it from her very body. Her mate's strength had been her rock the past few days but even his strength was wearing. They hadn't had a decent night sleep in weeks. Meals were scarce as they drifted from town to town in a desperate attempt to save their daughters' life.

They had been tipped off to a young human couple with a daughter who weren't able to have any more children and were looking to adopt. They had sent a letter to the family, praying to the God's that this would be their saving grace. The God's had bestowed a gift among their daughter, which meant they needed to trust the God's to protect her. Flora knew it was the God's who had led them thus far.

"We're almost there," Doran whispered as he tightened his arm around Flora's waist.

The horse trotted through the near silent streets. No one milled about, it was far too late for that. The sound of waves crashing sounded in the distance. The salt clung to their skin along with their sweat. Anxiety had taken root in their chests and had remained.

Flora clutched the bundled babe to her chest as she leaned into Doran.

"What if they're not there?" Flora whispered.

"They will be." Doran assured her as he rubbed his thumb in a slow circle across her hip.

Flora couldn't help the fear that had latched onto her and kept her prisoner. Her heart beat too fast, her breath came too quick. Her cheeks were flushed and she had constant bags beneath her eyes from lack of sleep.

The mage would be able to track their powers, which in turn would lead them to their babe. They didn't have another choice.

Every clack of the horse's hooves sent terror up her spine. She constantly glanced over her shoulder, waiting for men to jump out of the shadows.

Her heart lurched in her throat and Doran's hand tightened on her hip as a door creaked open. Her heart raced as an elderly woman hobbled out the front door of one of the homes ahead of them. She carried a broom and began to sweep off her porch.

"Take a breath, love," Doran whispered, his lips brushing the shell of her ear.

Her shoulders rose as she breathed in deep and they passed the elderly woman, who didn't spare them a glance.

Doran steered the horse through the alley like they had been instructed. The cobblestones turned to dirt and the buildings fell away from around them. Woods began to surround them. Flora hugged the babe to her chest and she tightened her arms around her. The branches of the trees loomed over them like sinister arms ready to pluck her from Flora's grasp and run off with the babe.

Finally, a small cottage came into view. There was a brimming garden on the side of the house and a large oak tree with a wooden swing hanging from it that swayed in the light breeze. Wooden toys littered the cobblestone walkway to the arched wooden door. On the other side of the house nestled between two trees was a chicken coop but surely they were in their roosts.

Doran stopped the steed before the walkway and dropped the reins. He hopped down first and reached back up for Flora as he lifted her to the ground. Doran ducked his head and placed his hand behind the babe's head as he leaned down and placed a kiss to her forehead. Flora felt tears prick her eyes but she swallowed them down as her mate placed a steadying hand on her back.

"May the Gods watch over you," he whispered as he pulled away and straightened.

The lump in Flora's throat only grew as he began to lead her up the walkway. She felt the tremble in her hands and knees but willed herself to remain upright. She knew they needed to do this.

As they approached the door, Doran raised his hand and knocked four times just like they had discussed in their letters. There was shuffling on the other side of the door and then a young woman opened the door. She smiled brightly at them as she stepped aside to allow them into the doorway. She was still in her work clothes with an apron dirty from tending to the garden.

"Flora and Doran?" the young girl chirped.

"Yes, you must be Eline," Doran spoke.

She nodded. "And this must be Alethea." She stepped towards them and extended out her arms.

Flora hesitated and would have fallen back a step if Doran hadn't been directly behind her. "Y-yes," her voice trembled as she released hold of her daughter.

Eline smiled down at the bundled babe as she rocked her softly. Alethea's wide eyes opened at the loss of contact from her mother. Flora's hands shook as she gripped Alethea's rosy round cheeks.

"I love you, my sweet girl," Flora whispered as she stroked her thumb down the side of her face. Her small fingers wrapped around Flora's thumb and as she stared down at the delicate fingers, she wondered how she was supposed to do this?

How was she supposed to leave her daughter? How was she supposed to miss her entire life? Even if to keep her safe.

She would miss her first steps and her first words. She would miss making her dresses as she grew, constantly growing out of the ones she made before.

She wouldn't experience the joy of watching her run away giggling, with Doran chasing after her. Flora would miss watching her mate love and cherish their sweet daughter the way he had always loved and cherished her.

Doran placed a hand on the small of her back as she squeezed her eyes closed. "How am I supposed to do this?" She couldn't stop the tears that leaked down her cheeks.

Doran offered the babe his pointer finger and she wrapped those dainty fingers around his large finger. "Because we love her and it's our duty to protect her," he responded, but behind his words she could hear the pain that laced through them.

Pain that he too would miss all of their daughters firsts.

Flora gripped the babe's fingers tighter as she leaned her forehead to Alethea's. "I love you so much, my sweet girl. Hopefully one day, we'll be reunited."

Flora heard Doran sniffle behind her and as she turned her head, she saw the tears that had broken free of his ironclad hold and flowed freely down his face.

"I love you," Doran whispered as he placed a kiss on Alethea's forehead. "If we are not reunited in this life then I will find you in the next life. And there I will give you the life we were meant to have. Even if I only get to meet you there, I will hold onto that hope that we will see each other again."

"We will protect her with our lives," Eline whispered as she clutched Alethea to her chest.

Flora's eyes fluttered to the babe clutching to Eline's dress that peeked out at them. She had to be no older than three or four. Her golden hair hung loosely around her face and her bright blue eyes were bleary.

"Laney, come here," her father, Wren called and scooped her up.

"We can't stay," Doran said as he bowed his head to Wren and Elise for the ultimate sacrifice they were making. They were putting themselves, their family, in harm's way to help *their* daughter.

"Be safe," Eline whispered as she stepped forward and tossed her arm around Flora's neck.

Flora's arms wrapped around her, tightening until her nails bit into Eline's shoulders but she didn't protest. "Please, take care of her," she whispered as a tear slipped down her cheek.

"We will," Eline agreed and Flora finally relinquished her hold.

"I love you," Flora whispered to Alethea again and her lips turned up in the slightest of a small smile at Alethea's wide eyes.

Oh how she would miss gazing into them. How she would miss watching the slow rise and fall of her breaths as she slept on her chest every night.

Doran leaned around Flora and placed a kiss to the babe's forehead, a final goodbye before he ushered Flora out the door.

As the door closed behind them, Alethea's cries echoed from behind it almost immediately. The sound reached out and latched onto Flora causing her steps to falter as she glanced over her shoulder at the closed door.

"Doran," Flora wept as she crumbled. She covered her eyes with her hands as her knees cracked off the cobblestone.

Doran dropped beside her, catching her before her body hit the ground. Sobs racked Flora's body as he held her to him. Even he couldn't deny the tears that streamed freely down his cheeks. Flora felt like she was ripping out a piece of her soul and leaving it behind.

Alethea's cries increased and in turn, so did Flora's.

"I can't, I can't do this," Flora sobbed as she clutched Doran's shirt. "I can't leave her here."

"My love, we can't. They've almost discovered us twice. We have to, we need to continue moving. We need to protect her."

"What if we find a way to mask it?" she cried.

"We can't risk her being with us until that is certain. Love, we've stayed too long." Doran extended his hands and gripped her face as he pulled it to him. "I'm so sorry, my love. I'm so sorry that my protection isn't enough to keep her safe."

Flora shook her head.

It wasn't his fault. She knew that. There were more sinister things brewing than even what they knew of. But she did know of one thing, if Alethea was caught then she would be butchered before even being given the chance to live a life.

That's what gave Flora the strength to push herself to her feet. Her hands clenched at her sides as Alethea's cries softened. She forced herself to put one foot in front of the other, putting her daughter's needs above her own.

She knew Wren and Eline would love Alethea. They would give her the chance at a life that they could not give her.

That spurred her as Doran helped her mount the steed. The steed nicked his feet against the dirt in anticipation.

"Ride, get us as far away from here as you can," Flora said.

She said the words firmly but felt anything other than strong. Doran would always have a part of her heart but the other part of it was left on Eline and Wren's doorstep. The wind whipped away any evidence of her tears as they rode into the night, the darkness and woods consuming them.

Chapter 1

Alethea

"Are you alright, lass?" an accented voice asked as they shook my shoulder.

I nodded my head but wasn't entirely sure the movement was up and down. It felt more zigzagged. His voice was muffled out by the rushing in my ears. The music that I had spent the night dancing to lulled around me. Before, it wrapped around me, coaxing me into its sweet embrace as I swayed and spun but now it caused a hammering migraine.

"Where is she?" a booming voice demanded, cutting off the music.

I groaned. Of course he was here to break up the party. My head fell against the wall and I closed my eyes.

"Alethea?" Mykill asked and I felt his cool hand on my shoulder. "Alethea, can you open your eyes?"

My mouth fell open as I shook my head. "The-they're not working." The words slurred as they fell from my mouth.

I could practically *hear* the annoyance rolling off of him.

"Bring me her tab and then I'll take her home," Mykill said to the bar keeper, not me.

"You got it, Yer Majesty."

I wanted to laugh at him and his accent. I managed a snicker as I pulled the bottle of rum to my lips and dropped my head back.

Empty.

Damn it.

I chucked the glass and heard it clatter and roll across the floor.

"Why did you serve her this much?" Mykill hissed as I whined over my empty rum.

"I need more rum!" I slurred/shouted as I pumped my fist in the air. "More rum for everyone!"

"I didn't serve her directly. Other patrons must have bought her drinks. I definitely didn't give her that bottle."

Mykill hissed something else at the bar keeper who argued with him.

"Hey! I was busy doing my job, if you want a babysitter for her, come with her next time or send someone else!" His tone was firm but still respectful.

"Here." I heard the sound of coins shaking. "And this too for the trouble."

"Thank you, Yer Majesty."

"On one condition, do not serve her again unless I am accompanying her. Am I clear?"

"Crystal, have a good night."

"Alethea, come on. I'm taking you back to the castle."

He refrained from calling it home because I had snapped at him the last time he had called it that. Because it wasn't my home. I didn't have a home anymore. Not here in Asgaith, not in Linterfame and certainly not in the human lands which were all but destroyed now.

"I'm fine," I grumbled as Mykill pulled me by my arm. "I don't want to leave yet."

"You're not *leaving*, Alethea, they're kicking you out." His voice was laced with annoyance as he slipped an arm beneath my knees and shoulders and hoisted me up.

My stomach immediately curled at the sharp movement. "Put me down, I'm going to retch!" I cried.

Thankfully he dropped me immediately and I sensed a bucket beneath my face as I coughed. The rum burned just the same coming up as it did going down. My eyes burned and watered as I held my hair in one fist and the side of the pail in the other. I continued retching until there was nothing left in my stomach and then groaned as I sat back. Mykill was crouched behind me, allowing me to rest my back against his chest as I closed my eyes.

"I think I'm ready now," I grumbled as I turned into him and raised my arm.

I didn't open my eyes as he slid his arms beneath me. The doors creaked as we exited the tavern and then I felt the rush of air around us as he shot into the sky. I rested my head on his shoulder as tiredness crashed over me.

The sound of the sea below me crashing against the rock was the only thing I could hear. I breathed in the smell of the salt and the water, the scent that reminded me so much of Mykill. I lost track of how long it took him to take me back to his castle and was alerted when he placed me down on my bed.

"This tonic will help," Mykill said and slid his hand along the base of my neck. I let him tilt my head up and felt the cool press of glass to my lips. I cringed as I swallowed the tonic, even more bitter than the alcohol.

"That's disgusting," I muttered as I dropped my head back on the bed.

"How did you get there?" Mykill asked, ignoring me and I heard clattering on the side table.

My head fell to the side, towards the sound of his voice, as he was surely moving my books and empty glasses around.

"A man flew me," I told him. "Don't touch my things!" I whined.

"A man flew you?" he snapped. "*Who* flew you, Alethea?"

I groaned and threw my head to the other side.

His voice was too loud.

His breathing was too loud.

Everything was too loud.

My skin was burning, sweat beaded my forehead.

I needed my clothes off.

"What are you doing?" Mykill snapped and grabbed at my hands.

I hadn't realized I had been unbuttoning my tunic until his hands caught my wrists. The cold air hit my overheated skin nonetheless. I didn't care that Mykill was seeing my chest naked, anyone could see me naked for all I cared, I just needed to cool off.

"I'm too hot," I breathed as I shoved against his hands and they brushed against my stomach.

His skin was like ice and I sighed in content. I wanted to be wrapped in him.

"Come on, let's get you into a cold bath," he said as pulled the blanket off of me but kept a firm hand gripping the front of my shirt. I slid off the bed and leaned into him. I heard the sound of the bath running before we even entered the washroom.

"Can you get in the tub on your own?"

I nodded as I peeled my eyes open. "I can manage."

Mykill's arm from around my waist fell away and I heard his soft footsteps as he retreated out of the washroom. I stripped quickly and stepped into the water. Bubbles covered the entire surface, shielding my body as I slid fully beneath the water.

"You can come back," I mumbled as I dropped my head on the side of the tub.

I closed my eyes again, keeping them open took too much concentration, but I heard his footsteps. He didn't say anything as he sat down on the ground.

"When will this feeling go away?" I mumbled.

"The tonic should take effect within the next twenty minutes."

"No," I groaned and shook my head as I pointed at my chest, at my heart. "When will *this* feeling go away?"

He was silent for several beats before his voice whispered, "It depends on the heartache."

I groaned again. I wanted him to say tomorrow. Although I wasn't entirely sure what I was feeling was heartbreak. Even before I had ended things with Eryx, I had felt my heart grow colder to him. Maybe the bond had made me see him differently, or the lack thereof.

"Would you have done it?"

"Would I have done what, love?"

Love?

I laughed. "Love? You've never called me that before."

"Would I have done what, Alethea?" He corrected himself.

I wanted to tell him to call me love but with the tonic beginning to set in, so did my rationality.

"Would you have killed the humans to save your kingdom?" I peeked my eyes open and found him staring at the ground between his legs.

His wings were folded behind him and his legs were drawn up but not taught to his body. His arms were wrapped lightly around his knees as he rocked slightly. His head raised and his eyes clashed with mine. That same icy breath chilling its way down my spine every time our eyes met.

"No," he responded, his voice deep and sincere. "No, I would not have. Fae have powers, where as humans do not."

Fae are never defenseless.

I had uttered those words to Eryx but he would not listen to me. If I was being truly honest, the moment I said those words he revealed himself to not be the person I thought he had been. He had always been loving and gentle towards me, but albeit controlling and lying. I didn't think he was a bad person at heart, but I think he had a lot of room to grow. Or maybe I was just the wrong girl for him. Maybe the Fates made a mistake.

"What is it that determines a mate bond?" I asked.

He cocked his head to the side as he studied me. "Abilities."

Eryx had the powers to summon shadows and darkness. I was light where he was dark.

Mykill's powers summoned lightning.

"Our powers are two sides of the same coin. Our powers compliment one another, bringing what the other doesn't have. Balancing each other out per-say."

I frowned. "But you control lightning?"

One side of his mouth slightly ticked up. "I could maneuver this water in the tub anyway I'd like, Alethea.

Would you like me to show you?" he raised an eyebrow at me, a challenge.

I rolled my eyes as that icy breath returned. "Stop flirting with me," I said and took a handful of water and splashed it towards him.

The droplets of water paused midair before they could hit him in the face and soak his shirt.

I scoffed and rolled my eyes again. But I still watched as the droplets moved through the air slowly, circling me. I realized all too late his intentions as they splashed into my face and I sucked in a breath of water and sputtered.

I surged forward as I spit out water and I swore I felt my ears heat.

"I feel better!" I gasped, my eyes going wide. "Get out!" I pointed towards the door.

Mykill laughed as he pushed himself to his feet.

"Hurry up!" I snapped as he sauntered towards the door.

I remained frozen gripping the edges of the tub until I heard the soft click of the door closing before I rose from the tub, my drunkenness gone.

After he left, I quickly dried myself and braided my hair in two braids so in the morning they'd be curled. I hated to admit it, but I missed Lira styling my hair for me. Even if she did yank on it harder than I liked.

I knew Eryx had treated his maids fairly but part of me wondered if after all that's happened between us, that could change. I feared for Lira's safety on a daily basis. Part of me wanted to go back for her but I wasn't entirely sure she would come.

Slipping on my nightgown, I sighed as I pulled the covers back and slipped beneath them. My eyes grew heavy as I stared at the now singular glass on my nightstand filled near to the brim of what I can only imagine was water. I fought the small smile that pulled at the corners of my mouth as I reached for it and drank before placing it back down and hunkering below the covers.

Mykill

I fisted my hands as I stalked down the hall. I passed door by door and hall by hall, but those glittering ruby eyes were the only thing I could see. The walls fell away around me as I got sucked into the chasm that was Alethea. She was mesmerizing, with her round eyes, and fair skin.

Her angry, piercing eyes haunted my every waking moment. Then even in my dreams. She was my walking daydream and nightmare. She intoxicated me more than the strongest alcohol. I found myself wishing I could be near her, always.

When I had found her in that tavern slumped against the wall with an empty bottle of rum in her hand, I wanted to throttle the bar keeper. Her skin had been coated in a sheen layer of sweat and you could smell the booze wafting from her breath before you even neared her.

She had been a mess.

Not that I could blame her. She had been through a lot in a short span of time, and I knew that I hadn't even been told the entire story. There were pains lingering beneath the surface that I was sure I didn't know of, and may never know of.

She had done well at concealing them, but there were times when her eyes were more haunted than others. I knew she had lost her family to the High Priest. I had witnessed her sister's death before fleeing from his kingdom. I had heard her screams as Eryx took to the sky on the back of his beast. Hearing her broken scream as Eryx held her back had halted my steps and panged at my chest. It had been one of the most chilling things

I'd ever heard. It was a sound I couldn't forget even if I wanted to.

But she carried her hurts unlike anyone I'd ever seen. Outside of me, she was kind to everyone, albeit sassy, but kind. The smiles she offered every guard she passed warmed a piece of my frozen heart. The more time I spent with her, the more I felt like I was melting. By the time it all was said and done, I'd be a puddle at her feet.

Heading into my study, I closed the door behind me as I made my way around my desk. My mind instantly went back to when we were in Eryx's castle and had been sitting across from one another reading. She had been enthralled in her book, but I had been enthralled in her. Her emotions when reading were written across her face, I could almost guess what was happening the entire time. I flipped through pages without reading them as I had watched her.

Sometimes I couldn't believe that she was a real, breathing being, even before she had become fae. Her beauty was unmatched, ethereal almost. It was a grace I hadn't been able to pinpoint until we were in Gild, when we retrieved the scrolls.

Petria was an old goddess who had long been forgotten. There were the Gods we worshipped now, and then there were the Old Gods that were a part of the Old Kingdom. The Old Kingdom was once a thriving kingdom until the Great War. After that, the kingdoms split and the Inner Kingdom was formed. Anyone who hadn't wanted to join, were pushed to the edges of the continents. Peace since then had come in waves. But I remembered when I was a boy I had visited the ruins of some older cities and Alethea's face had been on one of the crumbling statues. She looked older, more confident, but it was her. The same face and luscious locks.

I could tell Alethea still struggled with her identity. She was still trying to find her place in our world, her world, and I knew it would be a while until she figured that out.

Eryx had suppressed her, keeping her where *he* wanted her. It had been infuriating, especially after the realization began to slowly dawn on me that she was my mate. As her mate I wanted to stand up for her, pummel him, but I couldn't. I needed to let her stand up for herself, as long as it wasn't physically dangerous, because she'd accept nothing less.

I knew if she wanted to find her place in this world, she needed to learn to stand up for herself. Too much had happened *to her*, and now she *needed* to know what it was like to protect yourself. It was why I didn't go easy on her in training, I could see that need burning in her, and I'd do anything for her to feel safe in her own skin; And there were too many threats running around. With the High Priest, my ex-fiance, Freya, the barren and the Barren King and the Black Mage. It felt like everything was piling up, the load increasing to the point of overwhelming and crushing. There hadn't been a threat like this since the Great War, and too many lives had been lost during that time. But with the way things were progressing, and the stillness of our enemies, I was certain we'd lose many more lives before they were defeated.

Chapter 2

Alethea

"Again," Mykill commanded sternly with a heavy dose of annoyance.

I had moved sluggish all morning, which had earned me three kicks to the ribs and two jabs. I groaned as I planted my feet and raised my sword. Sweat made the hair at the base of my neck cling to my skin. I mumbled to myself as I shifted on my feet. Pain laced up the backs of both of my calves. Mykill said it was due to training everyday, he said my muscles were forming because he was sure I didn't have any before.

He was such an ass.

"How much longer?"

Not even a second passed before the words left my lips was he on me. The sounds of our sword clashing sounded and he advanced on me. I growled as I tried putting more force behind my blocks but he was slowly pushing me towards the edge of the mat. That would be another loss for me if I stepped off the mat. My arms shook with the effort to keep my sword up.

"Keep your sword up," he snapped as it began to droop.

He arched his blade through the air towards mine, and I grunted as I raised mine in defense. They slashed together and I spun in an attempt to keep off the edge of the mat. I moved to my left, moving back towards the center.

Our swords clashed again and with lightning fast speed, he reached for my wrist. I cried out as he wrenched me forward and used my arm to maneuver me. I cried out as he twisted it sharply behind my back and spun me so my back was to his chest. I growled as his blade raised, resting at my throat as his breath labored in my ear.

"Let's be done for today." His voice was cold as he released me and lowered his sword.

I didn't dignify a response as I dropped my sword at my feet and pulled away from him.

"I need a drink," I sighed as I gripped my hips and hunched over.

"None of the taverns here will serve you without me there," Mykill said as he picked up my sword and dropped them at the edge of the mat.

"Why would you do that?" I demanded.

"Because I will not let you sully yourself or your reputation. There is already talk among the kingdoms of you flitting around with one King and then moving onto another, they don't need any more reason to talk." He didn't look at me as he stalked by. "Now archery practice."

"Where are you going?"

"I have a meeting," he threw over his shoulder without looking at me. "When I get back I better see at least three arrows in the center!"

I grumbled to myself as he disappeared inside. He was always so damn bossy.

Stomping over to the rack of weapons, I pulled down my bow and sheath of arrows. I'd improved dramatically in archery since Mykill had brought me here. We trained every day, rain or shine.

He was as harsh as an instructor as I'd imagined he'd be. When he was training me in Eryx's kingdom, he had gone easy on me. Whether it had been because I was under Eryx's thumb or he just simply hadn't cared for my well-being, I wasn't sure.

One after the other, I notched an arrow, released and repeated. There were three targets propped up on wooden stands spread out in a line across the grass. Once I filled the first one, I lowered my bow and winced. Most of them were embedded in the white and black, the two outer rims.

Mykill would not be impressed.

Grinding my teeth, I stepped aside, moving onto the second target. After three shots, I managed to hit the blue stripe and lowered my bow as I stared at the arrow protruding from the target.

I could do better than that, at least that's what Mykill would have said.

Taking a deep breath, I readied another arrows and pulled the string back and froze as a twig behind me snapped.

"Alethea," a familiar voice called.

I yelped and instantly spun on my heel, notching the arrow. My eyes clashed with familiar cider ones and surprise flitted through at the anger that consumed his gaze.

"What are you doing here, Eryx?" I said quietly as I settled the tip of my arrow straight at his heart.

"You wouldn't shoot me," he said as he held up his hands.

"You don't know me anymore!" I snapped back as I tried to watch his feet.

He grumbled something beneath his breath and shrugged his shoulders. "No, apparently I don't."

I growled as that familiar fire flared in my palms. "What. Are. You. Doing. Here." I bit out between painfully clenched teeth.

"I've come to take you home."

"Linterfame is no longer my home." My voice was deathly even, much like the calm before the storm.

"I will give you one chance to return home with me, Alethea, or you will not like the consequences." He kept his voice low as he stalked towards me.

"If you move any closer I'll shoot," I threatened.

I felt the air shift around me but didn't look back over my shoulder. I wanted to breathe in relief because part of me knew that Eryx was much stronger than me and if he wanted to take me by force, he could.

"She'll do it," Mykill chuckled, his laugh coating my skin, soothing every frayed nerve.

"I will rain fury down on him and his men if you don't come home," Eryx growled and fisted his hands, ignoring Mykill entirely.

"Are you really that desperate, Eryx, that you would threaten the woman you supposedly love?" Mykill slipped his hands into his pockets as he slowly approached him.

I didn't move, I didn't even breathe as Mykill towered over him. I could feel the fury rolling off of him as he spoke his next words.

"Don't threaten her again." Goosebumps erupted across my skin at the low timbre of his voice. "You have crossed into my kingdom uninvited and have threatened my mate. If you do not leave now, I will rip. Your. Heart. Out. Now, this is your final warning. Leave."

Eryx's dark eyes slid over to me and my gaze didn't waver once as I glared back at him. My fingers tightened around the bow, itching to shoot him. Not fatally, but enough to harm him. Maybe then he'd feel a fraction of the pain he caused me.

"So be it." And he was gone.

All of my anxiety leeched out of me as I dropped the bow and arrow. The fear I didn't allow myself to feel slid over me until it felt like it was choking out all of my air.

Mykill swung towards me and gripped my arms as I slowly went down. He lowered to the ground with me.

"It's alright, Alethea. You can breathe now, love."

I nodded but still couldn't get words to form. His cool hands moved the hair away from my face as he tried to calm me.

"How did you know he was here?" I managed to bite out.

"I could feel your terror," he answered quietly.

"And you came?"

"Of course."

I nodded. Of course he would come. He was my mate.

I nodded again as I finally managed to take a calming breath and closed my eyes.

"I was scared he was going to take me."

Mykill nodded. "I will always be able to find you."

Relief spread over me, leaving goosebumps across my skin. I nodded again.

"Isn't there laws preventing him from entering your territory?" I raised my gaze to meet his.

Mykill nodded. "Yes, but I doubt that he's operating within the confines of the Treaty. I've sent the other kingdoms letters, informing them of his misconduct. I was reading their communication when I felt your terror." He paused. "Would you like to come back in and read it with me?"

I blew out a breath and nodded once as I slowly raised to my feet.

Mykill glanced around us, taking in the wooded line of trees before placing a hand on the small of my back. I let him steer me back towards the castle. The slight weight of his hand resting on my back calmed my racing heart.

"King Eryx just infiltrated our borders. He's gone now, but he threatened to take Alethea. Make sure it doesn't happen again." He stopped before a guard and I could see the anger that was hidden beneath his cool exterior.

"Yes, sir." The guard nodded fervently as he began at a brisk pace down the hall, surely to alert the other guards.

I followed closely behind Mykill as he led me to his study. He opened the door and stepped back, allowing me to enter first before closing the door behind him.

He stalked over to his desk and picked up a folded piece of parchment. He turned, extending it for me to take as his eyes remained glued to mine.

Taking the stiff parchment, I glanced over the edge at Mykill who slowly perched on the edge of his desk. He outstretched his legs in front of him and crossed them at his ankles. His large hands gripped the desk on either side of him and he stared down at his crossed legs.

As if he could sense my eyes on him, his head snapped up and a smirk pulled at his lips.

Clearing my throat, I threw him a glare before turning my attention to the parchment.

"King Mykill," I began to read aloud. "Thank you for informing us of what has been transpiring between your kingdoms. We have never heard of a mating bond being broken and then a new one forming. I will have my scribes look into the archives to see if there's a record of this in our history. In regards to Eryx partnering with the Barren, please forgive us as that is hard to believe. But my men will look into the matter to collect the proper evidence and when we have more to discuss we will contact you." The name Thillian was spelt out in a thick cursive signature across the bottom.

I handed the letter back to Mykill who folded it neatly and placed it on the desk beside his hip.

"They seem like a joy," I teased.

Mykill smiled lightly. "They won't take my word for it, that much I figured. Thillian has a seer in his army."

I cocked my head to the side. "A seer? I've never heard of one."

Mykill nodded. "Yes, she's quite gifted. She can see pieces of the past and future. But it's a heavy gift."

I nodded as he exhaled and dropped his chin to his chest. "I'm sure you're exhausted after training, but don't worry, if Eryx does step foot in my kingdom again he will be executed." He raised his head to meet my gaze. "He won't take you from here, I swear it on my life."

Slowly I nodded as my brows drew together. "I believe you. I'm going to go bathe and change."

He only nodded as I turned towards the door and as I stepped out into the hall. But my foot paused as it crossed the threshold into the hall. Slowly, I angled my head towards him. "Thank you."

He didn't say anything, like I'd expected. But I needed to say the words. Too much of me sometimes felt like I was taking advantage of him and his hospitality. Although sometimes I wouldn't call his frigid personality hospitable. The past couple of weeks living under the same roof was either extremely hot or extremely cold. He got under my skin, but I also *wanted* him there.

Maybe I was starting to lose my mind.

Chapter 3

Alethea

After a long bath, I rotted in my bed with a historical novel. It wasn't that fascinating but it was something that helped me pass the time. Without a word from Eryx, beside him appearing in the woods earlier, and nothing from the barren or the High Priest, my days consisted of nothing but training and reading. I had accumulated a stack of books that I had finished but had yet to return to Mykill. His study was a library in itself with two spiral bookcases behind his desk and I hadn't even made a dent in them.

He shared a love for reading as I did, though I noticed we read entirely different things. The books I'd noticed him read were informational, about war strategy, biographies written by who I'd assume were the Kings before him. I, on the other hand, chose fiction.

Stilling, I felt the chilling sensation of goosebumps prickling across my skin. I sat up straight and placed my book down on the bed. I couldn't pinpoint exactly what was making me react that way, but I knew it had to be deadly. I slid slowly off the bed as I made sure I had a dagger strapped to my hip, and made my way towards the door.

Peeking my head out into the hall, I didn't see a single guard in sight. Unlike Eryx, Mykill didn't find it necessary to send guards following me around every corner.

Mykill had to be aware of the danger that I sensed lurking nearby.

The blood in my veins and every hair on my head knew that Mykill was with whatever strange entity had me on alert. I took off at a run down the halls, letting that feeling that always lingered in the back of my chest lead me. The feeling that was Mykill and the bond.

"Dragon!" A guard shouted from within the halls, the sound echoing.

My mouth fell open and my eyes widened.

Eryx.

My breath heaved as I ran for the entry doors of the castle. I let the bond lead me towards Mykill, who I knew would face Eryx head on.

As I reached the doors, I shoved them open, but the scene made me trip over my feet as I halted. Mykill was standing before a slender man at least a foot taller than him with amber hair that fell in loose waves down to his pinched waist. His eyes matched his hair and my back stiffened as I noticed the slits in them.

That was why I didn't see a dragon in the courtyard. This man had been the dragon. We had met him once before when we had found the scrolls that were supposed to be the Mirror of Truth.

"Greetings," he spoke and the deep timbre of his voice vibrated my bones.

"To what do we owe the pleasure?" Mykill said cooley, but I could sense the distrust behind his words.

He saw this man as a threat and I didn't know how I knew, but I could sense he came in peace.

I stepped out into the courtyard and I sensed Mykill stiffen as his gaze shifted over to me. I felt him resist the urge to tell me to go back inside, but I knew he wouldn't treat me like a child. He would allow me to make my own decisions.

"I came to speak to your mate." The man's eyes drifted over to me.

"About what?" Mykill's tone sharpened as he blocked off his path. "Don't move towards her until you state your business."

The dragon's eyes slid towards Mykill and they narrowed in on him. "I've come in peace, fae King. I have no intention to harm you or your mate. This is a friendly meeting."

"Then state what it's about." I could sense Mykill reaching the end of his rope quickly but I wasn't sure how well he and his men would hold up against a dragon.

"It's in regards to the prophecy tied to her life." The dragon's gaze slid towards me and I felt my heart rate kick up as the full weight of his gaze settled on me.

My gaze slid over to Mykill who watched me. His eyes slithered down my arm as he took in the dagger in my hand. A small smile pulled at his lips momentarily before being tucked back away in the ice fortress beneath his skin.

"Follow me," Mykill said quietly as he brushed past him and headed towards me. He motioned for me to walk in front of him, keeping himself planted between me and the dragon.

I opened the front door, entering as I heard Mykill's footsteps behind me and then the dragons behind his. Anticipation itched through me as I led them to Mykill's study. Question after question danced around as the door came into view.

"We can speak in here," Mykill said as he waved a hand and the door floated open.

I resisted the urge to call him lazy as I entered and took a seat on one of the sofas. Mykill followed after me, sitting beside me, but not directly. He put enough space between us that was appropriate, but was close enough that he could grab me if anything happened.

The man slithered by us and took a seat in the armchair across from us. "My name is Vallant," he spoke as he lowered himself slowly and gracefully.

The elegance that oozed off of him made even Mykill seem like a barbarian.

"Nice to meet you," Mykill clipped. "Now please enlighten us as to what information you have that is so important you showed up at my kingdom unannounced."

I cast him a glare but Mykill didn't even glance at me as he leaned back. Ever the picture of ease and poise, but I could sense the monster that lurked beneath his skin, ready to defend me with his life.

"I've come to fill Alethea in on the matters of the prophecy that revolves around her. Your ancestor was a goddess who willingly gave up her powers," he said as he turned his attention towards me.

I frowned. "Why would she do that?"

"She was in love," he said simply as he stared back at me with his slitted eyes.

"She fell in love with a mortal," Mykill finished beside me.

"Indeed," he nodded towards Mykill. "But the blood of the Gods still runs in your veins."

"How was I born a human then?"

"That was part of the prophecy, it was a sign to the world that change was coming."

"Why did my parents have to give me up then?"

"Because there were those out there that thought slaughtering you as a babe would keep the prophecy from coming true and the Black Mage rising. There had never been a human born to fae parents before and news of it spread quickly."

"But what of her mate?" I asked.

"They were both cursed," he answered. "They were cursed to meet once every hundred thousand years give or take, but their love couldn't be. It was forbidden. They were always fated to love yet fated to fall."

I frowned as I glanced down at the carpet beneath my feet. "That must be referring to Eryx." I glanced back at Mykill before looking back at Vallant. "Now that we're not mated anymore, what happens?"

He shrugged. "That's the end of the prophecy, I don't know. The rest is up to the fates to decide I suppose."

I huffed in exasperation. "Why does everything have to be so vague?" I paused and then found the courage to ask the question that had been burning inside of me since he had shown up. "Why did my parents have to hide me?"

He cocked his head to the side and those slitted eyes of his narrowed eerily. I nearly shivered under the scrutiny of his gaze.

"Because your ancestors' love is what created the Barren," he merely said. "And those who didn't want to outright slaughter you to keep the prophecy from coming to fruition, wanted to slaughter you as punishment for what Petria did."

I frowned. "How?"

"Whatever is undone that was made to be permanent has consequences, it throws off the balance of nature. There are consequences to such actions."

"Why do the consequences have to affect so many?" I asked angrily, that had to be the dumbest thing I'd heard. "The Barren have slaughtered hundreds, if not thousands!"

"The Barren have touched as many lives as a Goddess would," he answered as if that was answer enough.

"How can that be possible? I can't say I've felt the touch of a Goddess in my life!" I snapped back.

He offered a small sympathetic smile. "I don't have the answers you seek, Alethea Divine. To find them, I suggest trying to search for your birth parents, they would know more of the curse."

"Why are you giving us this information?" I frowned as I cocked my head to the side. "It feels like the kind of information that would cost something."

Vallant's eyes narrowed into thinner slits. "Because I don't believe everything should come at such a high price and I still honor the Divine, whether you choose to acknowledge that you are or not."

I frowned and glanced down at my folded hands. "What do we do now? What is supposed to play out now?"

"Well, the Black Mage will rise again, and you will be tasked in defeating him."

My mouth fell open on a scoff. "Me? I can barely harness my powers as it is and I'm supposed to take down a being that is currently dead but will rise because of how *powerful* he is?" I laughed bitterly.

"You can be trained." Vallant glanced to Mykill. "I assume you're training her?"

Mykill nodded but did not speak.

"I still don't understand why you came to give us this information," I said, exasperated.

"Alethea, not everyone has ill intentions." Vallant's eyes slid back to Mykill. "Thank you for your hospitality, but I must be going."

"More scrolls to guard over?" Mykill joked half heartedly as he rose.

Vallant let out a laugh that sounded more like a grunt.

"Goodbye, Alethea, it was a pleasure to see you again. Most would consider it a blessing." He bowed with an arm across his waist.

"I'll walk you out," Mykill said and motioned for him to step out in the hallway.

I said my good-byes and followed them out into the hall but remained by the door as they headed back outside.

Mykill returned minutes later but I didn't have the energy to converse with him.

I waved Mykill off as I headed down the hall. "I just need some time, that is a lot of information to process." I didn't wait for his response as I continued down the hall. It was so rude of me, but my mind felt like it was jumbling. So much had happened in the last few short months, so much of my life had changed, it was all just so overwhelming. Even my looks had changed.

I closed my bedroom door behind me as I paced across the room. The weight of everything that had happened threatened to crush me. The prophecy, killing the Black Mage. How did all of this rest on me like it was my own doing? Yes, I was related to one of the Divine, but none of it had been my choice. How could her decisions affect my life so drastically?

Plopping ungracefully down onto the edge of my bed, I leaned over and gripped the sides of my head. There was a part of me that felt if I had just married Kirin like he had wanted, I wouldn't be in this mess. My family would all be alive, and possibly in the castle being taken care of.

I cut that thought off.

That was still wrong. The High Priest had said he had only used Kirin to find me and would have killed him off eventually.

I growled and tossed myself backwards and stared up at the ceiling as I willed for the bed to open up and swallow me.

***

I spent so much time sulking that the sun had set and I missed dinner.

But it was alright, I wasn't hungry anyway. The thoughts had eaten up all of my sanity, along with my hunger. All I wanted was a bottle of some rum, or anything that would burn my throat and help me forget the troubles of my world.

Which was how I found myself trying to sneak through the halls of Mykill's castle undetected.

Glancing over my shoulder, I paused, waiting for a sound to echo down the hall. I waited, Mykill always seemed to move silently. But the hall remained silent so I finally crept across the marble floors on my tiptoes. I scurried down the hall and clutched the flaps of my cloak to my chest.

I tiptoed down the halls. If I didn't risk exposing myself, I would have tried cloaking myself but my powers were still slightly unstable.

No matter how quietly I walked though, the sound of my shoes squeaked off the pristine floors. But Mykill didn't keep guards posted throughout the castle like Eryx had, so I didn't pass a soul. I wanted to ask him why. Eryx had said Mykill was a prideful person and part of me contributed it to that, but it also seemed like Mykill and his people lived a relatively peaceful life.

Finally, I reached the set of doors that would lead to the cliffside.

I sighed as I breathed in the fresh air as I broke through the doors. I could hear the sound of the waves lapping at the rocks hundreds of feet below me. Running down the steps, I glanced over at my shoulder towards the castle and then the woods behind it. The trees created the perfect wall, hiding us from the world beyond. If I didn't know war was coming, I would feel like I could stay here for the rest of my life joyous and carefree.

As I made my way to the edge of the cliff, I saw the railings for the first set of stairs.

My boots hit the wood and groaned beneath me as I hurried down the steps. Not too far down was the first stretch of shops. They were on the nicer side, cleaner. Soft music played from inside the apothecary. I was shocked they were open this late into the night. The shop owner's head popped up as I stopped before the open door. She offered me a warm smile and my heart tugged. She had the same honey brown skin as Medrina and the same warm smile. It must have been the power that healers possessed making the draw to them both so strong. I felt my feet step towards her.

A shoulder bumped into mine, drawing my attention.

"I'm so sorry!" the man exclaimed as he placed a hand on my shoulder.

I paused as I looked him up and down before plastering on my fakest, flirtiest smile. "It's alright! Maybe you'll be able to help me?"

He smiled down at me, his maroon wings tucking in behind him. "What can I do for you?"

"Well obviously, I am not blessed as you are." I motioned to my wingless back and then to his wings. "I was searching for a tavern. Do you have any in mind?"

"Sure, there's one a few levels down I don't mind flying you to." The male smiled even wider.

If I had just been any other girl, I would have swooned at his straight white teeth and glowing bronze skin. His brown hair ruffled in the wind and his emerald eyes glimmered beneath the moonlight.

"Are you sure?" I cocked my head to the side as I frowned up at him and placed a hand on my hip. "I really don't want to be a burden."

The male chuckled and outstretched his arms. "Not at all. I would be delighted."

"Thank you!" I beamed as I stepped towards him.

He outstretched his arms and then glanced up at me as I stepped in between them. I would pay to see the look on Mykill's face as he slipped his arms around me and then shot towards the sky.

"My names Lunnar," the man smiled as he kept his attention on our surroundings.

"Hi Lunnar, I'm Alethea," I answered with a smile.

His brows shot up at that. "Alethea as in Alethea Divine?"

"I'm not as divine as they say, Lunnar." I patted his chest as his boots touched down on a lower level of shops and taverns. "Thanks for the ride."

"Anytime." He shot me a wink and bowed his head before stepping backwards off the walkway. I would have gasped if I knew it hadn't been for dramatic affect. He shot by a moment later, stirring the hair around my face.

I laughed as I turned and took in the shops before me. The lower level was just as busy as the first couple of levels I had been on. I smiled as I spotted the tavern.

I could feel the burn already. The back of my mouth salivated as my hands fisted at my sides.

Pushing open the door, the face of the bar keeper snapped up and he shook his head. He was bounding towards me before I was even fully in the door.

"You've got to go," he waved behind me frantically.

"What?" I frowned. "How do you know who I am?"

"The King came through here and showed your picture to every tavern owner and instructed us not to serve you. You've got to go."

"Please, just one drink. It won't be like last time, I promise."

"You need to leave." He ushered me towards the door.

My shoulders slumped but also anger jolted through me. Who did that arrogant bastard think he was? He couldn't control me like that.

"Sorry, lass." He nodded sympathetically as he closed the door.

My hands fisted at my sides and my cheeks burned as I whipped around. I was going to give Mykill a piece of my mind when I got back to the castle.

Although I could ask someone to fly me back to the cliff, I decided to keep to the stairs. The fluid design of them was fascinating as they weaved beside and above and below each other. Most people didn't use them, even the children, so thankfully I wouldn't run into anyone.

My legs burned halfway up and I paused, glimpsing up at the top. I propped my hands on my hips and blew out a breath. I hadn't realized my chest was heaving so hard, or that climbing these damn steps would be so difficult.

Pushing myself to keep going, I lifted my foot to take the next flight of stairs up when something hit my shoulder. I gasped as I reached for the jagged side of rock but my fingers slipped away as I fell over the side of the stairs. My breath rushed out of me as I free fell and then I screamed. My arms and legs thrashed as I stared down at the waves crashing into the rocky shore.

I wasn't going to be killed by the High Priest, or a barren, or in a war. I was going to die in an attempt to get booze.

Hands clasped my upper arms, halting me midair and I felt the rush of wind stirring around me as the body shot upwards.

"I've got you," Mykill's voice drifted down to me and I snapped my head up in disbelief.

The wind ripped around me, whistling in my ears as he shot towards the top of the cliff. His fingers remained wrapped around my arms like miniature bands of steel. My heart felt like it was tumbling around inside of me, also looking for solid ground. Moments later, my feet were placed on solid ground and I tumbled forward.

"What the hell were you doing?" Mykill snapped as he landed before me.

I pushed up onto my hands and knees and waved a hand towards him. My chest was pumping twice as fast and I hadn't caught my breath in what felt like a lifetime.

"Did you do that?" I demanded as I pushed up to my feet, ignoring his question.

"Yes, I followed you the entire way. I was going to offer to fly you back to the castle but I could see the stubbornness in the set of your jaw and decided against it." He propped his hands on his hips as he landed before me.

Disbelief rocked through me as my cheeks heated. My teeth ground together as I resisted the urge to burst him into flames.

"You stupid, fucking, arrogant, asshole!" I shouted and shoved at his chest. He barely stumbled back a step, but I stormed past him. "I fucking hate you."

I heard his icey laugh follow me as I stormed inside and turned down the hall to my bedroom. Surprisingly, he didn't follow after me.

I waved a hand and my bedroom door blew open. I slammed it closed behind me and marched towards my bed. I didn't even bother changing, or removing my shoes. I jumped into my bed, wrapped the blanket around myself and tried to forget his equally beautiful and equally stupid face.

Chapter 4

Mykill

I blew out a breath as I heard her bedroom door slam behind her. I had caught her in the act of trying to sneak alcohol. If she would have asked me, I would have accompanied her. It was never my intention to cut her off from alcohol to control her, merely to keep the talk of her that was spreading down. She was using it as a crutch, I could see that, but it wasn't a healthy one.

She could have taken one of my guards with her for all I cared, I just didn't want her out there drinking alone.

The fact a man, *another man*, flew her down to the Coves made my blood boil. I clenched my jaw as I felt a slow tremble work through my hands. But I couldn't be jealous, she wasn't mine. She had made it very clear that she wasn't. She had made it clear that she felt nothing for me except disdain.

Even though she was mine.

The Fates had bestowed her upon me, as I'd been bestowed upon her. A mating bond though, was both a blessing and a curse. It meant that I had a walking and breathing vulnerability. Mates, even before the bond, were a liability to each other, a weakness. If something were to happen and she was taken from me, there would be nothing I wouldn't do to get her back.

My insides turmoiled at the thought. I shook my head, clearing my thoughts as I stopped before the foot of my bed.

She wasn't mine, she wasn't mine.

I had to constantly remind myself of that, because if I didn't, then I'd give into the urge that burned in my veins to claim every part of her for myself.

But I couldn't do that to her. She would never forgive me if I forced anything upon her.

I stiffened as a knock sounded on the door. I clenched my jaw as I turned. Stalking towards the door, I yanked it open. "What?" I snapped.

"Sir," Felix said after bowing his head. "There have been sightings of Barren in the area."

I stiffened as my fingers tightened on the door. "Where?"

"The Coves," he answered.

The Coves were where Alethea had attempted to get alcohol. They were the last couple of levels before the ocean. They were full of smaller shops, not many people ventured all the way down there. A few of the shops had been boarded up for a while now.

I frowned. "There's not normally a lot of people there."

Felix nodded. "I've sent men to sweep through the lower levels. We'll go through from bottom to top. If there are barren, we'll find them."

"I'll join," I said as I stepped out of my room. If there were barren here, that meant they had been sent here. Which meant, there were even bigger threats looming nearby.

Felix strode by my side as we made our way outside and towards the cliffside. We both leapt off the edge, letting our wings extend on either side of us and letting the wind catch us.

Men, women and children were being evacuated, ushered towards the top of the Cliffs. Clusters of men were swooping through the pathways, checking for danger. But below that was an even bigger group of my men readying to sweep every level on foot.

I watched from a distance as my men walked the edge of the Coves. They had their sword extended before them, ready to meet whatever threw themselves from the shadows.

My head snapped up as a scream sounded above us. I shot towards the sky, searching for where the screams were coming from. Clusters of my people were scattering and then I saw the gray bodies, *the barren.*

Shock radiated through me just as realization dawned on me.

They had let us see them in the Coves, and then waited at the peak of the cliffs for us to evacuate everyone. Someone was watching us, toying with us.

I threw a hand out, using the wind to shove a small cluster of people away from one of the barren. The barren shrieked as he clawed at the invisible wall separating him from my people. The ground trembled beneath my feet as I landed. The barren's head shot towards me and he gnashed his teeth. He was hunched over on his hands and feet like he was some kind of animal.

I growled in response as I threw a hand out and the barren was sent spiraling backwards. It screamed out as its back hit the ground with a 'whoosh', but it was back on its feet in a moment.

Gripping the hilt of the blade strapped to my thigh, I pulled it out and threw it. It glided seamlessly through the air before embedding in the side of its neck. The creature's loud hiss echoed around, blending in with the other screams.

I knew my people were blessed with powers, but it was my job to protect them. We should have anticipated something like this. But part of me wondered if the barren had acted so mercilessly and carelessly to trick us so that the closer war came, the more damage and the smarter they were. It had all been part of a grander game they were playing, but we were slowly catching up.

My men advanced quickly, swiftly ending the lives of the two or three dozen barren. Thankfully it didn't seem like there were many casualties. There were a couple men and women who passed by with a scratch or two.

"Sir," Felix spoke behind me, drawing my attention.

I turned, waiting quietly for him to speak.

"We lost some men," Felix said quietly with his head bowed.

I gritted my teeth, refusing to show an outward response. I wouldn't respond to him in anger, I knew it wasn't his fault. I had been just as fooled as he had, so it was mine. Their deaths fell on my shoulders and mine alone.

"Show me," I responded curtly.

Felix nodded, turning to lead me towards the bodies. I stilled over the sight of the three soldiers, *my* three men.

Bracken, who was an orphan whose parents died when he was only a boy. He had been a joyful person, always smiling, even in the toughest of times. Then there was Thomas, he was a father to two young girls with a loving wife. Then there was Rash, I hadn't known him well but I recognized a kind soul when I saw one.

They would all be missed.

"Take them to the gardens," I said softly, not tearing my eyes from the bodies.

Felix and a few other men began to move them, carrying them gently. I commanded another guard to find Thomas' wife. I had a private cemetery area for all of my soldiers who passed into the next life, but some families had more traditional ways to bury their loved ones, and it was their decision on how to handle that.

I wiped my bloodied hands on my sides, but it only smeared it across my skin. I could feel the blood seeping through my skin and into my soul. It was merely joining the sea of others' blood that ran through my veins, that I stolen from them.

My men cleaned up the ground and helped those who had been injured while Felix and I dug a grave for Bracken and Rash.

Thomas' wife wished to collect his body and bury him near his old family home, and I'd respect that wish.

My hands shook as I knelt down and gripped Bracken's ankles and Felix gripped his shoulders. "Ready, lift," he grunted as we lifted up his body.

We stepped over the grave and lowered his body into the hole. I knew it wasn't possible, but it was like his body felt lighter without his soul. Lowering his body into the dirt, I willed my erratic heart to slow. Guilt slowly gnawed away at my insides. So many had died. So many had died when I had promised that this would be a sanctuary for my people and it had turned into anything but. I couldn't focus on anything but the guilt that was slowly eating away at my chest as we continued covering his body until there was a fresh mound over Bracken's body.

Placing my shovel down, I let it clatter to the dirt.

I placed my fist over my heart. "May the Gods lead you home."

"May the Gods lead you home," Felix echoed the ancient prayer.

We both stood there as we stared down at the fresh mound.

Peace felt like it had evaded me my entire life. My soul craved for it, yearned for its comforting presence.

So I began inside and moved down the hall to the only thing, the only *person,* who could bring me a semblance of peace. I pictured her ruby eyes and her light strawberry blonde hair. I pictured the freckles that dotted her cheeks, what I wouldn't give to count each one. I wanted to run my hands over every part of her, until she was etched into the furthest parts of my memory.

Even if at the end of all of this, she decided to go off and build a home someplace else. At least I'd remember her for the rest of my lonely existence.

I stopped outside her door. I breathed in, smelling her familiar scent. I could feel her life form on the other side. Her tranquility was the first thing I felt, which could only mean one thing.

She was sleeping.

She never felt that peaceful when she was awake.

Lowering to my knees, I propped my head on the wood as I blew out a breath.

She wasn't mine. She wasn't mine.

I repeated that to myself over and over as I let the peace she was feeling wash over me. If I couldn't be right beside her, I'd let whatever piece of her I could feel comfort me. Just the fact alone that she was safe in her bed, bundled up and out of harm's way, was enough to calm my racing heart.

Keeping my eyes closed, I tried to imagine the sound of her slow breathing. I tried to picture the soft rise and fall of her chest. I could paint the picture in my head of her clearly. Head resting on the pillow with her hands tucked beneath her cheek. Her knees were drawn up, almost touching her chest as she puffed out soft breath after soft breath.

Placing a hand on the door, I imagined it was her skin beneath my palm. I imagined it was her hand as her fingers intertwined with mine and she leaned into me.

But instead of the peace I thought I'd feel, I felt a pang of sadness in my chest.

Because it was an illusion, because she wasn't mine and she'd never be.

Alethea

I sulked to the training grounds the next morning. Every time I recalled Mykill and his stupid stunt from the previous night, I felt the tips of my ears heat up.

As I headed outside, I fisted my hands as I prepared myself to see his arrogant face. Glancing up, I frowned as an unfamiliar man with icy white hair and clear blue eyes stood in the center of the mat.

"Who are you?" I asked as my steps faltered.

The man turned towards me and offered me a warm smile. "I'm the King's General, Felix."

I frowned and tilted my head to the side. "Where's Mykill?"

"In his chambers," he answered.

"Doing what?" I snapped.

Felix laughed and turned to face me fully as he continued stretching his arms above his head. "That I could not tell you, My Lady."

"Alethea," I corrected. "Please call me Alethea."

As Felix straightened, he bowed his head softly. "My apologies, Alethea."

I waved him off as I stepped onto the mat. "What are we going to be doing today?"

"The King asked we start on archery."

***

After I trained with Felix for hours, first with archery, then with dagger throwing, and then we practiced sword fighting, I headed back to my quarters to bathe and change. Then I began my way into the dining room for lunch.

My feet faltered as I came into the dining room. Mykill was seated at the table, across from where I normally sat with a plate of food in his lap. I gritted my teeth as I stalked towards the table.

I wasn't sure why him not being at training this morning grated on me so much, but it did.

"Did you and Felix enjoy yourselves?" Mykill asked and then frowned as I seated myself on the other end of the table. "What are you doing?"

I refused to look at him as I reached over and grabbed my place setting and pulled it in front of me. A bowl of granola with an array of nuts and a side of brown sugar. My stomach growled as I picked up my spoon.

"If you can avoid me, then I most certainly can avoid you."

"How exactly was I avoiding you?"

"You've never missed one of our training sessions," I pointed out.

I froze as thunder rolled around us and then Mykill reappeared with his plate and goblet across from me.

"I wasn't avoiding you," Mykill said softly as he continued buttering his biscuit.

"Then what were you doing?" I raised a brow at him.

His eyes slid up to meet mine and though his icy wall was present, I could see the haunted look in them. His shoulders fell a bit. "There was a barren attack last night."

My spoon clattered onto the table as I gasped. "Is everyone alright? Was anyone injured?"

"Three of my people were killed."

My mouth fell open as my cheeks heated. Shame and guilt and a whole slew of other emotions tumbled through me. My mouth closed as I sought to form a response but couldn't.

"I'm so sorry," I finally managed to say quietly.

Of course there had to be a reason he missed training. He had always kept me a priority.

"I'm sorry for accusing you of avoiding me," I added when he didn't say anything. "That was too hasty of me."

Mykill placed his biscuit down on his plate and placed his knife beside it as he stared straight at me. "There's no reason to apologize. I would've told you if I'd had the time."

"I know," I cut him off.

I knew that.

I felt my cheeks heat again as the silence between us spanned out and shame emanated in my gut. But his eyes never left mine. It almost looked like he was studying me as his head tilted to the side.

"Sir, our men spotted barren heading towards Grithel!" a breathless guard exclaimed, interrupting us, as he threw open the door.

Grithel? I frowned as I placed my fork down and finished chewing as I wracked my brain. I knew that name.

My eyes widened as realization crashed over me and my heart plummeted. "That's a human kingdom." Kirin had supplied troops to them when I was a teenager.

Mykill's face hardened as he shoved himself up from his seat. "Prepare the troops."

"Wait," I gasped as I scurried after him. "Take me with you, let me help you!" I stumbled forward in my attempt to reach him as he strode towards the door.

Fluidly, he spun towards me and gripped my arms before I stumbled to the floor.

"Thank you," I breathed as a flush spread across my skin as he stepped into me. "Please take me with you."

He merely stared down at me. His icy eyes narrowed and they bounced back and forth between mine.

"I can bring my bow and arrow," I said, making sure to keep my voice steady.

Mykill stared down at me, those icy eyes as cold and hard as glaciers. They narrowed as they danced back and forth between my eyes. I kept my mouth shut as the gears in his head turned before he finally nodded curtly.

"Get changed." He released me and angled his head towards the hall.

He followed closely behind me as I rushed down the halls towards my room. I slammed the door behind me and rushed towards my wardrobe. I yanked out the first pair of fighting leathers I saw and stripped out of my simple gown. I pulled on the pants first, then the blouse.

This one had a rather revealing neckline for my liking, but it was one of the more breathable sets. Reaching behind me, I began pulling at the strings to tie the blouse shut behind me. I cursed as the string slipped from my hand, not one, not twice, but three damned times.

I cursed and dropped my head back as I closed my eyes. My ladies maids hadn't come by yet and I wasn't sure where they'd be at this time and we didn't have the time.

Mustering a breath of courage, I cracked open the door and stuck my head out as I clutched my leathers to my chest. Mykill's head angled towards me as he pushed off the wall.

"Could you help me?" I asked softly.

He frowned and then realization dawned over his features and he nodded. I stepped back, allowing him into my bedroom and swung my hand, closing the door behind him.

The tips of my ears heated as I turned away from him and I felt him grab the strings that bounced off my back.

"Where did you get these?" His voice was low, almost like a whisper but guttural. His voice was absolutely menacing, promising retribution of the vilest kind.

My brows furrowed as I glanced over my shoulder and immediately halted.

My scars.

Closing my eyes and taking a deep breath, I pushed away the flickers of pain those memories brought on, mental and physical.

"I told you about my stay in the human lands when I was betrothed to Kirin," I explained, not willing to elaborate further.

A low growl followed my answer.

"You didn't tell me he *whipped* you," he responded.

"It wasn't important," I threw back and clenched my hands around the material at my chest. "Can you please just lace me up."

Mykill's hands immediately moved across the strings, pulling them gently. His fingers never made contact with my skin but I could feel the cold from his body. I could feel it in my bones. I could feel the breath he expelled as he stepped back. "Done."

Turning towards him, I dropped my hands and pushed my hair over my shoulders. "Thank you."

He nodded slightly but I could see his mind was somewhere else.

"I wasn't aware of the extent of your pain, but there were times when I could see the weight of it in your eyes," I flinched away from him as he spoke. "You carry your scars with a grace and resilience that I envy. I envy that through the pain you've endured, you've still remained the resilient, vibrant person you are. Your past may be full of brutality but it did not wipe the beauty of your soul."

I could only stare. All words evaded me as he stared down at me. I hadn't realized he had moved closer to me until I took a breath I hadn't realized I had been holding. My senses slammed into me as the breath I breathed consisted of the way I knew he tasted.

"I- I didn't know you could be so sweet," I managed to whisper but the smile I tried to put on faltered.

Those normally icy eyes were smoldering now. Searing me with that icy fire from the inside, almost like I could feel it deep within me.

"Let's go," Mykill finally spoke as he stepped backwards and turned for the door handle.

He stepped aside as he propped open the door and let me pass first. My feet remained glued to the spot as

I stared at him. His eyes slid back to mine again and that same fire returned. I felt myself intake a breath and I forced myself to step towards him. He closed the door behind me as we stepped out into the hall and then stepped towards me.

"Ready?" he asked as he outstretched his arms.

I nodded as I swallowed past the thump that had hardened in my throat. He bent slightly, slipping an arm beneath my knees and then the other beneath my back. I reached an arm around his neck and secured it there moments before clouds swallowed us. I covered my mouth as my stomach twisted and then dropped entirely.

Chapter 5

Alethea

As we tumbled out of the clouds, the sounds of screams rang up towards us. The scene below was gruesome. Bodies littered the streets, some dismembered. The barren ripped through humans like they were rag dolls. My hand flew to my mouth as I spotted a young mother with two babies on her hips running through an alley with a barren following behind her.

"Mykill!" I pointed and he immediately angled us that way.

I didn't feel my stomach dropping as the ground got closer and closer to us. The barren neared the mother who screamed as she tried shifting her daughter into her other arm and angled herself to where she was covering her daughters beneath her body.

A mother willing to give her life for her children.

My heart leapt into my throat as another barren began barreling down the alley as our feet hit the ground. Mykill dropped me immediately as he went after the barren looming over the family. Pulling out my dagger, I spun towards the second barren who bared his teeth at me. I gnashed my teeth back at him as I pulled out a second dagger.

I could feel the adrenaline and power coursing through my veins.

Flames licked at the edges of my wrists as I flung my first dagger. My aim wasn't perfect, but the dagger embedded in the stomach of the barren and then flames erupted around it. The flames engulfed the barren and he let out a heinous squeal as he fell backwards and began clawing at his own skin. I outstretched a hand, letting my flames consume every barren within my sight. The street erupted in squeals of the barren as their bodies shriveled.

I froze as the ground beneath me trembled as a roar sounded through the air. It had been quite some time since I had heard the sound of one.

Dragons.

Pulling out of the shadows, I searched the sky for the sound. If there were dragons, then that meant Eryx was here too. Maybe he had come to help us.

My eyes caught on a sliver of orange and then the bodies of dozens and dozens of dragons emerged from the clouds. The men and women on the backs of them sneered down at us as they swooped down. Screams erupted as more people tried to flee.

My mouth fell open on a scream as a dragon swooped above the tops of the homes and unhinged his jaw. Fire spewed from his mouth, engulfing the homes. I couldn't see the alleys before the homes but I could hear the screams as the fire engulfed human and barren alike.

Vomit worked its way up my throat.

Eryx was doing this. Eryx was helping in killing the humans.

My hands shook as I notched an arrow. I glanced at the tip of the arrow, envisioning flames and moments later, flames swallowed the pointed tip. I settled my gaze on the dragon rider and took a deep breath before

I let the arrow fly. I watched as it soared through the air and landed center in the back of the dragon rider. The man cried out as his back arched and he tried reaching for the arrow, but it had embedded just out of reach. He fell backwards, slipping off the dragon as he free fell. I watched as his body disappeared behind the buildings.

Fae or not, he would not survive a fall like that.

"You are getting better," Mykill spoke directly behind me.

I yelped as I spun back towards him.

"You need to watch your back at all times," he said between clenched teeth and then gripped my upper arms.

I cried out again and threw myself into him as clouds swallowed us. We reemerged moments later on the roof of a home on the edge of the city.

"Use your bow and arrows from here. Do not reveal yourself to those around you." Mykill's brows were drawn down fiercely over his eyes.

Although I knew he was trying to do this for me, I could see how much he hated it. Eryx would have never agreed to letting me do this, even if it meant jeopardizing our relationship.

I nodded and steeled my face. "I can do this."

He nodded and stepped back once. "I know."

Two words. Two of the simplest words. But they inflated my chest and made my skin heat and I felt a smile pull at my lips.

"Thank you for believing in me," I said genuinely.

"You could take on the world if you tried, although I wouldn't like it very much." A smile tugged at his lips too, matching mine. There was that playful demeanor of his.

I waved him off as I pulled an arrow from my sheath. There was a loud 'whoosh' and when I looked up he was gone, though I knew he wasn't far.

Glancing back towards the dragons, I notched an arrow as I followed them through the sky. I watched as an orange dragon swooped down, eyeing the streets before he took back up into the sky. I saw his throat begin to illuminate, meaning one thing.

Panic shot through me as my gaze fell to the people in the streets below me.

Running towards the edge of the roof, I glanced over the side. It was an angled drop, if I could just slide down the side, then I would probably be safe. It just depended on how I landed. But if I hurt myself, then my body would heal rather quickly.

Gripping my bow and arrow to my chest, I lowered myself over the side and took a deep breath as I released the ledge. My back slid along the roofing and regret filled me as I neared the ground. I had no idea how I needed to land.

Praying to the God's, I willed strength into my legs as I landed and then rolled forward, letting my entire body absorb the blow, rather than my knees and ankles.

"You need to take cover!" I shouted to the villagers in the street as I bounced back to my feet.

The man closest to me turned. He was holding a young blonde girl who didn't look a lick like him and then an even younger baby boy.

"I don't know what happened to her mother and father! She was wandering the streets crying, a barren almost got her!" he yelled frantically.

I nodded as I glanced up towards the sky. "Just hold onto her for now. Her life depends on you," I said back as I stared up at the sky.

The dragon swooped back towards us, its gaze locked on us.

"Get down!" I shouted as I threw my hands up towards the sky and a barrier of flames met the dragons. The children around me screamed as they clutched their parents. I used my body and flames to absorb the heat, keeping it away from them.

I screamed as the heat intensified. It felt like my skin was being flayed from my bones and my very bones would begin melting. Slowly, the heat subsided and I heard the beat of the dragon's wings as it continued down the length of the street.

My body sagged forward as I dropped my arms. But now was no time to tap out.

"Now run, get to the trees!" I commanded and turned towards one of the men. "Get them to the trees now!"

He nodded and began ushering the group around him towards the woods and away from the village. Turning back towards the carnage, a part of my soul died at the sight of scattered bodies, some brutally torn apart and others burnt beyond recognition.

The ground shook beneath me, tossing me to the side. I grunted as my side hit the ground. The ground thundered again and a roar filled the air.

Glancing around me, I saw the heads of two dragons just on the other side of the buildings before me. Shadows passed over me again, but only two. There were four dragons, which seemed like not many, but the damage a single dragon could wield was catastrophic. Shoving myself up from the ground, I took off at a sprint towards where the dragons were.

I reached the end of the street and pulled out a dagger as a barren ran by chasing a teenage boy. Spinning towards the barren, I flicked my knife, letting it sail through the air before it embedded in the back of its forehead. The young boy turned, his eyes landing on me.

I nodded my head once at him before he turned and began running through the streets again. Turning my attention back towards the dragons, I began running down the street. They were one more street over and I had to get to them before they lit the entire street on fire.

My heart beat erratically in my chest, and the adrenaline felt like it coated my skin. It made me feel stronger, invincible somehow. Maybe that was what had drastically improved my aim, because the last time Mykill and I had practiced throwing knives, I had not been that precise.

Reaching the end of the street, I didn't slow my run as I rounded onto the next street. The two dragons were biting at one another, almost like they were fighting. I frowned, I forgot how temperamental they could be. There were dozens of Mykill's men surrounding the dragons, throwing whatever powers they had at the dragons, but it was to no avail. They didn't even take a hit, they weren't designed to. They were a powerful ally if they partnered with you, but they were a more deadly enemy.

"Alethea!" Mykill shouted. "What are you doing? Take cover!"

I ran past him, avoiding his grabbing arms as I made straight for the dragons. Throwing my arms out, flames tumbled from my open palms and swallowed the dragons whole. The dragons shrieked, the sound making my ears feel like they were going to burst. Dragons were normally fireproof, but I reached into the part of me where I could constantly feel Mykill and pulled on his powers. Ice descended down my veins as the flames turned blue. The dragon's scream pitched higher and the flames spread to the second one. My vision blurred slightly but I shook my head, willing it away as I poured out the flames until it felt like I exhausted my reservoir.

A wave of exhaustion swept over my body and my knees buckled. I hit the ground on my hands and knees as I panted for a breath.

"Alethea," Mykill's astonished voice sounded above me.

I glanced up as I heard the sound of crackling, much like a fire. My mouth dropped open as I stared at the two frozen figures of the dragons and their riders. One of the dragons' head was dropped back in a scream and the other's head was curled under its belly in an attempt to get away from my flames, from me.

"I'm okay, I'm okay," I panted as Mykill's arms slid beneath my underarms and pulled me to my feet. My hands shook as he steadied me on my feet.

"I need to take you back," Mykill said as he stepped in front of me.

"What? I want to help, please let me help!" I said frantically as I shoved at his chest.

Mykill shook his head and ducked over me as another dragon swooped ahead. "No, it's too dangerous."

"Pleas-"

"We are outnumbered!" Mykill said as he gripped my face. His eyes were wide, wild. "I don't have the ability to protect you and you haven't fully learned to harness your powers. *Please*." His voice nearly broke on the plea. "If you keep exhausting your powers you'll pass out."

Everything inside of me froze as I took in his eyes. He was terrified. I could feel his terror rolling off of him in waves and I couldn't bring myself to argue. So I merely nodded.

Relief spread across his features and he stepped into me. I remained frozen as he slipped an arm around my waist and reached for the sky as lightning struck and swallowed us. I gripped onto his vest as the ground fell out from beneath my feet momentarily before we appeared in his throne room.

"Stay here, there are men guarding you here. You will be safe."

I nodded as I stepped out of his embrace. "Be safe."

He stepped away from me, his wide eyes resting on me for another moment before thunder sounded and he was gone.

I waited for what felt like hours as I paced back and forth across the room. I didn't realize my powers had heightened until I smelt smoke, and as I looked down at my feet smoke drifted from my heels. The carpet beneath my feet had been burned.

I tried to imagine Mykill's iciness to help me calm down and steel my emotions. But the longer he was gone, the more anxiety crept into my throat.

As I stalked down the hall, I traced my fingers across the marble walls as I tried to imagine the coldness of them was Mykill.

Pushing open the door to his sitting room, I closed my eyes as I breathed in his scent. The motion soothed me slightly.

Hopefully he wouldn't mind.

I closed the door behind me and threw myself onto one of his sofas. I closed my eyes as I tried to not imagine the carnage that was taking place. Guilt ate away at me, I needed to get stronger, I needed to learn to use my powers more if I was ever going to be of help.

Holding up one of my hands above me, I opened my palm and summoned a small ball of fire, then put it out.

If I couldn't help them, then I'd continue doing this, no matter how much it exhausted me.

***

After what felt like hours, I perked up as thunder rolled and Mykill appeared in a cloud of smoke.

"You're alright?" I gasped as I shot to my feet.

Although his body was dirty, he seemed unscathed. He nodded as he outstretched his hand towards me. I grasped his hand and his hand enveloped mine as he pulled me into his body. I threw my arms around his neck without thinking. He stiffened momentarily before his arms slowly slid around my waist.

"Careful, I'm beginning to think you're starting to actually care for me," he teased into my ear.

I groaned and shoved at his chest. "Just take me back there."

I ground my teeth at the bloodshed I was subjecting myself to. But I needed to see what Eryx and his men had done.

Mykill didn't object as he gripped my elbows, caging me in before him. My fingers curled into his leathers as the ground fell out beneath us and reappeared moments later.

Pulling away from Mykill, I turned to take in the damage.

The sight before me made my stomach drop and my steps falter. Practically every building that had been standing was now destroyed. Bodies littered the streets and they were piling them into two piles that neared my height.

"The remaining dragons retreated but there were mass casualties." Mykill's words echoed behind me as I stared at the men and boys dragging bodies to the ever growing pile.

"Almost all of them are women," I gasped and swung back towards him. "They killed the women?"

"All of them. The only men that died were those who fought back but they targeted mainly the women."

Tears flooded my eyes as I turned back towards the remains of the city. I watched in disbelief as a boy who was no older than seven or eight, carried a much smaller body covered in a sheet. There was a single circle of blood on the sheet, it stood out starkly against the light color of it. The body was too small to have died, too small to have been murdered so harshly. Tears burned the back of my eyes and I stumbled back a step.

I turned away and hunched against the side of a crumbling house as the contents of my stomach burned back up my throat. I coughed and sputtered as the food forced its way up my throat. Hands moved my hair away from my face and held it there until I was finished and I managed to wipe all of the bile from my mouth. I spit into the dirt once more before turning back towards Mykill.

"Thank you," I managed to say between short breaths as he released my hair. "I just-I can't-"

Eryx had done this. Eryx had commanded his men to slaughter women and children.

"Mykill-" I managed to gasp as my entire body began to shake. I felt my powers surging up beneath my skin and I cried out as my skin fought to contain it. My powers felt like they were flaying me from the inside.

"Take cover!" I heard Mykill shout but I couldn't tell if he was talking to me or warning others about me.

My skin burned and the smell of charred grass hit my nose.

"Just let it out," Mykill's voice said and I felt the sizzling touch of his cold hands on my shoulders.

"I don't want to hurt anyone, I don't want to hurt you," I said, my voice shaking.

My eyes wouldn't open as I shook my head.

"It's alright, everyone's protected, I can take it."

I dropped to my knees as I screamed. As I did, it was like the power rushed out of me. I felt the flames leap from my skin and rushed around me in an attempt to consume everything around me.

When I opened my eyes there was a wall of ice surrounding me, no, *us*. Mykill stood before me with his wings tucked in tightly behind him. He remained still as a statue as the flames around me licked at the wall of ice. But it remained tall and domed over us and whatever the flames melted, the ice merely replaced.

I had never hated so much in my life. Eryx had done this. *My* Eryx. The man I had trusted with my life. The one that had been kind, loving and had given me a home when I had nothing. How could he have done something so atrocious? How well had I known him? I had never thought he would have been capable of something like this. If only I had realized who he was sooner, maybe I could have prevented this in some way.

"Alethea," Mykill's cool voice broke through the haze of thoughts bombarding me. "You need to take a breath, love."

I nodded, but as I tried to breathe nothing would come in.

"Breathe," he commanded. "Again."

I sucked in another breath and focused on the feel of his heavy hand resting on my shoulder. I focused on the scent of the charred grass beneath me. I let the mixture of those two things ground me as I focused on breathing normally.

"I'm sorry," I shook my head. "I-". I gasped as he gripped my chin and forced my head back.

"Don't be sorry for having a heart," he growled as his fingers bit into my cheeks. "Your heart is what makes you shine so brightly to everyone around you, don't fear it, *use* it."

I nodded, his eyes bounced between mine before he released my cheeks. His wings were spread out on either side of him now, blocking me from the view of the soldiers who had been with us.

He gripped my hands and slowly raised me to my feet. When he was sure I wasn't going to collapse again, he released my hands. Steam wafted where our hands had just been.

I could feel my skin beginning to cool now that my emotions were steadying.

"Come help as I discuss with my General how we're going to accommodate the survivors." He motioned his head to the side, signaling to a small group of men all with their arms crossed over their chests.

"I'd love to," I nodded and followed after him as he turned away.

"More survivors!" A soldier from within the crowd shouted.

My head whipped towards the shout and as I did, my knees crumpled again. Coming from the line of trees were the men, women and children I had saved. All eight of them.

"Alethea," Mykill breathed as he caught me with an arm around my waist and slowly lowered me to the ground. "Alethea, what is it?"

I couldn't help the strangled cry that tore from my throat.

"Hey," Mykill said softer this time as he kept an arm secured around me as he knelt beside me. "It's alright, love."

"They listened, they ran to the trees like I told them," I sobbed as I turned into his chest and covered my face.

The three little girls and the mother with them were the only women to make it out alive. Four women out of a town of thousands.

The thought sent a tidal wave of tears as they rushed down my face.

"You saved them," Mykill breathed as a heavy arm settled around my shoulders and then another stroked down my hair soothingly. "You saved their lives," he said again, though it did nothing to calm the raging storm inside of me.

***

My eyes felt heavy as we continued helping with the damage the dragons had caused. We moved stacks of burnt and battered wood into piles, and then once we had done that, I had used my powers to burn them. Burning the piles of wood didn't take as much energy as the battle had. But by the time I was done, my hands shook.

Someone had assembled makeshift bonfires and had set up logs around them for people to rest. There had to be at least a dozen of them. I searched the crowds, looking for familiar faces. There was a makeshift line of tables set up that was serving beef and broth soup to everyone before we headed back.

Mykill's men would lead the survivors back home on foot. There were too many of them for the men to carry back. But the women and children that survived would fly back with us.

My arms and legs ached as I found the bonfire that was surrounded by those I had sent to the trees. The mother and her two daughters rested on her lap. One of them was only a babe secured to the mothers chest, and the other had to be four or five. She sat on the ground beneath her mothers feet and was resting her head against her mothers thigh. She stared at the fire before her, her eyes vacant and haunted. I couldn't image the carnage those young eyes had witnessed.

I shifted my attention over to the man who was holding his baby and the third young girl.

As I watched them, I noticed how different they looked. Heartbreak crashed over me as I realized.

The little girl had lost her entire family.

The man was trying to hold her in his lap while caring for his crying boy.

"Here," I said softly as I sat down on the log and patted my lap. "I have an extra leg."

The little girl gave me a tentative glance before she slid off the man's lap and hobbled over to me. She slid into my lap and wrapped her arms around me the best she could. She laid her head on my chest and puffed out a breath. I secured my arms around her, offering her the most comfort I could, though I knew nothing compared to the comfort of a mother.

My eyes met Mykill's over the tip of the flames from the bonfire and he offered me a soft smile before turning his attention back towards the guard he was speaking to. I ran a soothing hand down the girl's head as I rocked softly. Now that she had eaten, I was sure she was tired.

I glanced down at her soft form as I heard her breaths get heavier and heavier until I was sure she was asleep.

My heart broke for her. She had lost her entire family. Being an orphan was heartbreaking as an adult, but becoming an orphan as a child - it was a pain I couldn't fathom. I choked back the tears that threatened to spill.

Wrapping my arms around her, the best thing I could do for her was offer her a warm embrace, and somewhere safe to sleep. I rocked back and forth softly until my eyes grew heavy.

I hadn't realized I had drifted off until a cold hand shook me slightly, calling my name.

"Let's get back to the castle," Mykill said softly as he stirred me slightly.

I raised my head, my eyes bleary. "Don't wake her." I shushed and frowned.

He nodded and then glanced around him. His men were beginning to pack up, readying to move out.

"Can you help me stand?" I asked as I turned my attention back towards him.

He lowered slightly and gripped my elbows as he helped me stand. I stepped into him and he dropped an arm around my waist as I cocooned the girl between us. I didn't care as I dropped my head to his chest and closed my eyes and waited for the familiar feeling of the clouds swallowing us. I clutched the girl tighter as it did.

Thankfully it didn't wake her.

"Where are we?" I frowned as I stepped out of his embrace.

"This is another wing of the castle. They will all be given refuge here. We will have homes built above the cliffs for those who would like to remain here, but for now they can reside here."

My mouth fell open as I glanced back at him. "That's kind of you."

"It's the least I can do."

He moved around me and I took in the hall around me before I followed. This wing had a homier feeling. Instead of the sleek marble, the walls were a deep green with oak wooden flooring. There were gold accent tables lining the walls with overflowing vases with flowers and assortments of greenery.

"You can bring her in here," he said as he opened a door.

I followed behind him into the small bedroom that was clearly designed for a child. It had a small bed tucked into the corner, draped in a plush blanket and an array of colorful pillows. There was a large dollhouse on the wall across from the bed with a small wooden box beside it with a handful of wooden toys for the house. There was a small circle wooden table in the center of the room with a small cushioned stool.

On the table was a small stack of parchment and several jars of paint and paintbrushes laid out beside them.

The room was inviting and comforting. Carrying her across the room, I laid her down on the bed and stroked a hand down her unruly blonde hair. Mykill draped the blanket over her as I rose and simply watched as her small chest moved up and down.

Her face was peaceful, but when reality came crashing down on her, I knew those peaceful dreams would turn into perilous ones. It, unfortunately, wasn't something she'd be able to outrun.

"What will happen to her?" I asked as I stepped away from the bed.

I could feel the sadness clinging to my chest.

"Well there are the survivors that she was found with." My heart leapt into my throat.

"But there's only one mother, and she seems to have her hands full. The others are only men," I interjected.

"Then, she will be cared for by a woman," he answered instantly. "And for the time being, more than one until a good home can be found for her. I will have maids assigned to only caring for her."

I nodded as I crossed my arms over my chest, but I couldn't tear my eyes from her.

"Come on," Mykill said softly as he stepped up behind me and draped an arm over my shoulders. Clouds swallowed us and moments later, we were standing in the hallway outside of my bedroom door. "Please get some rest." His voice was soft, but firm, leaving no room for negotiation.

I nodded as I reached for the door handle. "Goodnight," I said softly before closing the door, but he and I both knew that I wasn't getting to bed.

Chapter 6

Alethea

Sleep evaded me, like I thought it would. I couldn't keep the screams and the sound of crackling flames from my mind. I tossed and turned, trying my best to get comfortable. But the longer I kept my eyes closed, the louder the screams became.

I kept the blanket wrapped around me and clenched the corners in one hand as I lifted off the bed. Slipping on my slippers, I stepped out into the hall. My footsteps echoed off the floors as I made my way down the halls. Sometimes the walls felt like they were going to suffocate me, the losses I had endured and witnessed were going to suffocate me. I could see every face of every dead body I had passed. Some of their faces had been frozen in terror, while others eyes were just closed. But I still could recall every single one.

Mykill's castle was darker and crisper than Eryx's but it didn't make it feel any less inviting. The space felt fresh and clean, not overwhelming.

There was also an abundance of sitting spaces. I had claimed a seating area outside as my own. It wasn't anything fancy, merely a small sofa with two chairs and a small table with a single candle on it to illuminate the space; Which I had all but nearly burned. As I found myself wandering outside on more nights than not.

As I stepped outside, I paused as a figure was draped across one of the sofas. His arms were crossed behind his head and his legs outstretched in front of him and crossed at the ankle. Dark wings were draped across the back, the moonlight reflected off of them.

"I figured you'd come out here," Mykill spoke as he lowered his gaze. "Would you like company?"

I nodded once before sitting across from him. "What are you doing out here?" I frowned as I stared at him.

His eyes were glued to the small table between us. But, though he was staring at it, I knew he wasn't seeing it. It was like he wasn't here.

"I feel like I lose a piece of me whenever one of my own dies," Mykill spoke; His voice was softer and more broken than I'd ever heard it before. It tugged at my heart as I watched him.

"You're a good King," I finally said.

His gaze snapped to mine and his brows furrowed.

"Most people just say thank you when they're complimented," I teased as I sat back.

The silence spanned out between us but I was okay with that. I dropped my head back as I propped my feet up on the small table. I smiled as the breeze kicked up and rustled my hair.

"Thank you," he finally spoke, but his voice sounded strained. "Thank you for helping me see the good when all I can see and think about is the way I've failed."

My heart panged as I raised my head to look at him. "It's not your fault that those people were killed. That was the Barren and Eryx, not you."

He opened his mouth to respond and by the look on his face, it was going to be to criticize himself.

"No, I mean it. Take responsibility for things you can control. You can't control the Barren or Eryx."

Mykill didn't answer as he continued to stare at the ground. I was more than happy to let him sit with his thoughts. He was always more than obliging to let me sit with mine. I leaned back in the seat and dropped my head back as I let my eyes trace the stars littering the sky. I tried to let myself get lost in the stories of the pictures painted above. Stories of bravery, love and heartbreak.

"What brought you out here?" Mykill finally prodded.

My face dropped as I felt the tears prick the back of my eyes. I took a deep breath in an attempt to keep my voice from wobbling but it did nothing as I spoke. "I just keep seeing all of their faces. All of those women and children who were completely defenseless, killed by the man I love. *Loved.*" I corrected and laughed harshly.

"It's alright for your heart to still be drawn to him," Mykill said softly.

I shook my head. "It's not," I answered. If I was being truthful, it hadn't been for a long time. Possibly longer than my stay here but I didn't need to tell Mykill that.

"He will pay," Mykill spoke. "If I'm not able to do it then the Inner Kingdom will make him pay. What he has done is considered a war crime and will not be tolerated."

I nodded at his words, at the words he had left unspoken. Eryx would be put to death for his crimes.

"Good," I answered and raised my head to meet his stare.

"I've never seen someone do that," Mykill spoke, changing the subject and I frowned. "I've never heard of a mate drawing from the other mate's powers," he clarified.

I smiled sheepishly. "How'd you know?"

"I could feel it, it was like a tug down in my stomach. Then when I looked over at you, your flames turned blue. But my suspicions were confirmed when the dragon was frozen."

"I'm sorry," I said as I ducked my head.

"Don't be," he answered. "Killing those dragons saved lives."

"Not enough," I breathed as I let my head drop. "Not enough lives were saved."

"What would you tell me if I said that?" he pondered.

I sucked in a breath and then cocked my head to the side as I looked up at him through my lashes. "I'd agree with you, but tell you that you did everything that you could. That you saved as many lives as you could."

Slowly, Mykill leaned forward and leaned his elbows on his knees as he pinned me with those icy eyes. "Alethea, yes, not enough lives were saved, but you did everything you could. You saved as many lives as you could."

I laughed bitterly as I wiped at a stray tear. "Would you believe me if I said that to you?"

Mykill didn't answer.

"I think you should get some rest," he finally spoke after what felt like several minutes.

At the words, a yawn slipped from my mouth and I stifled a chuckle. "You're right." I stood from my chair and turned to him. "Will you walk me inside?"

He stood before I even finished my sentence. Our walk back was silent, but not in a way that was uncomfortable. We were both engrossed in our own thoughts and our own pains, and sometimes it was nice to have someone who could sit with you in it and not try to make you see the best of things, because sometimes there wasn't a best.

Mykill opened the door for me and allowed me to enter first. I turned towards him as he followed and closed it behind him. His eyes narrowed as our gazes clashed. You could hear both of our breaths echoing down the hall, and the longer we stared, the more my heart rate kicked up.

"Goodnight," I breathed as I dropped my face.

"Goodnight, Alethea," he spoke softly.

I turned away first, fighting sleep the entire way. When I got back to my room, I slipped into a dreamless, but fitting sleep.

***

Letting out a loud yawn, I stretched out onto my side before pushing out of the bed. Sleep had claimed me effortlessly and I hadn't awoken, but it was the kind of rest that wasn't fitful. Although I had slept through the night, I still felt exhausted and drained.

Shoving myself out of bed, I drew myself a quick bath. My ladies maids were waiting in the bedroom with a dress for me to wear. They weren't like Lira, I could tell they only wanted to help me dress and then leave. Although, Lira was similar when we had met.

They dressed me in a cream dress with long puffed sleeves that tightened above my wrist and then flared out slightly once more. The corset was a deep maroon that pointed towards my feet before the cream fabric billowed around my ankles. They braided my hair down one side of my head and draped it over my shoulder. A few strands broke free from the braid and framed my face but I convinced them to leave them. After they left I used the tip of one of my fingers and summoned heat to it. I twirled a strand around it, coiling it tightly before pulling it away. The curl was tight and bouncy. I smiled triumphantly as I did it to the other stray pieces before standing and slipping on the matching maroon slippers they had laid out for me.

I headed towards the dining room, my stomach roaring the entire way. Mykill was already seated, looking wide awake as he reclined back in his chair.

He hadn't touched his plate yet, always waiting for me no matter how much I chastised him for it.

"You look rested," he observed as he cocked his head to the side.

Those glacier blue eyes felt like they were peeling back layers of my skin, seeping into my soul. I averted my eyes and cleared my throat. "I am, thank you."

I made my way towards my seat and paused as it pulled itself out. I couldn't help the nervous giggle that bubbled out of me as I took my seat, it pushing itself in on its own.

"What is so funny?" Mykill questioned, cocking an eyebrow at me.

I shook my head as I picked up the spoon for the porridge before me. "Nothing, your amount of laziness is astonishing," I joked as I began stirring it.

Mykill let out a sharp laugh and as I cast him a quick glance, his eyes glittered with amusement. We ate in silence, but the kind that wasn't strained. There was a certain comfortability to it. He didn't force me to be more than I was, allowing me to be silent when I felt like being silent. I never recalled feeling like that with

Eryx. There was always a constant pressure to be more, and there was always a fear that I wasn't doing what pleased him. Mykill never made me feel pressured in that way, and although Eryx had never spoke anything aloud that made me feel that way, there was always just a little tension.

I placed my spoon down as I finished and sat back in my chair. Mykill had long since finished and was merely watching me with that intense gaze of his. I wanted to ask him what he was thinking, I couldn't ever get a read on his emotions. I wasn't sure if he did that on purpose or if he wanted to shield himself from others, but it was slowly grating on my nerves.

"Sir," a guard spoke as he entered the room and bowed his head. "There's a man here requesting to speak with you and Alethea."

I frowned at the guard then glanced back at Mykill. He rose from his seat and I followed closely behind him. The guard led us down the hall towards Mykill's study.

"I believe he's King Eryx's General."

Cadmus? Longing filled me as I quickened my pace. Leaving Eryx had been hard but leaving Cadmus, my friend, had been equally as hard. He had become a comforting presence and someone I knew I could count on no matter what.

As the door to Mykill's study came into sight, I couldn't help it as I took off at a jog.

"Cadmus?" I gasped as I pushed open the door.

Cadmus' head swung towards me and his face fell in relief. "Alethea, I'm so glad to see that you're okay."

"What happened? What are you doing here?"

"Eryx relieved me of my duties when I told him I wouldn't lead his attack on your lands." He glanced back at Mykill and bowed his head. "I'm sorry to show up unannounced but I had nowhere else to go."

"You can stay here," I answered immediately and swept towards him. I threw my arms around his shoulders and embraced him.

He hugged me briefly before pulling away.

"Are you sure?" Cadmus asked as his gaze slid behind me. But I knew he wasn't asking me this time, he was asking Mykill who hadn't spoken since he'd entered the room.

"Of course, I'll have a room prepared for you." I sensed Mykill slip out of the room moments after he finished speaking.

"Did he really? Eryx I mean?" I gasped. "He was going to attack us?"

Cadmus nodded gravely and glanced behind me as the door closed behind us. I motioned for him to sit on the sofa across from the desk and sat beside him.

"Tell me everything," I prompted.

Cadmus heaved a sigh and rested his elbows on his knees. "After you and Mykill got away with the scrolls Eryx wanted to declare war against Mykill's kingdom. I tried talking some sense into him. If you and him were still mated, then he would have been able to. But now that you're no longer mated to him, it didn't give him the authority to do so and the Inner Kingdom would have had his head for doing so. But he wouldn't listen to me and when I told him that I wasn't going to do it, he relieved me of my duties."

"Cadmus, I'm so sorry. I know he was your friend." I placed a hand on his forearm.

"Thank you," he said as he covered my hand.

The warmth of his hand seeped into mine before he sighed and withdrew his hand. I offered him a small smile as I placed my hands in my lap.

"You can stay here as long as you need, you're welcome here."

Cadmus laughed. "We'll see if Mykill agrees with that statement."

I scoffed. "He will if he knows what's good for him."

Cadmus eyed me cautiously and I wanted to assure him that Mykill would be fine with him staying here. But the longer I thought about it, I knew that it couldn't be a safe choice. Cadmus was from Eryx's kingdom, and had supposedly been Eryx's second in command for hundreds of years. If I was a ruler, my first thought would have been that Cadmus was sent here to spy on us, or he was sent here to assassinate either of us.

It was probably a good thing I wasn't a ruler then.

The door opened, cutting off my thoughts and Cadmus raised quickly to his feet. "Mykill." He bowed his head to him as he entered the room.

I stood up beside Cadmus and cast a glance at Mykill. Like normal, I couldn't read his expression.

"We've prepared a room for you. I'm sure you'd like to take some time getting acquainted and freshening up." Mykill motioned for him to follow as he exited the room.

Quickly, we followed behind him as Mykill led us down the familiar halls of his palace. We stopped at the end of my hallway.

"Your room is down the hall, the last door on the left." Directly across from mine.

"Thank you," Cadmus bowed his head. "I'd like to go get cleaned up."

"Of course," I nodded and watched as he slipped past me. I waited for him to turn the corner before I whipped towards Mykill. "I'm sorry I didn't give you a chance to decide if you wanted him here or not," I said but Mykill shook his head as he stepped towards me.

"This is your home too, Alethea. You can invite whomever you'd like to stay here." His icy eyes bore into mine and I glanced down as nervousness flitted through me. "I just ask that if it's another man that you don't invite him to stay for breakfast."

A laugh bubbled out of me as I raised my head. "Jealousy isn't a good look for you," I quoted the words he had said to me on more than one occasion.

A smile tugged at his lips, showing his teeth as he dropped his head back and laughed. The sound made my chest spasm and warmth glided over my skin.

"Now, Alethea, you know that isn't true," he teased as he extended an arm to me.

Laughing, I slid my arm into his as he led me back down the hall.

***

"Come on!" I hissed to Cadmus as he followed closely behind me.

After much badgering, Cadmus agreed to come out drinking with me. I decided to withhold the fact that Mykill had ordered my usual tavern to not serve me, as Cadmus still seemed frightened of him throwing him out on his ass. I refrained against defending Mykill, his character spoke volumes enough.

After pulling information from a wandering pedestrian, I found that there was a smaller tavern further down the cliffs that I hadn't been to. I hoped that word hadn't spread to them as well in regards to me being allowed to drink too or I'd flick Mykill in the eyeballs.

We were down three levels before I felt a strange sensation wash over me, halting my movements.

"I don't know whether I should be offended that I wasn't invited and push you two over the side of the cliff, or ream you both to get back to the castle." I gritted my teeth at the cold voice behind us.

Cadmus' eyes widened and then slowly moved behind me. Spinning towards him, my hands fisted at my sides.

"What are you doing here?" I demanded.

"Well, I came searching for you, but when I found your room empty, I figured you made another one of your attempts at sneaking out again. But then once I knocked on Cadmus' door and found he too was gone, it confirmed my suspicions."

"Damn you," I gritted out. "We just want to have some fun!"

I heard Cadmus' intake of breath behind me.

Mykill chuckled as he landed on the deck before us. There were only a few stragglers around us, but they didn't bat a second eye at him.

"Can I not join you?" He extended his hands on either side of him in a questioning manner.

I frowned, cocking my head to the side. "You want to join us?" I knew my voice dripped with surprise, but I was.

Mykill's gaze narrowed on me as he stepped closer to me. "Would that be such a bad thing?"

"Terrible," I retorted instantly as I stepped back. "But if it's between you joining us or going back to the castle for another boring night, then I'd choose the first."

Mykill barked out a laugh as I spun away and resumed leading Cadmus to the tavern I had in mind. The pedestrian I had spoken to told me it was more of a dancing tavern, rather than just drinking, which I delighted in. The last time I danced was when we visited Gild.

I heard both Cadmus and Mykill following closely behind me, but one presence I felt was closer to me. I didn't need to turn around to see who it was.

Before I reached the doors, the sound of instruments playing a familiar song poured out of the closed doors. When I pushed them open, I fought to keep the grin from my face. There were men and women across the dance floor, following in unison as they performed the necessary steps to the dance.

"Will this do?" Mykill spoke.

I would have jumped in surprise if I hadn't known he was so close to me.

"It's perfect," I answered as I stepped inside and began towards the bar.

When I reached it, although he was unfamiliar to me, the barkeeper cast a look at Mykill behind me. I rolled my eyes when he looked back at me and leaned across the bar to take my order.

Once I got my drink, we claimed a small table off to the side of the dance floor and I spun towards Cadmus, gripped his hand and dragged him after me.

Turns out, we were both horrible at dancing.

I dropped my head back and laughed as I spun back towards Cadmus. I'd never done this dance before but I was awful at it. I held my hands out in front of me, keeping my hands inches from Cadmus' as we slowly spun in the circle I had so gracefully fallen out of previously.

"This dance is going to make me dizzy," Cadmus laughed as we stepped away from each other as the music kicked up and we tried following along to the jig the others were doing.

"Isn't it fun?" I laughed as I brought my leg up and tried to copy what the others were doing.

It ended in Cadmus and I choking in a fit of laughter.

"I'd like a turn," Mykill spoke behind me and I stiffened.

Cadmus bowed his head as he released my hands and stepped around me. I refused to turn towards Mykill, refused to show that there was any part of me that was partially excited to dance with him. I ignored the fluttering in my stomach and the uptick of my heart.

"May I?" Mykill asked as he extended a hand and bowed his head slightly.

"You may," I answered and took his extended hand.

I shrieked as he spun me around and pulled my back flush to his chest. He dropped a heavy arm around my stomach and the small flutters turned into a raging monsoon. Mykill swayed us to the music and I resisted a shiver as I felt his breath skate across my exposed shoulder and earlobe.

"What made you choose this dress?" his husky voice asked.

I merely shrugged as my heart lunged into my throat at the proximity of our bodies. "I wanted something I could dance in." I shrugged as I placed a hand on his arm that tightened once around my stomach.

His hand intertwined with mine and I shrieked in surprise as he spun me away from him. He laughed as he spun me back towards him, catching me easily.

"I thought you hated dancing?" I teased.

"I love what you love," he answered with a goofy grin.

A smile pulled at my lips and I couldn't help but laugh. He had never been this bold with me before. There was only one reason for it.

"Is the King getting drunk?"

"Tipsy at most," he replied as he turned to head back to our seats.

I barked out a laugh as his body swayed. "Tipsy my ass! Here." I grabbed his arm and draped it over my shoulder and slid an arm around his waist.

I had intended to help walk him over to our table but he began to sway to the music again. I laughed as his arm around my shoulders dropped to my waist and he pulled me flush to him. He dipped me backwards, his blue eyes twinkled with amusement as he raised me back up.

If I had to choose how to spend the rest of my days, it would have been dancing.

As the night grew older, the crowds got smaller, my feet grew sorer and Mykill only grew drunker.

When we decided it was time to head back, Mykill insisted I fly back with him, but I would have none of it.

"I'm not leaving Cadmus," I argued and stamped my foot, fully aware of how childish I looked as I did it. "Besides, I'm not sure you'll be able to control those things. You can't even stand up straight."

Mykill chuckled and rolled his head, cracking his neck. "Please, these are just as much a part of me as my legs are, I'll be fine."

I only stared and pursed my lips. "Yeah, you can barely control those, so my statement still stands."

Mykill laughed. "Fine, I'll follow after you."

He waved an arm, pretending to be a gentleman and I marched past him. By the time we made it up all the flights of stairs, my thighs were burning and I wanted to collapse in my bed.

"Good night, Cadmus!" I called as Mykill leaned into me when we finally reached our halls.

"Sleep well!" he called back before disappearing behind the corner.

Mykill's body began leaning on me more and more.

"And you tell me I'm an alcoholic," I teased as I gripped his wrist and secured my arm around his waist as we began walking to his bedroom. I shoved the door open with my foot and began shuffling Mykill forward towards the massive bed in the center of the room.

"I'm thankful to the Gods for giving me wings because I think if I had to walk everywhere as you do, then I'd surely die." He dropped back onto his bed, his wings flaring out on either side of him.

I laughed as I yanked his boots off and grabbed one of his arms as I tried to drag him towards the head of the bed. "Come on, your drunk highness. Get all the way up here."

He grumbled, but obeyed as he shimmied to the top of the bed and beneath the covers.

"Goodnight," I twiddled my fingers towards him and laughed. "See you in the morning."

Mykill grumbled something unintelligible as I closed the door behind me and headed towards my room.

Chapter 7

Alethea

After breakfast, I found myself out on the patio. Mykill said he had matters to attend to this morning, which left me to my own devices. I wandered for a bit before slipping into his study and nabbing several books. I hurried them to my room before deciding I wanted to sit outside.

Lunch was nearing, so I pushed myself up and began making my way into the dining room. Mykill and Cadmus were just seating themselves when I entered. The servants placed down a steaming bowl of boiled potatoes, steamed peppers and turkey legs. My stomach roared at the sight.

I heard Mykill's soft chuckle and I shot him a glare, but he feigned innocence. Rolling my eyes, I turned back to my food but as I reached for the rolls, I found Cadmus staring. I averted my eyes, buttering my biscuit.

The silence between us was strained. I knew Eryx had thought lowly of Mykill, which in turn meant Cadmus had. But now that they had separated, I wasn't sure what his opinion was.

"I can help with your training if you'd like," Cadmus said as he stirred his food around his plate, as if he was nervous to speak the words aloud.

"I'd like that," I offered him a smile and stilled as Felix entered the room.

"Cadmus, I'd like to introduce you to my General. Felix, this is Eryx's former General." Mykill waved to Felix who bowed his head, Cadmus followed in response. "Cadmus can be your second in command."

Cadmus stifled a cough, choking on his food. He pounded his fist against his chest as he coughed again, trying to clear his throat. "That really isn't necessary."

"Nonsense," Mykill waved. "It would be an honor to have you in my army."

Cadmus' expression remained stunned before he finally bowed his head. "Thank you." When he raised his head, his throat bobbed once before he picked up his fork and began cutting into the turkey leg.

"So I assume you weren't a part of the attack on the human lands?" Mykill questioned as he waved his hand and his glass filled with red wine.

My throat tightened at the sight and his eyes flew to me. With another wave of his hand, the glass was gone. I threw him a glare but turned my attention back to Cadmus as he answered.

"What attack?" Cadmus frowned as he placed his spoon down and glanced once at Mykill, then once at me. "What attack?" he repeated.

Mykill glanced at me and I took that as my sign to fill him in. "Eryx attacked Grithel and executed most all of the women and children. Male lives were lost in the battle as well, but there were only four females who survived."

Cadmus' eyes widened and his mouth fell open. He shook his head repeatedly. "No, no, I had no idea. Where are the survivors now?"

"In another wing of the castle. My kingdom is not exactly built for those without wings, as Alethea can attest to." He waved a hand lazily at me. "But we will be making necessary adjustments so that those who were harmed in that kingdom, can settle here if they'd like."

"What of their King and Queen?"

"The palace was set on fire, there were no survivors."

Cadmus swallowed as his gaze fell onto the table. "They have no home to return to." He spoke so quietly I wasn't sure if he was speaking to us or himself.

"No, they don't," Mykill agreed as he returned to his food. "But we will take care of them. They are being well fed I assure you."

Conversation didn't lull between them after that, but I tuned them out as I finished my food.

After we had eaten, I retired to my bedroom for the evening. So many questions just ate at me. Mykill and I hadn't discussed when we were going to broach the search for the mirror. We hadn't even been able to figure out how to find it because the scrolls were blank.

After we had stolen them from Eryx, Mykill let me keep them. I wouldn't have agreed to staying here otherwise. It was a small thing, but it was something that I was in control of. I wasn't willing to place my entire self in Mykill hands, as I had done with Eryx.

Pulling the scrolls out from the nightstand, I laid them out on my bed. The scrolls were supposed to contain a map, so I was told. But no matter what I tried, nothing revealed itself. Mykill was still researching to see if there's a missing piece, or if we didn't do something properly. But some nights, I felt them reaching for me, begging me to open them. At first I thought that was its way of telling me it wanted to reveal the map to me. I had been greatly disappointed when it hadn't.

I gently peeled the first one open, the crisp sound of the parchment stretching filled my space. I laid it out, and then set on opening the second. I recalled the way it had pulled on my powers, scrolling my blood across the letters that had been inked upon it, but shortly after, they had disappeared entirely.

Part of me wondered if we should have asked the dragon man, but with how ominous he was, he probably wouldn't have told us.

"I just want to know where my parents are," I grumbled to myself and chucked aside one of the scrolls. "Where are my parents?"

I tossed myself back on my pillow, blowing out an exasperated breath. Part of me wondered if Eryx would know how to use them, or why they weren't revealing the map to me. But given his cold greeting a few weeks ago, he would likely not share the information.

A soft hum filled my room. I bolted upright, searching for the source of the soft noise. But as I craned my head around, I found nothing. Then a soft light cast across my bed. Glancing down, I watched as the scrolls began illuminating something.

No, not just something, a place.

It had answered me.

Realization crashed over me.

The scrolls were supposed to lead us to the mirror, but instead they were the mirror.

The swirled writing stopped, revealing coordinates. I wasn't sure what that meant, but I knew Mykill would.

I dove off my bed, disregarding shoes, as I clutched the scroll to my chest and threw my door open. I took off at a run down the hall as the skirt of my dress swished around my legs.

My chest pumped as I ran towards Mykill's study. He said he had needed some time to go over some paperwork but I didn't care as I threw open the door.

"The scrolls! The scrolls are the mirror!" I exclaimed as I rushed towards his desk.

His head snapped up towards me and his eyes darted behind me, checking for danger. When he didn't find any, his eyes slid over to the scrolls I outstretched towards him. They were glowing with the inscription of the location I had requested.

"What did you ask it?" he asked slowly.

"Where to find my parents," I answered in a rush.

His eyes snapped up to mine and widened slightly. I thought he'd scold me, or ask me why I hadn't waited for him but instead he rose to his feet and said, "Let's go."

My eyes widened to his response as I stared at him. "Right now?"

"Yes. Go pack a small bag."

He took the scroll from me and frowned as he examined the map.

"This isn't a city," he said quietly. "These are the Outlands. We'll need to travel quickly so we'll stick to air travel. It should only take us two days to get there."

"Won't your arms get tired?" I frowned as he handed the map back to me and brushed on by.

His steps faltered as he swung back towards me and his mouth fell open in mock indignation. "I'm insulted."

I scoffed and shoved by him. "Oh shut up."

His chuckle followed me down the hall and then he shouted, "Meet me at the sparring mats with your packed bag within the hour!"

I didn't look back at him, I wouldn't give him the satisfaction of it. As I rushed to my room, I shuffled around in my wardrobe until I found a small sack stowed away. I stuffed a couple outfits that consisted of leggings and tight fitted long sleeves. Thermals, they were needed with the current weather.

Of course by the time I finished and met Mykill on the training grounds, he was waiting with a cocky grin on his face.

"Took you long enough," he scoffed as he shoved off the wall and grabbed his bag that was leaning against his leg. "Give me." He reached for my pack and I yanked it back as I stumbled away from him.

"You could ask like a gentleman," I bit out and one of those perfectly pruned black eyebrows raised.

"Alethea, my dearest mate, would you bestow me the honor of carrying your satchel?" His voice dripped with sarcasm that I couldn't ever recall hearing from him before.

I choked on a laugh. "I don't think I've ever heard you make a joke." I tossed him my bag and he caught it effortlessly. "Fine."

He slung my bag over his shoulder without another word as I stepped up to him. It was routine as I slipped an arm around his neck and his arms slipped beneath me as I leaned back into his arms. Then he took to the sky, and I clutched to him like I was going to hurl. The sun had begun to set and I wanted to ask why we didn't wait till sunrise to leave, but I knew what his answer would be.

"What if they're not there?" My throat bobbed at the thought.

"The scrolls said they are, so they have to be," he answered quietly. "Are you nervous?"

"My mind is running a million miles an hour," I answered bluntly. "What if they don't recognize me? What if they don't want anything to do with me?"

So many questions spiraled around inside of me, nearly making it hard for me to breathe. What if they really weren't there? What if they had somehow cloaked themselves and the scrolls were taking us to their last known location? What if they were prisoners somewhere?

"Why don't you ask me some questions," Mykill prompted.

I frowned as I turned to look at him. "Like what kind of questions?"

"Anything. Anything to take your mind off all the doubts I can tell are swirling through your head."

I nodded lightly, and paused, contemplating what I wanted to know most about him.

"What was your first year as King like?"

He frowned once and then chuckled lightly. "It was horrendous. I spent the majority of my time getting rip roaring drunk. I rarely attended any meetings.

I laughed. "It's hard to imagine you like that."

"Well, I like to think that I've matured a bit since then."

"Just a bit," I teased.

His smile grew ever so slightly and then his eyes shifted back to me. "Next question."

"Why did you make Cadmus your second in command?"

The smile slipped from his face and was replaced by that cool expression I was so familiar with. "It felt like the right thing to do. I know he's a great General and I wasn't going to throw him out in the streets and he hardly seemed like he would like living in a home on the edge of a cliff."

I laughed. "No, he probably wouldn't."

I paused as I contemplated my next question. Part of me felt like there was so little I knew about him, so I decided to start with the basics.

"What's your favorite season?"

"Winter," he answered. I couldn't say I was surprised though.

"Favorite color?"

"Gray." I rolled my eyes.

"I wouldn't consider gray a color, but alright. What about your favorite food?"

He frowned, his dark brows scrunching. "I haven't really thought about it. I'd have to say scrambled eggs with peppers or roasted duck."

I opened my mouth to ask him the next question when he interrupted me.

"What about yours?" I frowned, glancing at him. "What are your favorites out of the questions you just asked me?"

"Oh, well my favorite season is summer, my favorite color is yellow and my favorite food would have to be a biscuit with jam." He smiled slightly and I straightened as my frown deepened. "What are you laughing at?"

He shook his head and then his eyes slid over to mine. "I could've guessed that your favorite color was yellow."

"Oh could you?" I teased as I adjusted my arm, my hand sliding across the bare skin above his shirt.

It felt like his breath hitched as I did. But there was no way he would have reacted like that to me touching his skin.

I tapped my other finger against my lips as I contemplated on my next question.

***

After resting for a bit in the evening, we picked up our journey again the next morning. Mykill fed us each a cluster of grapes, cheese and crackers for breakfast, and then for lunch, some sliced turkey, with cheese, and some chopped vegetables. We chatted on and off throughout the day, and when evening came we rested again.

There were constant storm clouds the next day as we flew and I frowned, finally voicing one of my questions.

"Is that you?" I cocked my head to the side to look at him.

His eyes slid over to mine, so slowly, it was nearly breathtaking and those salt colored eyes latched onto mine. Then he dropped his head back as he examined the sky.

"No." He shook his head as he dropped it back to face me.

"Well what if it rains then? Can't you make it go away?"

The corner of his mouth pulled. "No, Alethea, I cannot. I can summon my own storms, rain, and thunder, but I can't control whatever nature decides to do."

I frowned. "Well you're pretty much useless then?"

He barked out a laugh at that. "I would hardly say I'm useless."

I shrugged, turning my attention to the land that we passed below us. I hadn't paid much attention, as the majority of it had been an unending forest. I had never heard of the Outlands before, I didn't know there was such a thing. But the further out we went, the thicker the trees and foliage became.

"We should be nearing the coordinates soon. We'll do a sweep over the area once, and then once it's deemed safe, we'll land."

I frowned as I turned back towards him. "They're my parents, they're not going to hurt me."

He didn't answer as he shifted his gaze before him. I knew no matter what I said, I couldn't talk him out of that. I knew it was just a precaution because he wanted to keep me safe, but I knew my parents would never hurt me.

I yawned and dropped my head to his shoulder. I didn't know how he had held me against him so firmly for the past two days, but his strength was astonishing. He said I weighed nothing, but that was a blatant lie. I was a full person. I was contemplating asking him how he had gotten so strong before I slipped into a short sleep.

Mykill nudged me some time later, and when I opened my eyes the sky had darkened significantly. Thunder rumbled in the distance, and flashes of lightning danced in the corners of my vision.

"We're almost there," he said softly.

I straightened in his arms, rubbed at my eyes and brushed my hair from my face. Anxiety crept up my throat, nearly making it hard for me to breathe. All the doubts I had thought of along the way spiraled around inside of me, each one fighting for dominance.

We swept over the area once, and I frowned when I didn't see a house, a tent or any form of life. Mykill's expression was blank as he stared down at the space before finally landing. I jumped from his arms, taking in the space around me. But what I saw made my heart trip over itself.

I wasn't entirely sure what I had been expecting. A cottage draped in vines and flowers, shaded by a willow that swayed in the wind? Or a shack with nothing more than a bed for the two of them?

But what I didn't expect was to see two makeshift gravemarkers.

The ground before the gravemarkers were probably mounded at one time but they had been flattened. The grave markers were worn, surely from the elements.

I felt my knees wobble as I stopped before them and read the names that had been carved into the stones.

"Flora and Doran," I whispered to myself and swallowed past the lump in my throat.

At least I had finally learned their names.

I wish I could have met whoever cared about them enough to bury them. Maybe they could have told me about them.

Slowly, I lowered myself to my knees as thunder sounded above us. But it wasn't Mykill, it was the natural kind.

Raindrops began to pelt my shoulders, first slowly, then they intensified until I could barely see beyond the gravemarkers.

"I never got to meet them," I whispered as the rain slid down the sides of my face, slicking my hair to my cheeks.

The ground crunched beneath Mykill's boots and I heard him crouch behind me. "I'm sorry." He kept his voice soft, sympathetic.

Tears burned my eyes and throat as I turned my face away and closed my eyes. Somehow I had thought that meeting them would fill the hole my adoptive family had left behind but losing them too just tore the hole into a chasm.

I covered my face with my hands and before my throat broke on the first cry, Mykill's arms wrapped around me. I leaned into his side, needing something to ground me as the grief hit me. I should have known better. They had been hunted. I should've expected this but the smallest part of me hoped that I would have showed up and they would have walked outside and greeted me with open arms.

I hated the stone slab and the cold graves. They served as another reminder of all that had been taken from me and simply added another pair to that list.

"I'm so sorry, love," Mykill said as he stroked a hand down my soaked hair.

A shiver worked its way up my spine and then something warm draped itself around my shoulders. I didn't have to look to know it was Mykill's wings.

I didn't have words to speak as the grief threatened to swallow me.

Chapter 8

Alethea

The rain finally subsided, not long after, so did my tears. I finally relented, walking away from my parents' graves. I couldn't look back at them as the trees swallowed us once more. I insisted we walk for some time, sticking to beneath the trees so we could not only stay out of the rain, but also so I could walk off some of my grief.

Every single person that had loved and cared for me, outside of Eryx, was dead. Every one of them.

Mykill had spoken words of solace when we first began our walk, but after a while, they died down. I appreciated him letting me be alone with my thoughts. It gave me the opportunity to accept the fact that I would never see them, I'd never know what they even looked like. I could put together images of what I thought my life with them would have looked like, then I would feel guilty for yearning for that when I had two parents who did love and care for me as a child.

This was all so wrong, and so unfair. I deserved to have my family go with me through my life, walk me through it, and guide me. But now I didn't have anyone that I had known for more than a few months to turn to, and it wasn't the same. It wasn't the same to turn to someone who hadn't walked through life with me, like Laney. It would never be the same. Even if she didn't have advice, she was still a comforting presence in a way no one could replace.

The sun had long since set and I knew Mykill was following behind me and wouldn't stop me until I felt too tired to continue. But he had spent two days carrying me, and I knew he needed rest. My body ached from just sleeping on the forest floor, so he must have been in some pain.

I stopped and turned towards him. He was a few feet behind me, and had stopped before I fully turned around.

"Where should we stop for the night?"

He cocked his head to the side, his fingers twitched slightly at his sides. "Here is fine."

I nodded as I crossed my arms against my chest to ward off the chill that hung in the air. Mykill dropped both of our packs at his feet and I found a relatively dry patch and lowered myself to the ground.

I watched as Mykill arranged the leaves, and dried twigs he could find. Then I outstretched my hands and started a small fire. The flames had bounced from my hand into the pile of leaves and caught fire immediately. If it had been a normal fire, it wouldn't have caught due to the moisture that was in the leaves and air, but I didn't have the energy to ask Mykill how it was different.

He arranged our sacks, our only comfort on the ground, then laid down on his. He had picked the driest spot he could find. But he had arranged our sacks closer together than normal, to help keep us warm through the night. The air was bitingly cold, and I wasn't experienced enough to use my powers to ward it off.

I laid down, resting my head on my sack and stared up at the forest above us. The sky was barely visible, even as the trees swayed. Droplets of water still slipped through the leaves and branches, dripping all around us.

Rolling towards him, I tucked my hands beneath my cheek and frowned. "What about your family?"

He sighed as he gazed up at the branches above us. "My parents were murdered when I was eight."

I stifled a gasp. "Gods, that's horrible. I'm so sorry. Were you there?"

"Yes," he answered quietly. "Everyone always asks me that."

"Do you remember it?"

"Yes," he answered again. "Every detail of it."

His eyes went vacant as he spoke.

"We were visiting another kingdom and my father insisted that we carry on through the night. One of my mothers wings had been broken when she was a child, so we rode in a carriage. I had fallen asleep with my head in her lap when the carriage lurched forward and she screamed. It had been a group of thieves that pillaged through the entirety of our things. They took every last thing that could make them some money. They had rounded us up beneath the trees and killed off the guards."

He paused and his lips pursed. I nearly asked him to stop but it seemed as if he hadn't told the story to many.

"They tortured both of them and left me tied to a tree to watch after they broke one of my wings so I couldn't fly off. They ripped the earrings from my mothers ears. I remember the blood dripping down her neck and all she ever asked was for them not to hurt me. They found me wandering the woods a few days later. Thankfully they were able to heal my wing but my Uncle became

Regent until I was old enough. He died fifty years ago, leaving me by myself."

I hadn't noticed my breath had stalled until I sighed. "I'm so sorry."

"It was a long time ago," he responded and waved his hand, silently commanding the flames to die down.

"That doesn't take away the brutality and horror of it."

"I suppose," he murmured and rolled onto his side to face me. His eyes darkened as they studied my face. "How are you doing?"

I sucked in a quiet breath and resisted the urge to roll onto my back. I sucked my bottom lip in between my teeth to keep it from trembling.

"Sometimes I think the Fates must hate me," I whispered so quietly even I couldn't hear myself.

"I think the Fates chose someone they thought would be easy prey." His voice was soft as he answered.

My chest stung and I laughed bitterly and rolled onto my back. "Wow, thanks." I wiped at one of the stray tears.

"But I think you continue showing them that you're not," he finished.

I stilled as I contemplated my response. But I didn't have one. I felt his eyes on me, but I couldn't bring myself to look at him. Something had shifted between us. There was something like longing that spanned between us, but it had been something neither of us wanted. But it was becoming more and more distracting.

"Get some rest, Alethea," he said softly, interrupting my thoughts, and I heard the sound of him rolling onto his back.

I didn't answer him. I merely let the bad thoughts consume me, until they pulled me into a deep sleep.

***

"Alethea," a voice called, shaking my leg. "Wake up, we've got to get moving."

I grumbled, rolling away from the gruff voice.

"Get up," Mykill said as he nudged my leg. "If you're still tired, you can sleep while we fly."

I grumbled beneath my breath as I rolled onto my side. "Can you give me like twenty more minutes?"

"No," he snapped and nudged me again. "You have till I count to ten to stand up or I'll toss you in the creek."

My eyes snapped open and my palms instantly heated. I shoved myself up into a sitting position and tossed my now messy braid over my shoulder

"Why are you such an ass?" I grumbled.

"I think you're just used to being coddled," he threw back and my mouth fell open.

He blew out a breath and his head dropped. "I didn't mean it like that."

"No," I said as I stood and brushed by him. "Let me relieve myself and then we can go."

"Alethea!" he called after me but I disappeared into the shrubs.

I wasn't necessarily angry at him, but more at myself. I was more angry at myself for allowing myself to get used to being coddled.

Mykill wouldn't meet my gaze fully when I reemerged from the shrubs. He lifted me up into the sky easily. I could feel the tension between us. I could sense he wanted to speak, but wasn't entirely sure what to say.

"You're right," I said quietly without raising my head.

"About what?" I smiled lightly as I listened to the sound of his voice rumble through his chest.

"I am used to being coddled." I could sense him opening his mouth to speak but I cut him off. "I am, and I appreciate you treating me like your equal, even if you are an ass about it."

"I was only joking, Alethea. I'm sorry," he said again.

We continued on in a strained silence. I could feel the guilt from what he had said this morning washing over me. But no matter how many times I told him it was okay, he didn't seem to believe me. I tried to distract him later with some more questions, which he unwillingly answered. Some of them were like prying teeth. Like when I asked him about his first kiss.

He very reluctantly told me it had been with a girl he had grown up with when he was fifteen. But once she was of marrying age, she was married off to a wealthy fae in another kingdom.

After I pried some more answers from him, I finally let us fly in the silence it seemed he so desperately wanted. The sun would be setting soon, which meant we only had one more night of sleeping on the forest floor.

Oh how I yearned for my bed back at Mykill's castle.

"What are we doing?" I frowned as he began to descend from the sky. I knew we still had at least a day before we reached his castle, but we had never landed for the night before the sun had set.

"Staying at an inn," he said without looking at me. "I assumed you'd like to sleep in a bed tonight."

"I would love to sleep on a bed," I grumbled as I leaned back dramatically.

He chuckled lightly and then dropped quickly. I curled my fingers into his shoulders, biting down on my tongue and the curses I had come up for him. I wouldn't give him the satisfaction anymore. Once we were on solid ground, I hopped from his arms and glanced up the street.

I took in our surroundings. We were on a small street that was bustling with people. No one paid attention to us, their only focus on wherever they were headed.

"Let's stop here for dinner first," Mykill said, drawing my attention.

He placed a hand on my back as he steered me towards a small tavern.

It wasn't loud like the others I had been to. It was much smaller, with tables laid out evenly, and waitresses bustling from table to table, serving the largest bowls of soup I'd ever seen.

"Sit wherever you'd like!" one of the servers shouted at us with a smile. "I'll be with you in a moment!"

Mykill nodded and led me towards a table in the corner. He sat in the corner, it was the only space large enough for his wings to stretch out behind him.

"I'm sorry about the lack of space, we don't get very many winged folk in here." The waitress smiled at him, then at me. "I assume you folks aren't from around here?"

Mykill nodded, offering her a small smile. "No, we're from Asgaith."

"Asgaith?" she beamed as she placed waters in front of both of us. "That's quite a ways from here."

Mykill only nodded to her.

"What can I get both of you?" Mykill's gaze slid over to me, pinning me to the spot.

"What would you like?" he asked deeply.

I frowned. "Why don't you figure out what you'd like first."

"I'm getting whatever you are."

His voice was gruff, but so serious. I wanted to laugh at him, but the fire that burned in his eyes froze the sound. I stuttered, my eyes flying around the space before pointing at the table beside us.

"Can we just get what they're having?"

"Of course! They're having the cook's special, it's a bone broth veggie stew."

"It sounds delicious," Mykill answered with a small smile.

"I'll be right back with those." She gave us a quick wink and rushed off.

I frowned at Mykill, wanting to ask him why he wasn't ordering for himself. But when I looked over at him, that fire was gone and back was that vacant expression. The one where I couldn't tell what he was thinking. The one that made me nervous to ask questions, for the fear that I would sound like a fool.

"Where are we?" I reached for my glass and took a large gulp of water.

"This is a small human village called Ropland. It's mainly unincorporated, so they don't get very many visitors."

I nodded as I downed the remainder of my water before placing it before me. Our waitress returned a few minutes later with heaping bowls of steaming soup and a large basket overflowing with biscuits. Mykill stirred his soup around, blowing on it. I didn't pay it any attention, I fixed my sights on the basket of bread she had given us. I thought I saw a semblance of a smile pull on Mykill's lips, but when I glanced at him, it was gone.

As I waited for my soup to cool enough for me to eat, I buttered and ate two of the biscuits. They were some of the fluffiest ones I'd ever had. They were still a little doughy in the middle, just like I liked them. By the time I began on my soup, Mykill was already finished with his. He didn't hurry me though, he leaned back, dropping his arm across the chair beside him as we struck up light conversation.

After we finished eating, Mykill settled the tab and we were back on the street after taking a recommendation for a reputable Inn for the night. Mykill didn't seem up for conversation. Everytime I looked at him, storm clouds brewed in his eyes. His brow was drawn down, and his face a little pinched, as if something was wrong. I wanted to ask him what was bothering him, but I thought better of it. Knowing him, he would tease me, avoiding the question entirely.

"Hello!" The Innkeeper hollered as Mykill pushed open the door.

A bell rang as we stepped inside and the rickety wood creaked beneath our boots. A pudgy man appeared moments later through an arched doorway.

"We've got one room left for the night if ye'd like it." His short red hair stuck up in all directions, like he'd run wet hands through it and he was chewing on what looked like a grain of wheat.

"We'll take it," Mykill said softly as he approached the chest height counter. "It has two beds I assume?"

The Innkeeper shook his head. "It doesn't, I'm sorry, Lad."

He glanced back at me and I shook my head nervously. Butterflies erupted in my stomach at the thought of us sharing a bed.

"That's alright," Mykill answered. "We'll take it."

The Innkeeper smiled and began discussing the terms for payment. But I drowned them out as I stared at Mykill winged back.

"It's the last door on the left up the stairs and down the hall," the Innkeeper said and gave us a key before disappearing back through the doorway he had appeared from.

We both used the small shared washroom at the bottom of the stairs. Separately, of course, before readying to head towards our room.

Turning towards the set of stairs he referred to, I began climbing them. I heard Mykill follow behind me, and as I climbed the stairs, I could feel how close in proximity he was to me.

"Don't worry," he whispered, his cold breath brushing across my shoulder. "I'll sleep on the floor."

I only nodded as I continued up the steps. My breath quickened and my hands shook from nervousness. Would he hold true to that? Did I want him to?

The room was smaller than the Innkeeper let on. He said there was plenty of space but when we got in the bedroom, we learned how much he had exaggerated. There was nothing in the bedroom besides a bed, a rickety night table and a small dresser pressed up against the wall.

"Well, it'll do for tonight," Mykill said softly.

"It'll be better than sleeping on the floor," I countered jokingly, but my pulse was still pounding.

He placed both of our sacks on the dresser as he offered a small chuckle. He opened his, pulling out a fresh shirt and a pair of sleep pants. My breath hitched as I turned away. I kept my back turned from him as I heard the sound of him removing his trousers, and then his shirt before dressing again.

"You can turn back around," Mykill said softly.

I was surprised at how he didn't tease me as I looked at him. But there wasn't an ounce of amusement in his gaze. I thought I saw a trace of agony, but when he caught me looking too long, he slammed that icy expression down.

After he turned so I could change, I hurried over to the bed and slid beneath the covers. I didn't pay attention to Mykill as he arranged his bed on the ground beside the bed. I wanted to ask how there was going to be enough room for him to sleep but I couldn't bring my voice to work. Not only was nervousness crashing through me, but also guilt at the thought of him sleeping on the floor.

"Goodnight, Alethea," he spoke softly below me.

"Goodnight," I answered, my voice a higher pitch than I intended.

Rolling onto my side, I huffed out a breath and felt my brows slam down.

"What is it?" he asked, although I wanted to ask how he knew something was wrong when he couldn't see my face.

"I can't possibly sleep up here knowing that you're sleeping on the *floor*." I pushed myself up slightly. "Let's switch."

"*Absolutely not*," he said, clearly appalled.

I grumbled again and threw myself onto my back. I knew I shouldn't offer this, this could very easily blur the line of the friendship we had established. But I couldn't let him sleep down there on the wooden ground.

"Just lay up here," I breathed and began scooting towards the wall.

He was silent for so long I thought he was going to say no, or ignore me. Either one was a very possible outcome.

"Are you sure?" he asked, a slight pain hiding behind his words.

"Yes," I grumbled. "Just get off the damned floor."

He shuffled around, lifting off the ground, then his pillow dropped on the bed besides mine. Then the bed creaked as he lowered onto the side. He moved slowly, as if he expected me to change my mind. I scooted further across the bed, giving him and his wings the space he needed.

The bed shifted as he moved closer to me and then something large draped over me, sealing in the heat. His arm brushed mine as he stopped beside me. I tucked my hands beneath my cheek as I closed my eyes. His wing trapped in the heat around us and it helped lull me to sleep.

***

I wasn't sure when I awoke again, but when I did the sun wasn't even up yet. But the steady sound of Mykill's breathing wasn't beside me. Opening my eyes, I searched through the dark and stilled as I saw his still form perched on the edge of the bed. His wings were folded behind him and he was hunched forward with his elbows resting on his knees.

"Is everything alright?" I asked as I shifted on my side.

He was silent for several long moments before he blew out a soft breath.

"I came to your room," he whispered.

I frowned as I rubbed my eyes with one fist and pushed myself up onto an elbow. "What are you talking about?"

He glanced down at his open palm, like there was something on it. But when I glanced at it, it was clear.

He didn't raise his head as he spoke. "I came to your room the night that I lost those three men."

My body stiffened and it felt like I was instantly awake. I sat up, clutching the blanket to my chest as I pulled up my legs.

"What were their names?"

His shoulders stiffened and I heard his breath hitch. "Bracken, Thomas, and Rash."

I paused, waiting for the words I could sense he wanted to speak.

"My men spotted the barren at the Coves and as standard protocol, they evacuated everyone so we could do a sweep through each level. But the barren were smart, they waited for us to evacuate everyone before attacking at the top of the cliffs, when most of my men were doing their sweeps and my people were the most defenseless," he paused as his breath hitched. When he spoke again his voice was so pained it made my eyes nearly water. "I just wanted to see you, the one face that can bring me even a semblance of peace. But when I got to your door, I could sense you were sleeping, and for once, you finally felt like you were at peace, so I wanted to give you that."

I opened my mouth to say something, his name, something comforting, anything. But it felt like my heart had leapt into my throat, silencing me. His words shocked me, stunned me to near speechless.

"Mykill," I finally managed to rasp.

"It's alright." He waved a hand to me. "I don't expect anything from you. I just wanted to be truthful with you-"

"Lay with me," I interrupted.

His head snapped towards me, his eyes wide in surprise. "I wasn't expecting anything of you-"

"I know," I interrupted again. "Just lay with me."

He remained glued to the spot for several long moments. Part of me grew uneasy, nearly expecting him to turn me down. But finally, he nodded and began moving towards me. He slipped back beneath the blankets as I laid back on the bed, resting my head on the pillow. I peered up at him through lowered lashes as he settled in beside me.

His arm slipped beneath me, curling around me and securing me to his chest. I rolled easily, letting him move me how he'd like. When he was settled fully on his side, he dropped his other arm around me, locking me into him entirely. I breathed out a sigh of contentment as I let my head rest on his chest. His chin rested on the top of my head, and he let out a deep sigh as I felt his body relax.

His scent engulfed me, wrapping me in its embrace. The scent of him, and the feel of him coaxed me into the best, most fitful sleep of my life.

***

Letting out a yawn, I stretched an arm over my head and went to roll over, but found I was constrained. A large head was resting on my chest and large arms were wrapped entirely around my middle. Looking down, the first thing I saw was a head of black hair sticking up in all directions. Then as my gaze travelled down, large feathered wings draped over my legs and over the side of the bed.

One of my arms was draped over his shoulders, with my hand tucked into the back of his shirt. I could feel the corded muscles running through his back even in his sleep.

The scene was peaceful, serene. I couldn't bring myself to breathe heavily, or even move. As I stared down at his face, it was the most relaxed I'd ever seen him. Usually he had a pained expression, or a neutral one whenever he'd put up that icy wall. But now, he looked almost boyish. I could imagine him as a mischievous child as he ran around with that single dimple in his cheek. I could imagine the heartbreak that ensued following it. Although he was stunningly handsome, he didn't seem like an intentional heartbreaker.

I didn't want to leave this moment, I didn't want it to end.

So I let my head fall back against the pillow, closed my eyes and slipped back to sleep. When I awoke again, Mykill was gone and there was a steaming plate of food beside me on the night table. Pushing up onto my elbows, I frowned, glancing around. Mykill's boots were gone and so was his pack, it was like he hadn't even been here.

Sitting up fully, I dropped the blanket as I slid out from beneath the covers. I noticed fresh clothes were set out on the dresser, as was a bowl of water and a washcloth. I stood, heading over to the bowl. I pulled my hair away from my face and dipped my hands in the cool water and washed it over my face. After I did that a few times, I used the rag to wipe at my face, drying it and I folded it back and placed it on the dresser.

Changing quickly, I stuffed my clothes back in the sack and sat down on the bed as I finished my food. It wasn't more than an egg with a fresh biscuit and jam, but it was enough to appease my hunger.

I perked up as the door opened, and Mykill slipped inside.

I placed my plate on the night table and stood. "Where did you go?"

He glanced over at me, but there wasn't an ounce of *anything* in his eyes when he did. It was like they were emotionless. "I was using the washroom and struck up a conversation with the Innkeeper."

He was lying. I didn't know how I knew, but he was lying.

"Oh," I said lightly, frowning. "How did you sleep?"

"Well, and yourself?" He didn't look at me as he took my freshly packed sack from the dresser and turned towards the door.

"Good," was all I said as I stared at him.

He nodded. "I'm glad, are you ready to be on your way?"

Shock radiated through me at his cold reaction. I wanted to ask him what was up his ass, but I refrained as I brushed by him and began down the hall. I didn't wait for him as I flew down the stairs, nearly taking them two at a time. I felt a heat set over my palms as anger burned through me.

I could see that icy wall settling between us, sealing me out as he followed me down the stairs. He paid the Innkeeper and we were on our way. He didn't stand too close and didn't let his gaze linger too long on me. He insisted we wait to take flight until we were at the edges of the city, so I followed behind him as we did just that.

"Are you ready?" he asked as we reached the edge of the city. His voice was almost clipped as he stared down at me.

As I stared back up at him, I swore a piece of me shriveled up, curling in on itself. We had come so close last night, so close to whatever this was between us. But now he was slamming that wall back up, and in the process cutting me off from him.

I tempered back my glare as I looked away and bit my tongue. "Yes." I stepped towards him as he outstretched his arms and slid them around me.

This time, his touch was nowhere near as comforting as it had been. It was tentative almost, nearly unwanting.

The remaining hours of our flight were strained. I kept my arms crossed over my chest the entire way, refusing to speak to him, or even look at him.

I nearly groaned in relief when the spires of his castle came into view. We dropped into the training grounds and I couldn't have headed to my bedroom quicker. With a brief goodnight and thank you, I was in my rooms, changed and hunkered beneath the blankets as I let my anger stew.

Chapter 9

Mykill

I paced across my study as I recalled the soft touch of her hands as she placed them on my chest, then the feel of her body pressed into mine. Then the sound of her soft breath as she lulled off to sleep in my arms. I had laid awake for what felt like hours, in awe of the feel of her against me, of the care and tenderness she had shown me.

Even now, it baffled me. But it had also scared me nearly out of my skin. She had been there for me, cared for me, and in turn, I had shut her out. I had taken every ounce of that trust and care and slammed it back in her face when I lowered that wall between us. I could feel her anger when we flew home. I could feel it through her hands as she placed them on me. I wouldn't tell her, but her hands had burned into my skin the entire time.

But I could also feel it through our bond. She didn't know how to shut down her emotions through the bond as I did. So I felt every single one of them the entire flight home.

First, confusion flittered down the bond. Then, shock, more confusion, and then anger. She was so, so angry with me.

I wanted to apologize, I *needed* to apologize because my actions had been childish.

But since we had been home, I only seen her briefly at breakfasts. She was usually finishing hers as I came in to start mine. She had requested Felix and Cadmus keep training her.

So like the coward I was, I gave her the wide berth she requested. I made sure I didn't hear her stepping through the halls before turning a corner. I would give her the space she wanted, if that would make her happier. But the more space I let grow between us, the more anger I felt radiated through the bond. But whenever I saw her, that anger was still there.

My thoughts were cut off as a knock sounded on the door. I spun around and gripped the handle as I nearly ripped the door off its hinges.

Felix stood on the other side with wide eyes. He had noticed my restless attitude and the anger that loomed so close to the surface without interacting with her. He remained still, waiting to see if I'd snap at him or not for interrupting me.

"Yes?" I asked, forcing myself to be slow.

"I just came to report that Alethea fell and bruised her arm today." His eyes were wide, as if he expected me to lash out at him.

But I knew it wasn't his doing.

"Come in," I breathed as I stepped away from the door.

I heard Felix close the door behind him as he stepped inside to give us privacy. I walked over to one of the sofas and dropped onto it as I let my head hang.

"How badly was she injured?" I tried to keep the growl from my voice as I pinched the bridge of my nose.

"She just tripped when we were headed inside," Felix started. "She banged her arm up pretty bad on one of the steps and it immediately started bruising. She waved me off though and went back to her room. I'm sorry sir, no matter what I tried, she would not go see a healer."

I waved a hand, silencing him. "I know it wasn't your fault, and I know she's not one to be easily forced into doing anything."

I ran a hand through my hair, and lounged back on the sofa.

"Has she said anything to you?" I asked.

Felix and I didn't have a casual relationship, but I felt comfortable enough with him to ask about her.

"Honestly, sir, she seems tired. I don't think she's sleeping well." He lowered his gaze. "But no, she hasn't said anything."

I blew out a breath and dropped my head. She didn't want me anywhere around her, I knew that, but I didn't know how much I should push her.

"What do I do?" I asked, exasperated. "I mean, how do I get her to talk to me?"

Felix blew out a sigh. "I think you should speak to her. Give her a piece of yourself, that will show her you value her friendship."

I nodded.

He was right.

"Thank you," I said softly.

"Of course." He bowed his head. "Is there anything else?"

"No," I replied. "But I will pick up with her training tomorrow." I wasn't going to give her much of a choice.

"I can still join you two to help keep the fighting to a minimum," Felix teased.

"That's not a bad idea," I chuckled as I scrubbed my hand down my face.

After telling Felix to meet us at her normal time, I headed back to my room.

The sun had set hours ago, and I had gotten a sliver of sleep, but she haunted my dreams. So I resorted to pacing in my study to ward off the sleeplessness.

She would be getting up for breakfast within the next couple of hours, though I wasn't sure when exactly. I could wake one of the maids and ask them.

I walked quietly down the hall towards the dining room, debating on when I thought she would be coming to breakfast. But instead of waking up a cook to ask when she normally came down, I decided to head to the dining room and wait for a cook to bring out breakfast, they would have adjusted her eating schedule after the first day of her showing up early.

So, I sat at the table and waited.

She came in within the hour, and the cooks had served our food just minutes before.

Her face lit up in shock as she turned the corner and then skidded to a stop. Her mouth fell open, and her eyes nearly bugged out of her head as she stared.

"What are you doing?" she breathed.

"Having breakfast." I motioned to my untouched food, still steaming. "Join me."

She shook her head. "I'm actually not hungry." She spun around, heading towards the door.

I could feel the anger rippling through the bond again. I made a mental note to teach her how to block that off if she didn't want me to feel it.

"Alethea, please," I called softly.

But she didn't stop, she disappeared from the dining room entirely. I shoved away from the table and chased after her.

"Alethea!" I called again as I rounded the corner into the hall.

"Why did you act so cold after the Inn?" she shouted as she spun towards me and cocked her head to the side.

I hated when she did that. I also hated it when she looked at me like that, like she was close to berating me, or slapping me.

"What do you mean?" I said coolly.

I saw her teeth grind as her shoulders strained, preparing for a fight. "Why did you act so cold after the night at the Inn? Are those words not clear enough for you?" She bit every word out on a growl.

I should've known playing dumb would bring out her angry side. I had only brought it upon myself.

Sliding my hands into my front pocket, I strolled towards her. Her back straightened as I neared her.

"Why, love? Did you want me to continue holding you? Caressing you?" I smirked as I saw her shiver.

She stepped back, away from me, only for me to match her steps. She jumped slightly in surprise as her back hit the wall behind her. When she looked up at me, it looked as if she was biting her tongue.

I could feel every ounce of desire that rolled off of her body and into mine. I wonder if she could feel mine?

I wanted to ask her, to tease her, but she wasn't one that took to teasing well. If I pushed her too far, she might make good of her promise and castrate me.

"I just want an answer," she bit out. "A truthful answer."

I froze. I had already been truthful once before with her, and I had pushed her away by the next morning. The words had been painful to get out even then. I hadn't wanted to share with her, that's why I had waited until she had fallen asleep to drown in them. But now I wondered if she had felt them, even in her sleep, and woken up because of how strong the emotions were.

I hadn't realized how long I had been silent until she spoke.

"I should've known you were a coward." Her words hit me square in the chest as she slipped out from between the wall and I.

I couldn't move, I couldn't even breathe as I let her words settle over me. They suffocated me, choking off my breath because she was right. I was a hateful coward.

Spinning towards her, I strode after her. I hadn't realized I had remained frozen so long, so long that I'd almost let her slip away and down the hall. I reached for her, gripping her elbow as I spun her towards me. Her eyes widened as she stared back up at me. I was sure my gaze was feral, *she* was driving me feral.

"I've never shared those feelings before with someone else," I said before she decided to smack me. "I've never even spoken those words aloud before. You were the first, and if I'm being honest with you-" I paused as I sucked in a breath. Whatever she was doing to me was going to have me bearing my whole heart before her. I would rip it straight from my chest and hand it over to her to do with what she pleased.

She cocked her head to the side and I felt my knees almost wobble at the sight. She could nearly get whatever she wanted with that look. It could wither away any form of self control I contained.

"I'm not deserving of your friendship, Alethea," I finally spoke the words aloud, voicing one of my largest self-doubts. It loomed over me night and day, threatening to suffocate me. I thought of it every time she smiled at me, every time she even looked at me.

I was not worthy to be in her presence.

Her face fell.

"But you are deserving," she whispered as she stepped up to me.

She placed a hand on my chest, and I sucked in a breath. My body remained frozen, waiting for her next move as she pushed up onto her toes. Her other hand fell on the side of my face as her brows furrowed. I wanted to rub my thumb between them to coax them upwards. She shouldn't be frowning over me.

"You're more than deserving," she whispered again as her lips brushed mine.

Disbelief rocketed through me as she pulled closer to me, resting both of her hands on the sides of my neck as she kissed me. We had kissed once, but that had been fear fueled. She had almost been murdered. I had been coated in her blood, and heard her rattled breath. It had been wrong at the time for me to kiss her.

But this time, it was purer. Our friendship had strengthened, and I hoped her fondness for me had too.

I surged forward, the tight hold I had on my self control snapping in half entirely. We moved backwards until her back hit the wall. She moaned into my mouth as her arm slid around my neck as she pushed up onto her toes. She flattened her chest to mine and I curled my fingers into her hips to the point of near bruising. I wanted to brand her taste into my mouth, I wanted to wear her scent as my own personal cologne so I smelt her wherever I went. Everything she was, I wanted.

She made another breathy sound that had my heart tumbling in my chest as her other hand gripped onto my bicep. I slid a hand up her curves, gripping her cheek, my grip softer this time. I angled her head backwards, deepening the kiss.

This was what our first kiss should've been like. I could feel her care pouring out of every touch and kiss.

She had done well hiding her feelings from me, but now that we were mouth to mouth, there was no denying it.

But although it was so right, it was still so, so wrong. I didn't want to consume her, I wanted her to grow into her own person and there was a part of me that felt if I did claim her, she'd halt. Not because I would smother her, but after her experience with Eryx, I feared that it would leave a permanent impact on her, a permanent fear that she could never measure up, she was never strong enough and she was never good enough; And I didn't want her to feel any of those things. I wanted her to want me, I wanted to be with her, but most of all, I wanted to build her up. I wanted to watch as she took on the world, claiming who she was. I wanted to watch as her smile grew more confident and the pain that haunted her became something she used instead of feared.

Pain could become a great weapon when wielded properly. It could fuel us to do better, be better. But for some it became a crutch, one they used as they halted, basking in it in a way that affected them entirely.

So I did what I knew I needed to do, but hated.

I pulled away.

She gasped for breath as I dropped my forehead to hers. My thumbs stroked across her cheeks, taking in her smooth skin before I had to inevitably release her, before I had to put that wall back up between us. Because in order for her to continue growing, I needed to stay back, giving her the freedom to do so.

"Felix is probably waiting for us," I whispered.

Our lips were so close that they brushed as I spoke. I pulled away more, opening my eyes as she did. Those ruby eyes glittered with questions as I dropped my hands and stepped away. I ran a hand through my hair as I continued putting distance between us. I straightened as I cleared my throat.

"You should probably change, I'll send your food to your room."

Hurt flashed across her features and I wanted to gouge out my own heart at the sight. But she nodded. "Okay," she spoke, her voice nearly breaking. "I'll be out there in a few minutes."

She spun on her heel, not giving me another chance to speak before she disappeared around the corner.

Alethea

Slamming my door behind me, my breath pounded in my ears as I leaned back against the door. My lips still tingled from his kiss, and I could still feel the ghostly touches of his hands as they cradled my face. My cheeks heated as I touched the tips of my fingers to my lips.

We had kissed once before, but it had been nothing like that.

But as I stared up at him before retreating, I could see that damned wall forming behind his eyes again. The wall I wanted so desperately to pick at until it shattered.

Grunting, I shoved off the door and moved towards the wardrobe. I changed into a pair of tights, my boots and a fitted long sleeve. We were merely practicing with my powers today, so I had the option to dress more comfortably rather than in my leather fighting gear.

As I laced up my boots, I contemplated how I was supposed to act when I faced him. What were we? Were we friends? Lovers? Enemies?

No, we hadn't been enemies for a long time, though he grated on my nerves most times.

Pushing up from the bed, I tightened a sheath around my thigh for my dagger before heading out towards the training grounds. Both Felix and Mykill were waiting for me, their heads bowed together in quiet conversation.

Their heads perked up as I cleared my throat.

"Alethea," Felix greeted.

"Hi," I smiled lightly and then my gaze slid over to Mykill.

"I was just informing Felix that we'll be heading to Emerald Mountain in the morning," Mykill spoke, straightening.

It felt like my heart deflated. "Oh, and when will you be back?"

He cocked his head to the side, his gaze narrowing on mine. "We all will be going, Alethea, including you."

I perked up at that. I offered him a small smile. "What will we be going there for?"

"To form an alliance with them."

I briefly remembered Eryx telling me about their powers. I mainly remembered the shadow blades and how it had been used to kill his father.

"Are you trying to get shadow blades from them?" I probed.

His eyebrow shot up in surprise. "Now how did you know about those?"

"Eryx told me about them. He told me how one was used on his father." Mykill nodded and watched me, waiting for me to continue. "Can they be used on the barren?"

"And mages," he answered. "They will be our one advantage if we have to go to war."

"I was told that mages are stronger than fae, is that true?"

He nodded again. "Yes, infinitely. It takes at least three of our strongest to defeat one of their mediocre."

My jaw dropped in disbelief. "How are we supposed to go to war with them if they are that much stronger than us?"

"We've beat them once before. We were nearly wiped out but we did win."

"Why do they hate us so much?"

"They think they're superior to us, with their powers and their immortality."

"I thought fae were immortal?" I asked, cocking my head to the side.

Mykill shook his head. "In comparison to a human life, we are. But there are some fae who die and wither of old age, while others live for centuries, it's not really known. But mages will live for eternity unless killed."

I frowned, mages, fae, elves, they were all so similar yet so different. It was all a little overwhelming to understand, especially since I had only heard of fae, and the stories I'd grown up hearing were gravely wrong.

He inclined his head towards me and gestured to Felix to begin. There was no warmness in his gaze, not a welcoming feature. I was met with cold, hard ice.

We started off with the basic, summoning balls of fire. At first it had been easy, but the more we practiced, the more tired I became. We had started practicing regularly since the attack in the human lands, but I had only had my powers for a few short months, compared to other fae who had them since birth. Mykill said it would take quite a bit of time before using them repeatedly wouldn't tire me out.

His presence behind me was distracting. I sensed every move he made. I could sense the distance between us, and hear his every breath, reminding me of his heavy breathing in the halls of his castle. Then I'd see glimpses of his hands on me and I'd lose focus, the flames sputtering out as I did so.

I glanced at Mykill once and I swore I saw the semblance of a small smirk on his face.

"Again," Felix commanded.

Taking a breath, I planted both of my heels into the dirt and outstretched both of my hands. Flames unfurled from my palms, engulfing the mass of trees before us that were already burnt from the hours we had already spent practicing. The amount of flames I was able to summon kept diminishing.

We had been practicing since after breakfast. Mykill said that practice would help the exhaustion I felt after I used my powers. I withdrew the flames back into my palms and heaved a breath.

I dropped my arms and hung my head as my breath labored in my chest. My hands shook as I placed them on my bent knees as I hunched over. My hair stuck to the back of my neck, the frosty air coming from Mykill was a welcoming reprieve.

"She's exhausted," Mykill said as the icy breeze chilled the air around us. Goosebumps rose across the back of my neck as I shivered.

"I'm fine," I shook my head as I brushed a strand of hair behind my ear.

"You don't want to push yourself too hard, you'll collapse," Felix said. "We're done for the day, get some rest."

Felix turned, headed back towards the castle and I grumbled as I swung towards Mykill. I tried to glare, but even that felt hard.

"I could have kept going!" I argued.

Mykill cocked an eyebrow at me. "Throw a ball of fire at me."

I frowned and then raised my hand in front of me. I summoned a ball of fire and as I went to cock my arm back, it flickered and sputtered out. My mouth fell open in indignation as I stared at my empty palm.

"Go get some rest," he said as he turned from me.

I huffed out a breath as I followed after him. My legs felt like they quivered as I stomped behind him. Damn him for reading me so well and being right.

"Can I borrow your arms?" I grumbled as I slunk behind him.

Mykill stopped walking and turned towards me. He didn't say anything as I draped an arm over his shoulders as his arms slipped beneath me. My eyes slipped closed as he lifted me to his chest. I rested my forehead against his neck and listened to the sound of his breaths as he began walking again.

The lull of sleep nearly pulled me under entirely as we made our way inside.

"It will be easier the more you practice," Mykill said, stirring me.

"I feel like I've been running for days." My arms and legs burned and my heart rate had yet to slow.

"It's harder to learn your powers when you're older," Mykill merely said. "We grow up harnessing our powers. We grow up with them being apart of us, so it will take some time for your body to adjust from the force of them. Think of them as another life force."

"So you're saying that I operate on the same level as a child?" I grumbled.

Mykill's chilly laugh echoed through the hall and then I heard the sound of my bedroom opening. "I'm just saying it will take some time, and lots of rest."

I grumbled again as he laid me down on the bed. The thick mattress was a godsend as it enveloped my aching body. Rolling onto my stomach, I mumbled a thank you as he pulled my boots off. I heard them drop onto the floor and then a blanket was draped over me. I swore I felt the ghostly remains of a hand that skimmed up my back longingly before it disappeared. I didn't stay awake long enough to say a word.

Chapter 10

Alethea

Grumbling, I rolled onto my back as I blinked against the sunlight. I frowned as I rubbed at my eyes. The sound of my roaring stomach made my eyes widen as I pushed myself up onto my elbows. I surveyed my room. It was empty but there was a tall glass of water on my nightstand.

I nearly toppled over the edge of the bed as I reached for it. I pulled the glass to my lips and threw my head back as I downed the entire thing. I gulped and set the glass down on the nightstand and shoved the blanket off. I was still in my fighting leathers, but my boots were propped up at the foot of my bed.

The memory of Mykill taking them off flitted back to me.

I glanced at the window again and frowned. It had been mid afternoon by the time we were done practicing which meant I slept until the next morning, or I hadn't slept long at all. The rejuvenated feeling flitting through my limbs hinted at what I thought, but disbelief rocketed through me as I hurried into the washroom.

I drew myself a warm bath and poured in the healing salts before slipping beneath the water. I groaned as the ache in my muscles instantly soothed. I hadn't realized how draining training would be on my body. It took more out of me than physical training.

After bathing, I changed quickly and braided my hair in two braids on the side of my head that I conjoined at the base of my skull and draped it over my shoulder before heading to find Mykill. But it was no mystery where I would find him, he was always in his study.

My legs burned as I made my way down the hall. But the burn was a welcoming feeling. It reminded me that I was learning something new, that I was growing into who I was meant to be. It was also a reminder that I would be able to protect myself no matter the circumstances, that I wasn't a helpless human anymore.

"Good morning," Mykill greeted as I pushed open the door to his study without knocking, and then cocked his head to the side, still without looking at me. "Or I should say good afternoon."

"Good afternoon?" I frowned at him.

"You've been asleep since yesterday afternoon."

"You let me sleep an entire day?" I nearly shrieked as my stomach roared.

"You obviously needed it," he answered.

"What if I was dead?" I demanded.

One corner of his lips tipped up as he turned the page, still not looking at me. "Do you think I would have let my mate go more than a couple hours without being checked on?"

I felt the color drain from my face, much like it did every time I was hit with the realization that we were mates.

"So you came into my room?" I asked, my voice carried less of a bite that time.

His head finally lifted and his gaze met mine. "I did."

"Hmm," was all I said.

His eyes remained glued to mine. The tension built between us, making me slowly bounce from foot to foot.

"What about going to Emerald Mountain?" I finally asked.

He didn't answer for a moment, his face remained unreadable before he finally cleared his throat. "I was waiting for you to get rested."

"Thank you," I said softly as I ducked my head to watch my conjoined fingers twiddle. "Thank you for not leaving me here."

"Your welcome," he simply responded and then cocked an eyebrow at me as my stomach roared again. "I would suggest going to the dining room so you can appease the beast residing in your stomach."

My brows slammed down and my hands fisted at my sides. Irritation prickled beneath my skin as I flung around and stalked out of the room. I could feel him follow behind me. But he was right, I headed straight for the dining room. I took a seat at the table as he slipped into the kitchens. He reappeared minutes later with a bowl in one hand and a plate in the other.

He placed down the bowl first and it was brimming with a deep brown broth with chunks of hefty meat, potatoes and vegetables like carrots and celery floating near the surface. He placed the plate down next with a large slice of bread and a dollop of butter rested in the center of it.

"Thank you," I said as I quickly picked up the spoon.

Mykill didn't say anything as he regained his seat across from me. I took a small bite and nearly groaned as the broth hit my tongue. Rosemary, pepper and a slew of other spices danced across my tongue and down my throat as I swallowed.

"Did a maid make this?" I said as I lifted the spoon to my lips again.

"I did, actually."

I snorted, the spoon slipping from my fingers. "*You made this?*"

He frowned, offense crossing his features. "I'm offended that you think so low of me."

"All I ever see you do is train me and read, how else was I supposed to know?"

"I'll have you know I cook meals for myself regularly. The kitchen staff is there for me when I don't want to."

I rolled my eyes. "Of course, they're there to serve you at your beck and call."

Mykill stiffened. "They're there so they have a constant flow of income for them and their families."

My mouth fell open, partly in shock, partly in guilt.

"That's kind of you," I finally said and turned my attention back to my bowl.

There I went again, constantly thinking the worst of him when he had shown me time and time again that he wasn't that kind of ruler. He didn't use his status to belittle people, he used it to help others in every way he could.

"It's heavenly," I added on as I brought another spoonful to my lips and refocused on my food before me.

The silence between us that normally came so naturally, was taut with tension. I was aware of every breath he took and every move he made. I didn't tear my attention away from my food as I drained the bowl and finished off the slice of bread. I hadn't noticed the glass of water he'd placed in front of me until I looked up, and I downed that to cool down my throat.

"Thank you for lunch," I breathed as I pushed up from my seat.

I heard his chair scrape along the floor as he followed after me. "Alethea, wait."

I turned slowly, but I couldn't bring myself to look at him.

"I'm sorry," I whispered as my gaze remained rooted on the floor. "I don't know why I always assume the worst of you when you've done nothing but continually show me the best."

My entire body stiffened as his cold thumb stroked across my cheek. I hadn't heard him breathe, much less move. The tips of his fingers danced across my jaw and he slowly tilted my face up. Our eyes clashed, electricity thrummed in the air around us. Then I felt the familiar heat of my skin as a fire ignited beneath my skin.

"I'm not angry with you," he breathed as his thumb stroked across my cheek again.

My eyes snapped up to meet his and it felt like his eyes froze me to the spot. There was the slight sound of hissing around us and I knew it was his ice and my fire meeting. He always seemed to do that to me.

Everything that had built between us, the glances, the touches, the flirting, all of it had built and built and built. We were fools to think it wouldn't eventually explode in on us, especially with our last kiss neither of us seemed to want to acknowledge.

My breath came out in wicked short breaths as his hand cupped my face entirely. He inched closed, our noses brushing before his lips brushed mine once, then a second time, prodding me. But I wasn't as timid as I once was, there wasn't an ounce of me that was nervous to kiss him back as I slid an arm around his neck and pulled his chest into mine. He groaned into my mouth as I opened my mouth to his.

I groaned back into his mouth as our tongues clashed. His hand cupping my jaw became firmer, possessive almost as it curled around the back of my neck, keeping me to him. His other hand slid around my back and rested on my waist before pulling me closer. As our bodies made contact, I slid an arm around his neck as I pushed up onto my toes.

His hand around the back of my neck slowly slid around until it gripped my jaw firmly and tipped my head back. His mouth peppered kisses across my cheek and jaw before moving beneath it. I dropped my head back as his mouth descended down my neck, leaving goosebumps in its wake. My fingers curled into his shoulder as I melded more to him.

"We can't be doing this," Mykill whispered.

My eyes fluttered closed as his tongue stroked across the shell of my ear. "Then why do you keep touching me?" I gasped.

"We can't do this, neither of us want this." His hand slid down to the side of my neck and his fingers curled around the back of my neck.

It felt like a knife slid into my chest at the words and every ounce of courage in me deflated. I stepped away and only nodded.

"Good afternoon, King." I bowed my head and before he could get out another word, I swung around and slipped into the hall.

I didn't hesitate to let the door slam behind me. My feet stomped off the marble floors as I made my way back to my room. I waved my hand and the door flew open and bounced off the wall as I stalked inside. I closed it behind me, softer this time, and leaned my back against it.

I growled out a string of curses as I pushed off the door. He made me so damned angry. My hands fisted at my sides as I began pacing. If he didn't want it, why had he kissed me?

Glancing out the window, I cursed and threw the door back open. I would rather die than eat dinner with him later.

I found a stray guard and requested dinner be sent to my room. I wasn't sure how Mykill would react, but I also didn't care. He made it clear that he didn't want this, when it had been more than obvious that I did. How had I let this stupid man affect so much of my emotions? I grumbled to myself as I stalked over to my bed, plopped down on it and buried my face in my hands.

My heart longed for another soul to talk to. I missed Lira, she was a grumpy, but loving soul. I missed my sister so badly. She had always been the first one I'd run to when problems arose. I wanted so badly to tell her of Mykill and the way he had acted. She would swoon after I told her how he looked. Then she would jokingly tell me to suck it up because of how attractive he was. But then she would tell me not to settle.

I sniffled lightly as I raised my head and squeezed my eyes shut against the onslaught of tears. Rising from the bed, I headed into the wardrobe and pulled out a pair of leggings and a tighter long sleeve blouse, they weren't leathers, but I wanted to be more comfortable. I changed quickly and slid on my training boots.

Pushing open the door, I glanced up and down the hall before stepping fully out. I prayed to the gods that Cadmus wasn't in some study somewhere and was in his room. Knocking on the wood, I crossed my arms in front of me as I waited for him to answer.

I breathed a sigh of relief as the door cracked open a moment later. Cadmus was wearing his glasses, which meant he was reading. I cringed inwardly.

"Oh I'm sorry, I didn't mean to interrupt. I'll just go back-" I started.

"It's alright," Cadmus said as he opened the door fully and peered down at me. "Is everything alright?"

"Yeah everything's fine. I had simply come to ask if you wanted to train with me for a bit?"

"Of course," he answered immediately. "Let me just get changed."

I nodded and stepped back. He closed the door and emerged minutes later dressed in more casual training gear like mine.

My entire body felt taunt as we strolled down the hall towards the training grounds. "I heard you had a strenuous day yesterday?"

I laughed. "I nearly drove myself into the ground. I wasn't aware that training my powers would be so difficult."

"Oh, I'd assume it's brutal," he responded as he stepped aside and held the door open for me.

Stepping out onto the balcony, I breathed in deep, breathing in the crisp fresh air. We walked the remainder of the way to the training grounds in silence. I listened to the sound of the waves crashing at the bottom of the cliffs, and the sound of chatter that got carried with the wind up to us.

"What would you like to do?" Cadmus asked as he stepped onto the training mat and turned towards me and propped his hands on his hips.

I sighed. "Let's just do some basic sparring."

He nodded and then raised up his fists. "Let's see what you've got."

I chuckled lightly as I copied his movements and we fell into a rhythm of jabs, spins and kicks. Fighting was slowly becoming more and more similar to dancing. It was all just footwork and being agile. When I jabbed, he ducked, when he spun, I jumped. We fell into a perfect rhythm with one another.

"How are you liking it here?" I asked as I ducked his blow and rose again, rearing back with a strike of my own.

"It's definitely an adjustment," he answered truthfully.

His shoulder absorbed my blow, but he stepped back, clearly unaffected.

"Do you like being here?"

I sucked in a breath as my steps faltered. Cadmus caught up quickly, dropping his arm, that would have been a crushing blow if I hadn't moved.

I opened my mouth to respond, but then snapped it closed. I wasn't entirely sure where our relationship stood anymore, so I decided on, "It's been welcoming."

Cadmus' lips picked up into a side grin. "That sounds like you have a lot of unspoken words."

My shoulders sagged as I heaved out a sigh.

"I don't want to talk badly of him because I know he is your friend."

Cadmus' eyes glistened with grief lightly before hardening again. "You can speak freely, Alethea. I know he didn't treat you as you should have been. You can be honest with me. I may be his friend, but I also know his downfalls."

"I just feel lost," I admitted as my shoulders sagged. "After everything with Eryx, and the secrets and lying, I find it hard to let someone else in."

"But Mykill?" he prompted.

I whooshed out a breath and nodded. "Yes, but also no at the same time. It seems even harder to let him in, but then sometimes I feel like he's already there."

"It's because of the mating bond, it will tell you things about each other," he interjected.

I nodded understandingly before continuing. "But now he seems like he doesn't want it either, like he doesn't want me, and I don't know what to do."

"Well I would say that's a lie," Cadmus chuckled as he picked up a set of daggers and extended one towards me. "If you want my true honest guess, I would say he's just as terrified of letting you in too."

I didn't answer, unsure of what to respond with. Part of me felt like he was right, Mykill had expressed that he hadn't felt deserving of my friendship, but what if it was more than that? Or worse, an excuse?

"Do you want to know my true honest opinion as *your* friend, Alethea, not Eryx's?" Cadmus asked.

"Of course," I breathed as I palmed the dagger and waited for his next words.

"I think he treats you well, better than Eryx did. I think you've grown into a fuller, more confident person," he paused, contemplating his next words. "I think that he didn't know how to handle you being able to defend yourself. I think he wanted you to rely on him more than what was healthy, and when you wanted to stand up for yourself, it made him question his masculinity. It's something I think he's always struggled with and that's all he's ever known. He's been the protector of his people for hundreds of years and instead of letting you be his partner for him to lean on, he wanted another subject and I don't think you deserve that. I think you deserve someone who pushes you, challenges you and applauds your growth."

My mouth fell open as I processed his words. True shock emanated across my features, I was sure, as his words truly sunk in.

He raised his dagger in a fighting stance, prepared to move on to another part of training.

"You're a good friend, Cadmus," I finally breathed as I readied myself for his attack.

***

Grudgingly, I rolled out of bed and into the washroom to bathe quickly and dress. My ladies maids were waiting for me by the time I emerged from the washroom to help me dress. One of them braided my hair from the top of my head down to my waist. Not a single hair strayed and she didn't adorn it with any pearls or berets like I thought she would.

As I stood from the vanity, I stood admiring myself. I looked like a warrior. My body had filled out, I could feel the strength coursing through my body and you could see the muscles, although slight, that adorned my arms when I wore my dresses. My face was slimmer but somehow fuller. My red eyes didn't appall me every time I looked in the mirror anymore. They were once a sign that I no longer looked like my mother, but now they were a reminder of the strength I possessed.

They were the eyes that had frozen two dragon, saving hundreds of lives.

Turning away from the mirror, I thanked my ladies maids. I shoveled down the hefty strips of bacon and the muffin they had left for me before heading down the hall to join Mykill and the others.

As I exited the front doors to the castle, my feet paused as I laid eyes on Mykill. He was speaking to one of his men. But it seemed he sensed me too as I noticed his back stiffen. My hands clenched at my sides as I marched towards the crowd preparing to leave. I knew Mykill expected me to go to him since he was normally the one who flew me, but I couldn't think of anything worse.

Mykill waved the man he had been speaking to away as he turned towards me.

"We don't need to speak of what happened yesterday," Mykill said quietly as I stopped before him.

I merely nodded. I didn't have it in me to keep up a conversation with him, not after he had rejected me.

"I'm going to fly with Felix," I said and then brushed past him.

I wasn't going to give him the space to respond, not after how he acted last night. It was clear I had wanted him. We had danced around each other for long enough. Last night we had come toe to toe with our affection for one another and then he practically slammed the door in my face. I wasn't feeling particularly friendly.

Felix stiffened as I stopped before him. "Can you fly me?"

He bowed his head. "Of course." I nodded and turned, staring out at the cliffs before me as I waited for the remainder of our group to make an appearance.

I could sense Mykill's gaze lingering on me from afar, but I refused to look at him. If this was the choice he was going to make, then he had to live with the consequences of them.

"Are you ready, Alethea?" Felix spoke behind me.

I turned and nodded as I stepped up to him.

Chapter 11

Alethea

Emerald Mountain was exactly as I'd imagined it. With rolling green hills surrounding the mountain. The city was what I'd imagine the heavens would look like one day. All of the buildings glistened in the sunlight, sparkling like none of them had ever once been dirtied. Cream colored spires loomed far up into the clouds with flocks of birds floating past.

In the streets below, I could make out the bodies of the elves that strolled through the streets, though they were too small to describe their appearances.

Felix angled, circling one of the spires as we neared it. Mykill followed behind Felix as he swooped around one of the spires. I shrieked as I clung to Felix. The air ripped at my braid, pulling strands free that whipped around in the wind. I clenched my eyes closed as I gripped onto Felix's vest. His arms beneath me tightened and then I felt him straightening and then his feet hit the ground.

My eyes peeled open as they did and I nearly launched out of his arms. I would never get used to the feeling of my stomach dropping out from beneath me.

I froze as Mykill stopped before me. His face, which normally remained unreadable, displayed irritation. His hands clenched at his sides and I watched as his jaw worked. If we were alone, I was sure he'd speak. But as his eyes slid behind me to Felix, that mask of cool indifference set across his features. Mykill brushed past me without another glance and I ground my teeth.

I turned as the massive set of double doors opened. The deep groan rumbled beneath my feet and blew my braid over my shoulder. Three men walked in a line towards us. Each one of them wore a lightly braided crown on top of their heads and all had identical orange pin straight hair that rested on their chests. Their amber skin glowed in the sun, making them look like the Divine. The man in the middle stepped forward. He was dressed in a flowing tunic that reached his knees with golden bands around his biceps. Rings adorned his fingers with jewels so large they looked like they were more annoying to wear than anything else.

"King Mykill," the tall man bowed his head with his palm on his chest. "And this must be Alethea, daughter of the Gods."

I paled and shook my head. "Please, just Alethea."

The corner of the man's lips tipped up and his eyes narrowed but he nodded. "*Just* Alethea, it's a pleasure. I'm Valdom." He bowed his head again and turned back to Mykill. "It's been a few hundred years at least. Your letter didn't explain much."

"We can discuss the details I left out in private," Mykill responded.

I bowed my head in respect towards Valdmon and as I met his eyes, I felt them devouring me even though I was fully clothed. My skin felt like it was crawling as I stepped partially behind Mykill who met Valdom's gaze head on, understanding my uncomfortability.

"Where would be a good place for us to discuss the details?" Mykill asked but his voice dripped with a promise of violence if Valdom didn't avert his eyes.

Valdom's beady gaze slid away from me to Mykill and his lips tipped up in a cruel smile. "This way," he said softly as he stepped aside and motioned for us to follow.

One of the two men behind Valdom watched me with an intensity I couldn't read. I stared back until he turned away, following Valdom as they led us down the long hall.

I kept pace besides Mykill as we followed the trio down the hall. Popping up onto my toes, I leaned into his side and Mykill angled his head down for me.

"Who are the other two?" I whispered.

He glanced down at me and then back towards the three men. He pointed a finger at the one on Valdom's right. "Those are his younger brothers. That's Broncrias, the second oldest and Heliar, the youngest."

I nodded. "Are they all King's?"

Mykill bobbed his head up and down. "Yes, they rule together but Valdom is the deciding head."

Valdom waved his hand and another set of doors opened into what looked like a meeting hall. The table was long enough to seat at least twelve people on either side.

"Is there a place my men can rest?" Mykill asked as he stopped at the threshold.

I continued walking past him but stopped as his hand brushed the back of mine and he gently pulled me back towards him. Valdom turned towards us and his eyes shot to our conjoined hands. A small smile pulled at his lips.

"Yes, if you continue further down this hall there is a sitting room with lounge chairs. I can have the wait staff bring your men food and drinks."

Mykill bowed his head and released my hand as Valdom turned and took up residency at the head of the table. I watched as his brothers silently flanked him. I frowned as they crossed their hands behind their backs. They acted more like guards than Kings.

I turned towards Mykill as he addressed his men, instructing them to wait down the hall. Only Felix would remain with us. Finally Mykill turned back towards the table and didn't look down at me as he strode past me towards the table. He took the seat on the right of Veldom. I sat beside him with Felix on my left but he remained standing, much like Broncrias and Heliar.

"I must say, you're quite the union," Valdom smiled as he leaned back. "Tell me Alethea, how is it jumping between Kings?"

I cringed inwardly but didn't answer. Mykill's head cocked to the side and I could feel the roll of his emotions as his anger heightened.

"We are not here to discuss Alethea's love life, that is no one's business but her own." Mykill crossed one leg over the other and draped an arm across his knee.

"Even if it involves you?" He responded and I felt the ice descend upon the room.

"I am involved with no one," I bit out before settling in my seat.

Valdom's eyes slid over to me and he seemed to contemplate my answer before looking back at Mykill.

"So what do we owe the pleasure, Mykill? I have to say the last time we met it wasn't for good circumstances."

I made a mental note to ask about that later.

Mykill sighed and his wings flared on either side of him, surely for dramatic effect, before they settled behind him. "I'm sure it is not lost on you that the threat the Barren pose has grown."

Valdom only nodded.

"Then you surely must know that war is coming. So I've come to offer an alliance with the elves."

"Elves haven't partnered with the fae in centuries. Your kind is reckless!" Valdom spat back.

I watched as Mykill cast him a look of pure disdain as he admired the rings adorning his knuckles. "And elves are cowards."

I felt my face pale.

"I can promise you that if we don't partner, Eryx and his men will tear through here and crumble every semblance of peace your kind has made. My men can offer you protection."

"King Eryx would simply be appeased if you gave him his mate back," Valdom answered and then sneered in my direction.

"Their mating bond was broken," Mykill answered coolly.

"What does that matter? The Fates destined them to be together and that stands regardless of their mating bond being intact or not."

Mykill clicked his tongue and then chuckled. "Valdom, I have to say I think your old age is catching up to you."

Valdom's face nearly went red as he sputtered.

"*They're* mates," Broncrias said.

Valdom glanced back at his brother who was staring at us in wonder. "Impossible! That's never happened before!"

"Smell them," Heliar answered this time.

Valdom stiffened at the command but I saw his nostrils flare. His eyes widened as his gaze bounced back between Mykill and I.

"Impossible," he whispered breathlessly. "How did this happen?"

"As you know Alethea was human when their mating bond was broken. She is no longer human and the bond set in after she was changed." Mykill explained quickly, refusing to hash out the details of everything that shifted when I was changed.

I picked at the end of my braid but refused to look down at the light orange of it.

"Then it's true then," Broncrias spoke softly.

"Quiet, brother," Valdom hissed as he threw him a glare over his shoulder.

Broncrias shook his head without looking at Valdom. "I will partner with you. Even if Valdom does not, I know there are elves here who will. This prophecy is an omen from the Divine."

Mykill watched Valdom for a moment before he bowed his head. "Thank you."

Valdom slunk into his chair and grumbled. "Will you please leave us? We have matters to discuss."

Mykill nodded once and rose from his seat. The sound of his chair scraping along the floor echoed throughout the room, then the sound of my chair followed.

"We will summon you when it's time for dinner," Valdom said without looking at us. His heated gaze was pinned on his brother behind him, who was not cowering.

I wanted to watch them. I wanted to know why they thought so differently.

"Come on," Mykill said quietly as he placed a hand on the small of my back.

I cast him a quick glance before ducking my head and turning. I followed behind Felix, my eyes finding themselves focused on his wings as we walked.

Felix broke off as we entered the hall, joining the other men who were lounging in the sitting room. Their roaring laughter echoed down the hall and I smiled as I peeked in.

"Walk with me?" Mykill's voice caused me to jump.

I whipped towards him and balked. "What?"

He extended his arm towards me. "Walk with me?" he asked again.

I frowned and glanced down at his arm and then back up at his face, but there wasn't a hint of insincerity in it. Still with a frown, I stepped up to him and slipped my arm in his.

"Most elves are cowards," Mykill explained as he began to lead me down the hall.

I didn't know what to say as I followed his lazy stroll. We passed a couple more sitting rooms before he waved a door open and ushered me inside. The room was simple with a lush green carpet and cream colored walls adorned with paintings of fields and flowers. There was a golden circular table in the center of the room flanked by two chairs with cream cushions. I walked over to the table and ran my fingers across one of the place settings. The door clicked shut behind Mykill causing me to stiffen.

"Alethea?"

I didn't look at him. "Yes?"

"Look at me," he said softly.

"Why?" I demanded and then frowned.

"What is it?" he asked.

"What is it?" I repeated and then scoffed as I spun towards him. "You rejected me. You kissed me and then *you* rejected me. You can't just expect me to act normally."

"I thought you didn't want this," he answered as he tilted his head to the side.

"I didn't at the time, but times have changed." My voice dropped as I answered and then I stared down at his chest, needing to look anywhere but his eyes.

I heard him blow out a deep breath but I interrupted him before he could get a word out. I was too anxious to hear anything he had to say.

"We should go train for a bit."

"I'm sure we can find some sparring mats." He didn't look at me as he made to leave the room but my feet remained rooted to the spot as the question I'd been pondering on ate at my insides.

"Why do you keep pushing me away?"

Mykill's shoulders stiffened. Then he sighed and turned to face me. His gaze was pained as his mouth pinched.

"I don't want to be loved because a prophecy says so, or a mating bond says so," he said as he stepped closer to me, facing me fully. He paused, cocking his head to the side as he seemed to contemplate what he would say next.

"I have always danced between the lines of good and evil. I don't want a mating bond to determine what you will think of me. I want someone to love me on unbiased terms, to *choose* to love me, to *choose* me for who I am."

"But by not telling me, you took *my* choice from me," I responded.

"Just leave it Alethea," he sighed and went to turn away from me. "Come."

I didn't move and he paused as I remained frozen. My hands fisted at my sides as anger stirred in me as I glared up at him. He wasn't going to get me to obey so easily. He slowly turned back to face me fully and stepped up to me.

"I said, come." It was a command.

He towered over me, his brows drawn down in a glare.

"I am not your pet!" I growled at him.

Quicker than he could track, I brought my fisted hand up and my knuckle cracked as it came in contact with his cheek. Mykill let out a harsh laugh as his head was thrown back and he stumbled.

My breath quickened, adrenaline took over my body as his head snapped towards me. Steely cold fire danced in his eyes and they narrowed as he massaged his jaw.

"Do it again," Mykill growled as he stepped dangerously close to me.

My heart leapt into my throat and I took a step back into the table. I gripped the sides as he stepped into me. Our chests brushed as he leaned in and placed a hand on either side of me.

"Do what?" I stammered.

"Do it again," he repeated. "Defy me, insult me, laugh at me, roll your eyes at me. I can promise the repercussions will be rewarding."

His voice had dropped to a whisper and he had leaned in so close that our noses brushed. One of his hands moved as quick as a viper and gripped my chin roughly.

"Do. It. Again."

A ball of fire formed in the bottom of my belly. I should've cowered. I could see the demon lurking inside, readying to be set free.

But instead I said, "Don't tell me what to do."

I couldn't prepare myself for the brutality of his lips. All the air was sucked from my lungs as his hand tightened on my chin and he pushed me onto the table. He shoved himself between my legs and plastered our bodies together. One of his hands snaked around me and fisted in my hair at the base of my scalp. I hissed into his mouth which he then took advantage of as his teeth hooked on my bottom lip. My fingers dug into his biceps as they flexed beneath the leather.

I needed his shirt burned.

"Let's go to my room," he breathed against my mouth and tugged my head back as his lips continued their trek down my cheek and jaw.

I merely moaned in response.

An arm slid around my waist, pulling me closer and then he lifted me. My legs locked around his waist as he began to move towards the door. I wanted to ask how he knew where his room was or how we were going to get there without anyone seeing us. But my voice couldn't seem to work other than unintelligible moans.

Every ounce of the feelings we both had been fighting, surged to the surface and threatened to consume us. I clung to him as he began to climb a set of stairs, but his assault of my mouth never wavered.

I groaned into his mouth as he slipped a hand beneath my blouse, splaying his icy hand against my burning back.

I wanted to devour him like I was starved.

His hand fisted in the back of my hair, wrenching my head back. I hissed as my back slammed into the side table and things clattered to the ground - very expensive things. I gripped either side of his neck and hauled him to me as my lips claimed his.

I wanted him, needed him like I needed air.

My skin heated at his touch, my powers surging to the surface, in response to him. A clap of thunder sounded outside and I smiled against his lips as his teeth tugged on my bottom lip.

A crack of lightning lit up the foyer as we scuttled across the room in a tangle of teeth and limbs.

We weren't going to make it to his room and he knew it too as my hands traced down his chest. I undid his belt and shoved his trousers down and he gripped the backs of my thighs and lifted me against him. I finally got his shirt off and tossed it over my shoulder. His teeth moved down the side of my neck as I clung to him. My back hit another wall and he mumbled something under his breath - then my clothing was gone.

I smiled again as my fingers curled into the strands of hair at the base of his scalp. His hand did the same as he tipped my head further back. A shiver made its way up my spine as he dropped his face into the crook of my neck. His teeth skidded across my skin and one of his free hands palmed my breast.

My moan filled the room as he slammed into me, filling me. I cried out as fire sprung from my hands, catching the curtains on fire. But a gust of wind ripped through the room, blowing it out.

He didn't even have to look up.

"Let's not burn the castle down, love," he teased breathlessly as his lips found mine.

"Shut up," I hissed into his mouth, swallowing his chuckle.

A hand slid up to grip the curve of my breast while the other dug into my hip. The touch was bruising, imprinting me - just like he had. This kind of love was consuming, claiming, and damn any soul that tried to take him from me.

"Let me hear you," he growled into my ear, sensing my unraveling.

My chest heaved, the fire burning through my abdomen. The tension built and built until I couldn't take it anymore. Time seemed to still as I tried biting into his shoulder to stifle my cry. But he would have none of it as he gripped my throat and shoved my head to the wall. My head fell back and thudded against the wood as he moved into me again and I cried out, this time shattering. My breath came in labored pants as my fingers curled into his biceps, and he went crashing over the edge with me.

Chapter 12

Alethea

I felt my skin burning into his. His skin returned like the touch of ice. A cloud of steam floated around our bodies.

The light reflecting off of his eyes made it seem like his eyes were glowing, illuminating every silver fleck in them. He seemed to still as the pad of my thumb brushed beneath his cheekbone. He was so beautiful, so god-like.

His next kiss was tender against my lips. I closed my eyes as I relished in the feel of him, his scent engulfing me as he exhaled loudly.

"That was my first time as a fae, is it always like that?" I said between breaths as I dropped my head back against the wall.

Mykill's responding smile was something truly devious as he leaned his face to mine. "That was just your first time with me," he said and then *licked* my bottom lip into his mouth.

I couldn't help but laugh against his lips as he began kissing me again, before I could call him an arrogant bastard.

Placing me on my shaky legs, I clutched his arms to remain upright. He laughed and within a moment, swept me back up into his arms. I shrieked as I wrapped legs back around his waist and draped my arms over his shoulders.

"What if someone sees us?" I asked.

"No one will see us, I've glamoured us." He didn't look at me as he answered.

He began moving down whatever hall we had stumbled into. His eyes remained glued behind me for several moments before they slowly slid back over to me. All of my senses went on alert as he angled his face towards mine, our noses brushing. His lips pressed to mine again, but softer this time. I wanted to pull away and ask how he knew where he was going if he couldn't see, but I couldn't pull my lips from his.

This kiss was lazy, explorative as his tongue probed my lips. It swept into mine as I yielded to him. With an arm secured around my waist, his other hand slid up my spine slowly before resting on the back of my neck. His fingers curled around the base of my neck and I let out a breathy moan. He answered with a chuckle before pulling away. The hand that rested on the back of my neck, pulled away and brushed down my hair once before he stopped.

I glanced over my shoulder, taking in my surroundings. We were in one of the most elaborate washrooms I'd surely ever been in. It had golden walls with vines and florals engraved from floor to ceiling. There was a gigantic clawfoot tub behind me.

"What are you doing?" I asked as he placed me down on the bathmat before the tub.

"Drawing you a bath," he said as he gently nudged me to sit down on the lip of the tub. "It will help with the shakiness."

I couldn't muster a response as he reached over me and turned on the faucet. The sound of water running filled the empty space around us. I watched as he checked the temperature before pouring soap from one of the many bottles resting on the ledge behind the tub.

"Here," he said softly, drawing my attention.

I stared down at Mykill's extended hands before me. So many thoughts and emotions spiraled around inside of me, it made it hard for me to grasp that this was truly happening. First, we had gone from kissing and him rejecting me, and now this man was drawing me a bath. It was all just so confusing. *He* was just so confusing.

Steeling a breath, I took his hands and he helped me to my feet. He spun me slowly around as his hands dropped to my hips and he led me towards the bath.

I watched as he first stepped into the water, and then turned, extending his hands to me. He helped me as I stepped over the side of the tub, and then I watched as he lowered himself down. My body reacted instinctively, following his movements as I lowered myself. I turned, laying back against him. He picked up the rag that was draped over the side of the tub and dipped it into the soapy water.

"So we're taking baths together now?" I raised an eyebrow but didn't elaborate as he wrung the rag out.

The water ran down my chest, causing goosebumps to rise across the surface of my skin. He dropped an arm around my waist, pulling my back flush to his chest. His knees jutted above the water on either side of me. I had thought that this bath was gigantic, but with Mykill, it didn't seem that large after all.

"You were right," he finally sighed.

"Right about what?" I prodded.

I felt his breathing stall for a moment. "It was wrong of me not to tell you about our mating bond, and to continue pushing you away. I truly didn't know what to do because you were with Eryx and you hated me-"

"You annoyed me," I corrected.

I sensed his smile which caused me to relax in his embrace. I let myself recline fully against him and felt the soft kiss he placed on my bare shoulder. The light touch traveled down to the tip of my toes, making me feel fuzzy.

"But you were right. I should have told you and I'm sorry." He heaved another sigh. "I feel like I'm sometimes still coming to terms that we're still mates. Not because of you, but because of me. I'm not a kind person like you, Alethea. I am selfish and rude-"

"And arrogant and prideful," I finished for him as I sat up and turned towards him.

His wings were draped over the side of the tub. The sight of them still marveled me.

I straddled his hips and placed my hands on either side of his neck. "But you've saved my life on more than one occasion. You've also been my friend as I navigated everything that this treacherous prophecy has thrown at me."

I felt a hand settle on the small of my back, and smiled lightly as his fingers played with the ends of my hair.

He merely stared. He stared as a storm brewed in his eyes. I could see so many pent up emotions raging war in his icy eyes. Guilt, regret, sadness, all of them fighting for domination.

"I saw what Eryx's love for you did to him and I never want my love for you to do that-"

My eyes widened as I cocked my head to the side. "You love me?"

His eyes focused on mine again and for just a moment, they softened as he nodded. "Yes, Alethea. Very much."

Disbelief coursed through me as I stared at him with wide eyes. "How?" I breathed as my mouth fell open.

He raised an arm from beneath the water and placed two fingers beneath my chin and pushed my mouth closed. "I can't tell you for certain when because I was not expecting it. But I fell in love with the voracious woman who punched me because she didn't like that I bossed her around. I fell in love with the woman comfortable with the silence sometimes and wasn't pushed away by it. You showed me what it's like to be a kind person even through all the misery you've endured. You, Alethea, are what I aspire to be."

His words settled over me like a coat and as he leaned towards me, the mask that was always there fell and I saw his true self. The tortured, lonely soul who had spent a lifetime searching for his kindred spirit.

One of his arms tightened around my waist as he pulled me closer and placed a dripping wet hand on my cheek. "I'm so thankful for the woman you are, Alethea."

Woman, not girl.

That replayed in the back of my mind as his lips met mine in a searingly tender kiss. I felt another piece of my heart, of my soul, mend as he tightened his hold on me and moved his lips softly against mine.

I shivered as the tip of his finger traced across the peak of my breast.

"We should probably leave our room," I laughed as I swatted his hands away.

Another smile pulled at his lips and my heart nearly crumbled at the sight. I couldn't help but smile back as I leaned into him and draped my arms around his shoulders. He leaned into me, his lips brushing mine once more. I sighed in contentment before pressing my lips to his. He laughed against my mouth before pulling away.

"Let me grab you a towel," he said quietly and slid his arms out from around me.

I scooted off of him as he rose out of the water and stepped out of the tub. I watched his powerful body as he strode across the washroom. Water dripped down every curve and indent of the muscles that rippled through his body but I couldn't bring myself to care as I followed each and every one.

He smiled knowingly as he extended his arms towards me. I reached up, his large hands enveloping mine as I stood. He helped me out of the tub and I watched as he knelt down. He grabbed my left ankle and gently lifted it. He lifted his head, his eyes finding mine as he ran the towel up my leg, absorbing the water.

It felt like my heart did a somersault in my chest as he leaned towards me, placing a kiss to the inside of my knee. My heart kicked up in my ears and if I could have swatted the damn thing, I would've. Slowly he set my leg back down and did the same with my other leg. This time, he let his fingers slide across my skin, and by the devious smirk that pulled at his lips, he had done it on purpose.

Rising up, I lifted my arms as he wrapped the towel around me. He knotted it at my chest and then brushed my hair over my shoulder. I offered him a smile before he leaned into me and dropped a kiss to my forehead.

Then, he grabbed the second towel for him and dried off.

I made my way into the bedroom and dropped onto the bed. I watched as he dressed and then draped the towel on the counter. His eyes slid to mine and I felt myself inhale as those icy eyes burned into me.

He stalked towards me slowly, his eyes never losing their intensity.

"You can't stay in here forever," he teased.

He pecked a kiss to my cheek as I pulled the towel tighter around me. "I'll meet you out there soon. I just want to dress and braid my hair."

"I can stay if you'd like." He offered me a smile that I knew was more devious than he tried to play it off to be.

"No," I laughed as I shoved at his chest. "Go, I'll be out soon."

"Fine," he receded but winked before spinning around.

The door thudded shut behind him and I chuckled to myself as I headed over to the wardrobe against the wall. As I opened it, I shuffled through the dresses until I found one that didn't require a second set of hands. It wasn't anything fancy, just a simple satin gown that cinched around my waist and long sleeves that billowed around my wrists. It was a deep brown, and I found a pair of matching strappy sandals that I made a note to ask Mykill who could make these for me in every color.

I braided my hair on either side of my head and then conjoined the two braids into one, before draping it over my shoulder. Pushing up from the vanity, I checked myself in the reflection once more before heading towards the door.

I pushed open the door and jumped in surprise as a large body crowded me backwards.

Everything moved too quickly for me to track.

Something cold pressed against my neck and then the sound of it locking into place echoed throughout the room.

I stumbled back as I gripped the lock of the collar that rested around my throat. Disbelief rocked through me as I yanked on it to no avail. My mouth fell open as my gaze stared up into all too familiar cider eyes.

"Eryx?" I gasped as my hands flew up to the steel now resting around my neck.

I raised my hands to throw him backwards but nothing happened. He merely stared at me as I tried again. I tried throwing flames but it was like I was empty.

"What did you do?" I gasped.

He merely glared.

Every muscle in my body tensed as I spun on my heel and ran towards the door. He was on me in a second. He flipped me around and slammed my back into the door. He smashed his palm over my lips to silence my scream and pressed my wrists into my chest. My eyes widened as I fought against his hold. Shadows emerged around him and trailed up his arms and wrapped themselves around my wrists. They cinched around my wrists and Eryx dropped his hands but before I could shout, a band of shadows wrapped around my mouth silencing me. I shrieked as best I could as I fought against the shadows. Another one wrapped around my waist, lifting me off the floor as he turned his back to me. As I was lifted off the door, he opened it and began out into the hall.

Mykill appeared in a doorway with his hands chained in front of him. There was an identical band around his neck, rendering his powers useless. One of his eyes was swollen shut and I felt like my heart stopped as I noticed the spikes that protruded from his wings. His mighty, beautiful wings were coated in his blood as he was shoved forward.

"Alethea," he gasped as his gaze fell on me. "Eryx, I will kill you."

I couldn't call to him as the shadows dragged me behind Eryx. Eryx didn't even spare him a glance. I shrieked as Mykill disappeared behind me.

Eryx didn't glance back at me as he continued down the hall. I tried twisting and turning but no matter how hard I struggled I couldn't free myself of the shadow bindings.

Eryx stopped and as my gaze snapped towards him, Valdom smiled back at me. "I see you've got what you've come for."

"You upheld your part of the deal, I shall uphold mine. Four of my men and their dragons will remain constantly posted around your borders."

Valdom nodded but his gaze didn't leave mine. "She's truly a beautiful creature."

My eyes snapped to Eryx as a low growl emanated from his throat. "Watch it, Valdom."

Valdom's eyes slid over to Eryx and his lips grew into a smile. "Apologies, Eryx." He bowed his head without looking back at me. "Safe travels back to your kingdom."

Eryx brushed past him without another word. As he exited the castle, my eyes fell on Adrius. I hadn't seen him since I'd left Eryx's kingdom. His scales glistened under the sunset.

The shadows dropped me to my feet and I turned to run, but Eryx dropped an arm around my waist and hauled me back. With my back flush to his chest, he mounted Adrius, who shifted unsteadily as he glanced back at us. This would be the first time he witnessed us like this, with me as Eryx's prisoner.

The word settled over my shoulders like a ton of bricks.

"Let me go," I demanded as I pulled against Eryx's arm.

"Quiet," he answered gruffly.

I shrieked as his hand gripped my jaw and titled my head back.

"Eryx, you better let m-" I was cut off as he dumped the remains of a vial in my mouth.

I hissed as he covered my mouth and then pinched my nose closed. The liquid pooled at the back of my throat as I fought my best to not swallow it. I coughed and sputtered but as I tried inhaling a breath, I swallowed it.

Panic took over my body as I thrashed against him. The shadows banded around my chest, stilling me as Eryx released my face. My mouth fell open to berate him but as it did, my words slurred out of me. I slumped into Eryx's chest as my heart rate slowed and my limbs turned into what felt like liquid. My head fell back on his arm as he took to the sky. I couldn't even feel my stomach drop out from beneath me as the sky above me grew fuzzy.

**

My coming to was not as peaceful. Pain felt like it was splitting my head in two. I tried mustering strength to speak, or call for Mykill, or even just a grumble, but I couldn't muster a thing. My throat was so dry that it was almost painful to swallow.

"You promised that once the mating bond was completed that she belonged to me," a muffled voice argued.

I groaned as I forced my eyes open. My vision was watery, everything danced as I tried to force myself to focus. Rolling onto my side, the effort nearly draining me, I stared at the form beside me. Mykill. His eyes were closed and he too had an iron collar around his neck. His eye was swollen and there were bruises peppering his cheeks, jaw and neck and more that disappeared beneath the fabric of his tunic.

"Mykill," I managed to rasp. "Mykill, please wake up."

He stirred at the sound of his name and his eyes flew open but they were heavy. The collars around our necks had to be keeping our bodies from burning through whatever sedative or poison they had given us.

"Alethea," he gasped and grunted as he extended his arm towards me.

I reached for him and linked hands with him. The touch comforted some of the fear in me. His head fell back as his eyes slipped closed again and mine followed. All I could hear was our heavy breaths as whatever was in our system slowly began pulling me under again.

Someone grabbed my wrist and I winced as the tip of a blade dragged across it. I forced my eyes open again and a set of hands grabbed onto Mykill's wrist and held it down as they cut it open. "What are you doing?" I mumbled as I was dragged closer to him.

No one answered as they lifted up my wrist and placed it to his lips and did the same thing with his wrist. I felt the droplets of his blood hit the back of my throat.

They were completing our mating bond.

I couldn't fight it as the warmth cascaded down my throat and traveled to the tips of my toes and fingers. I could feel *him* in every fiber of my body. I could sense every breath, every heartbeat and every minor movement in his body.

I gasped as my chest tightened. I heard Mykill gasp beside me as I was sure the same thing was happening to him.

My back arched off the ground as a new sensation filled my body. It wasn't painful, more comforting as a strange warmth filled my body. Emotions bombarded me from every direction, but they were mine. They were *his*.

I gasped as I flattened back on the ground, and Mykill's emotions and entire being washed over me. It was the purest form of ecstasy.

"The bond is complete," someone spoke above us.

My fingers found Mykill's again and they tightened reassuringly around mine.

I whimpered as a blade dug into my arm again, but deeper this time. It tore from my elbow down to my wrist. I heard the sound of a second blade brandishing and as I opened my eyes, I saw another man leaning over Mykill as they did the same on his arm. They used the tip of the blade to draw three circles down the first line. My eyes fell closed as they continued. I felt my blood pool over the sides of the cut and down my arm.

Something tugged in my chest as the ground beneath me began to rumble. The blood loss made me too weak to search for Mykill. My mouth fell open on a cry as I rolled onto my back. My back arched off the ground as my mouth fell open in a silent scream. I could feel something tethering itself to my blood, using it as an amplifier. Mykill's pain laced groan sounded beside me.

I dropped my head to the side and turned it towards him. His back arched off the ground as he cried out. His eyes were scrunched closed, his face contorted in pain.

There was something that resembled a low moan, and then the ground stilled entirely. Everything around me was eerily quiet, and then I heard soft footsteps approach above me.

"This is the girl the prophecy speaks of?" an unfamiliar voice said and I groaned as they nudged my ribcage with their boot.

"Don't touch her," Erxy growled above me.

"Do what you want with them," the unfamiliar voice laughed.

A set of arms scooped me up against a plated chest. I knew it had to be Eryx's plated chest, he wouldn't stand anybody else touching me.

"No," I groaned as I felt the distance between Mykill and I growing. "No, please."

"Alethea," Mykill grumbled and I heard him grunt and then the sound of chains.

"Bring him with us," a barren spoke and I felt my heart lurch into my throat.

"Mykill," I groaned as my head fell backwards. "Mykill, I love you too. I love you, I love you," I repeated over and over until I slipped under again.

Chapter 13

Alethea

I gained consciousness with a blistering headache. My throat felt like I had swallowed a handful of sand full of shards of glass. I coughed and then winced as I forced myself up on my elbows.

I heard the rattling of a chain and felt the weight of one around my wrist as I pushed myself up fully.

I blinked, letting my eyes focus in on the oddly familiar space around me. Cream walls, cream bedspread, golden vanity with a cream cushion. Memories of the space assaulted me. Me asking Eryx to hold me through the night after I conquered the Isle of Mirrors. I couldn't breathe through the terror that clogged up my throat as my fingers curled into the comforter beneath me.

My eyes snapped towards the doors as they creaked open. Cider eyes greeted mine.

"What are you doing?" I demanded as I scurried back until I was pressed against the headboard.

Eryx looked a heady mix of furious and exhausted. His hair was in a ratted bun and there were bags beneath his eyes. His jaw was colored with stubble and I could see the muscle clenching in his jaw.

"I brought you home," he finally said as he closed the door behind him.

I glared. "This is not my home."

Eryx laughed as he approached the end of the bed and placed his massive hands on the comforter. "This will always be your home, Alethea. Your mate will be killed and if you survive the bond shattering a second time then you'll stay here."

"If you harm him I will murder you," I growled and knew if I had my powers, my skin would have heated. Eryx laughed and reached for my ankle but I yanked it out of his reach. "Don't touch me."

"Believe me, Alethea, if I had taken him, his fate would have turned out much better. His death would have been swifter."

"Why do you want to kill him so badly?"

"Because he stole you from me," he growled between what I could have guessed were painfully clenched teeth.

"You pushed me away! Don't blame your actions on anyone but yourself. You chose to be a self-serving bastard and decided your secrets were more important than our relationship. Where we are now is your fault."

His jaw clenched and his eyes churned as he stared down at me.

"Who took him? What do they want with him?"

He shrugged and began to move around the bed. I could hear my heart hammering in my chest as I scurried across the bed as far as the chain around my wrist would let me.

I yelped as he lurched towards me and dragged me towards him. I clawed at the blankets as I tried crawling away on my stomach. He growled as he gripped my sides and flipped me onto my back. His shadows leeched out around him and circled around my wrists, effectively pinning them down on either side of my head.

I stiffened as he lowered down on top of me, pressing me into the mattress beneath him.

"You can learn to love me again," he purred as he ran the tip of his finger down the center of my chest until it hit the dirtied hem of my blouse.

I bit down on my lip as anger flooded me. I had been so fooled by this man. His pretty face and eloquent speech had fooled me once, but I could see what really lurked beneath the surface. A cunning, deceptive, self-seeker.

"I will *never* feel anything for you other than hatred. *You* took my mate from me and you better pray that the Gods protect you because once I'm free there's a death warrant over your head and I will come to claim it." There wasn't an ounce of fear in me as I spit the words.

That was what had changed first after separating from him. I didn't feel as timid and nervous like I'd always felt because deep down I had known if he had truly known me without the mating bond, he wouldn't have been attracted to me. He may have even left me in the dungeons in Kirin's kingdom from the beginning. Mykill had never made me feel like that, he encouraged me to better myself, to challenge myself and to stand up for myself. I just hadn't realized how soon I had begun to feel like that.

Eryx's eyes darkened as his face turned into a deep glare. I could hear the sound of his teeth grinding together. I waited for him to make his move.

"How do you feel now?" I smirked up at him as I taunted. "How do you feel now that you've turned into the very thing you promised to protect me from?"

His eyes turned murderous as he shoved himself off of me. I couldn't help but chuckle as I pushed myself up. The wall shook as the door slammed shut behind him. Pushing myself up, I looked towards the nightstand for anything that would help free myself. I slid off the bed and opened the drawer but it was empty. Cursing, I slammed it closed and stomped towards my - *the* vanity. I shrieked as the chain yanked me back.

"Lira," I gasped as the door opened and she slipped inside. Her lips were pressed in a grim line as she hurried over to me.

A cry slipped out as she threw her arms around me. "I'm so sorry, girl," she whispered as she kissed the side of my head.

"What's going on?" I asked as I pulled away. "Why is he being like this? What happened?"

"I don't know much. All I know is that he's broodier and partnered with the Barren King."

The Barren King?

My teeth ground together, if he were here I would have slapped him across the face.

"Can you free me?" I asked as I held up my shackled wrist.

Lira tsked her tongue and placed the pitcher she was carrying on the night table. "I'm sorry, girl. I'm not able to."

"What's going to happen? Where have they taken Mykill? Is the Barren King here? What of the Black Mage?" The questions all poured out of me as I continued yanking against the damn shackle.

Lira shook her head as she handed me the small plate with a slice of bread lathered in butter and jam and the small cluster of grapes still on the vine. My stomach roared at the sight of food and I snatched the plate from Lira's hand.

"How am I going to get out of here?" I shoved a couple grapes in my mouth. "Please come with me!" I exclaimed.

Lira nodded as she glanced back at the door. "I will figure something out. In the meantime, keep your head down and do whatever he says. I can't stay longer, but I will be back."

I nodded, although I wanted to beg her to stay. It was comforting having someone I knew was on my side. I watched as Lira retreated, closing the door behind her.

I ate the food Lira had left within minutes before settling back on the bed. I wasn't sure how much time had passed as I watched the room around me, searching for unknown threats. I had been hounded and attacked in this castle on more than one occasion, and I hadn't felt safe when I had lived here. But now that I was the enemy, I didn't trust a soul outside of Lira.

I perked up at the sound of the door opening. Two unfamiliar guards glided into the room and headed straight towards me. My fingers curled into the comforter as I began sliding backwards on the bed.

"We've been told to bring you to the dining room," one of the guards spoke as he gripped the end of the chain attached to the headboard and began undoing it. I watched as he pulled a key out, unlocking the lock, and shoved it back in his pocket.

"I'm not hungry," I retorted as I moved as far back on the bed as I could.

The guards ignored me. The one who had unchained me, gripped the length of the chain and then wrenched it towards him. I yelped as I tumbled forward until they were both gripping my arms and lifted me off the bed.

They kept their grips on my upper arms firm as they began leading me towards the door, not giving me much of a choice. I dragged my feet as they opened the door and led me out into the familiar halls. If I had thought the guards had been bad before with their side glances and sneering, they were even worse now.

Once they pulled me into the dining room, I saw Eryx sitting at the head of the table. He donned a neutral expression, as if this was any normal day. I tried halting as they continued bringing me forward, but in the end I lost. They pulled me over to the seat beside Eryx and shoved me down in the chair.

They pushed the chair in, sealing me in as I felt a power latch onto the seat. Eryx didn't look at me, but I knew it was his doing. He picked at the peppers and eggs sprinkled with a light orange cheese. He had a steaming cup of tea resting beside his plate and a biscuit resting on a napkin.

My blood felt like it was boiling as he continued ignoring me, as if I was nothing to him. I glanced down at my full plate, but I couldn't bring myself to eat any of it, even if I knew it was the right thing to do.

"Let me go, Eryx," I finally said. "You can't keep me here."

He cast me a quick side glance before continuing with his breakfast.

"Let. Me. Go. Eryx."

The sound of his knife echoed off the crystal plate as he set it down.

"Eat or you can go back to your quarters." He didn't look at me as he lifted the biscuit to his lips.

"I don't want to eat!" I shouted as I slammed a fist to the table. Glasses and silverware trembled, clinking off each other. "I want you to let me go."

"I'll wear you down eventually." He glanced at the guards stationed behind me. "Take her back to her quarters."

"Eryx!" I shouted as my chair was wrenched backwards and then rough hands clamped down on my arms before lifting me from my seat.

Spinning towards one of the guards, I let the small knife I had tucked in my sleeve slip into my palm. Gripping the handle, I aimed for his neck. He cried out as the knife embedded in the side of his neck. Blood spurted, spilling over the sides of the wood and coating my hand. I ripped the blade out and advanced on the next guard. I ducked beneath his arms as he reached for me. As I ducked, I swung my leg out in a large sweep. I caught him by the ankles and he went down in a heap.

Shadows slid up around me, sliding around my waist, pinning my arms to my sides. I screamed as the knife slipped from my fingers and clattered uselessly to the floor.

"Stop, Alethea," Eryx commanded.

I nearly laughed as I watched his jaw work from side to side as he ground his teeth. He towered over me, glaring down at me, as if willing me to obey.

"I will never stop. Every chance I get will be spent trying to escape from you. I will never love you, I will never call this place home, I will never be yours. I will always fight back." I raised my head a bit as I glared back at his glaring face. "You're going to have to kill me."

I could see the tremble working its way up his body. The temper he had done so well at hiding was so close to erupting on me and part of me wanted it to.

"Take her back to her quarters," he said gruffly as he stepped away and turned from me. "Now!"

The shadows from around my waist dropped but before I could fall to the floor, guards arms were encircling me. They dragged me backwards as I thrashed.

"I will get away!" I screamed as the arm around my waist tightened. "You won't succeed in keeping me from my mate!"

Eryx didn't turn back towards me as I was pulled out of the dining room. The guards grunted as they dragged me backwards as I kicked. I clawed at the guard's arm around my waist, but it did little to no good as he was wearing long sleeves.

As soon as they got me in the room, they shackled my wrist back to the headboard. I bit down on my tongue in outrage as they swept out of the room once they were sure I was secured.

I slid off the bed and screamed as I ripped the drawer out of the nightstand. I turned towards the door and chucked the drawer. It shattered as it hit the door. Splinters of wood exploded around me and I grabbed the nightstand and threw it too. It didn't shatter quite the same way but it still cracked in three pieces before falling in a heap on the ground. Turning back towards the four poster bed, I gripped the comforter and ripped it off the bed. It fluttered around my feet and I jumped up onto the mattress as I gripped the chain that connected to the headboard. I planted a foot against the head of the bed and threw my weight back. The sound of wood cracking sounded at my first attempt. I grunted as I gripped the chain tighter.

Wood splintered and the door was thrown open. It bounced off the wall, my spine stiffened as my head snapped to the side.

"Get down from there!" the guard exclaimed as he threw himself at me. An arm wrapped around my leg and yanked me down. My back hit the mattress and I rolled. The guard hadn't anticipated my strength, which gave me an advantage as I wrapped my arms around his neck.

As they did, so did the chain. Anger seeped into every fiber of my body. If I had access to my powers, I would have burnt his skin from his flesh and relished in it. Every moment here was a moment Mykill was in trouble.

As I tightened the chain, the sound of bone breaking sounded throughout the room. I didn't give the guard a second thought as I shoved his dead body off of me and stood to my feet. More guards poured in, their eyes wide as they took in the body at my feet.

A guard lunged towards me and threw their arms around my middle, pinning my arms down.

"Let me go!" I shrieked as the guard fell back on the bed with me.

I felt the prick of something in the back of my neck and a wave of nausea washed over me.

A shadow lingered in the doorway. A glint of black hair and tattoos revealed themselves and another wave of energy surged through me.

"Face me you coward!" I shouted.

He stepped out of the shadows, his wide eyes meeting mine.

Eryx's prone form was the last thing I saw before the darkness claimed me. He stared at me with wide eyes and his chest heaving. He looked at me like he didn't know me anymore.

I had warned him.

***

After I had awoken, I sat on the ground where the mess had been previously. I pulled my knees to my chest as I sat on the floor. The wreckage had been cleaned after they had sedated me and everything that was near the bed was now shoved out of reach. The splinters that had cut my skin had healed over before I had awoken.

I wasn't sure how much time had passed since I had woken up, but I could still smell Eryx's scent, which meant he had stayed in here after they had sedated me. The thought made my skin crawl.

I perked up as the door opened and a guard shuffled into the room. This time instead of him being accompanied by a single guard, he was accompanied by three. The side of my mouth tipped up in a smile as he knelt before me. I could see the hint of fear that lingered in his eyes but he didn't speak as he unchained the shackle from the headboard and used the length of the chain to wrench me to my feet. I didn't object as he dragged me down the hall behind him, passing guards who sneered wordlessly at me. They had hated me when Eryx had first brought me here, all because I was a human. But this time I had killed one of their own. If any of them were given a moment with me, they'd likely kill me.

The guard led me into the dining room. Eryx was seated at the head of the table with a half cleared plate before him. The guard led me to the place setting on the right of him, like I had sat when I had resided here.

I nearly scoffed as he pulled out my seat. I glanced down at Eryx, then at the brimming plate of food. My stomach roared at me to sit down quietly and play nice. Eat the food, and then go back to my vendetta.

"Sit," Eryx's voice echoed through the dining room as an invisible force pushed me down into the seat.

I grunted and clenched my teeth as I placed my hands on the table. That invisible force that I knew was Eryx, pushed my chair in. All without glancing up at me.

Staring down at the food before me, I picked at the eggs. I was only able to shovel a couple spoonfuls in my mouth before I dropped my fork. It clattered off the glass plate and Eryx's head snapped up, our gazes colliding.

"What do you expect from here, Eryx?" I asked calmly. "Do you expect me to be your Queen? Do you expect me to bear your offspring?"

His jaw clenched as his glare deepened.

"Eat your food," he growled as he picked up his fork and resumed eating.

I simply stared, waiting for an answer.

"If you don't eat, I will feed you myself," he growled.

I couldn't help but laugh as I slowly turned my face back towards him. "The High Priest did that to me once."

Horror splashed across Eryx's face as he physically recoiled. His mouth fell open, trying to find words, but I knew he'd find none. What I had said when he first brought me here continued to ring truer and truer. He had become everything he promised to protect me from, and he knew it.

He shoved himself up from the table, clearly rattled. He stared down at me as his chest heaved at the realization. His hands shook as he stepped away from the table, his eyes glued to mine. But I would not cower, he was the one who had done this, not me.

"Is something wrong?" I prodded as I cocked my head to the side. "You seem a little out of sorts."

His mouth fell open again, searching for the words. But like before, he found none. He stepped back once more before spinning away from me and stormed from the room.

The moment he was gone, a guard ripped my chair backwards, sending me stumbling to the floor. I grunted as I landed on my shoulder.

"Get up," one of the guards hissed.

Rough arms lifted me off the floor and to my feet as they began dragging me from the dining room.

"I thought I was supposed to eat!" I objected.

"We weren't given such instructions," the guard growled back as he wrenched my arms behind my back.

I cried out as he continued yanking me down the hallway. But with the grip he had on my arms, I didn't have the ability to fight back. I decided against fighting them and let my body go slack in his arms. We arrived in my room quicker that way. They tossed me inside and made sure my wrist was chained to the headboard securely before slipping from the room.

I paced as best I could with the chain still around my wrist, but the longer I paced, the hungrier I became. I rubbed at my stomach, willing the feeling to go away and then laid across my bed. I stared up at the ceiling adorned with intricate carvings of golden stems and roses that stood out elegantly against the cream wallpaper.

I hadn't realized how tired I was until my eyes grew heavier. Closing my eyes, I pulled my knees to my chest and drifted off.

Chapter 14

Mykill

My heavy breath echoed around me and bounced off the cell walls. There didn't seem to be much I could do to calm my breathing. My hands and arms had lost feeling ages ago.

I glanced up at them, noticing the blueish tint of them.

I was on my knees with my arms chained up above me on either side of me. There was a chain around my waist that was secured to the ground before me. But it was my wings that made it impossible for me to move.

Three hooks.

There were three hooks embedded in each of my wings. One at the bottom of them with a chain attached to the ground beside my knees. The second one the end of them, outstretching them to the point of near breaking, and then the third embedded at the top and securing them to the ceiling.

Three days. It had been three damned days since someone had come in here. My stomach had stopped growling, the hunger had slowly become part of me.

I raised my head as the dungeon door opened. My cell was at the end of my cell block, so it took a few moments before the light from the torch illuminated my space.

"Oh King Mykill," the Barren King smiled as he dragged a taloned finger across the bars separating us. "You look positively dreadful. Tell me, is there anything I can get for you? Some water, food, your mate perhaps?"

I dropped my head. "You don't have her."

He let out a deep chuckle. "And how would you know that?"

"I would feel her."

"Hmmm," was all he said.

"What do you want?" I growled

The cell door opened and I watched through slitted eyes as a barren slithered into the room like the animal it was.

I dropped my head back and screamed as the barren yanked on the chain connected to the tip of my wing. I felt the cartilage ripping. Fresh blood poured from the wound, pooling on the ground that was already stained brown from my blood.

"Nothing, just thought you'd like some company," the Barren King laughed.

"She will be rescued," I huffed. "My men will do everything in their power to rescue her. Eryx will not be able to keep her."

"We'll see," the Barren King laughed and then I stiffened as I saw another figure form from the shadows behind him.

The purple robe was the first thing I saw, then blonde hair. I recognized him. He had been Alethea's captor, the High Priest.

My blood boiled in rage as I remembered the first time I had laid eyes upon her. She had been in a skimpy outfit, I was sure had been for his liking. Her body had barely been concealed from me. But she had looked up at me with a mix of shock and bewilderment, but that had quickly changed once I spoke.

"I recognize you," he cocked his head to the side as he entered my cell. "You were the one who rescued Alethea, who took her from me."

"She isn't a piece of property," I spat back.

The High Priest stuck out his bottom lip in a mock pout. "Aww, love, how sweet." He stopped before me and lowered himself into a crouch. "We have great plans for you."

"Do with me what you will," I breathed as I dropped my head forward, succumbing to the pain once again.

Alethea

A clammy hand slammed over my mouth as another hand shook me vigorously.

"Alethea!" the voice hissed. "Wake up, girl!"

My eyes shot open, squinting in the dark. Lira's beady eyes gazed down at me.

"Wake up!" she hissed again. "We don't have much time!"

I sat up, my eyes adjusting to the dark space around me and then stared at the figure behind her.

"Lira, who is this?" I asked as I glanced at the maid behind her with her head still bowed.

Lira stuck her hand in her pocket and I gasped as she pulled out a key.

"Lira, what is that?" I whispered and then gasped as the maids body disappeared, the clothing falling at her feet.

"It was a glamour, I brought you a maid's uniform. Hurry, put it on. Cadmus is waiting for us in the woods."

"Cadmus?" I frowned.

"Hurry, girl," she hissed. "We will sneak out through some servant tunnels that lead to town."

Lira took my arm, yanking it towards her as she undid the lock. I nearly groaned in relief as the weight of the iron fell away. I pushed off the bed as I stripped my clothes and she helped slip the cream shirt over my head followed by the brown dress identical to Lira's. I slipped on the slippers and then tied the apron around my waist.

I didn't ask questions as she braided my hair in a crown around my head, pulling it from my face. She opened the door softly, and stuck her head out, searching for guards. When she didn't find any, she turned her head towards me and outstretched her hand. I reached for her and took it as I followed her out into the hall.

"Where are all the guards?" I whispered.

"Shift rotation," she answered without looking at me.

"Where are we going?"

"There are some tunnels near the servants quarters that lead out into town. We take them when we have to run out."

The servant quarters were on the other side of the castle. We would have to be quick if we wanted to get there undetected. Since Eryx had kept the guards posted on the outside of my room, I hadn't been able to learn of their routine, so I wasn't sure how much time we had.

We made our footsteps near silent as we scurried through the halls like two mice. We kept out breathing shallowly and refused to let go of one another. I felt my heart kick up in my chest as we neared the dining room, which would be near to Eryx's office. Thankfully we passed both undetected and were just passing the kitchen, when we rounded a corner.

My steps faltered as my eyes clashed with cider ones. But they were void of any warmth. Eryx was covered in an array of weapons, ones I was sure he wouldn't hesitate using on me if the time came.

His gaze narrowed in on Lira who stood behind me. My hands fisted as I took in his size. I could take him out if I was quick.

"Lira, run," I growled.

Eryx's gaze snapped back towards me.

"I'm not going anywhere," Lira responded and I could see her step up beside me out of the corner of my eye.

Eryx's jaw clenched and his hands fisted as his shadows billowed out from behind him. Lira threw her hand out just as his shadows pounced. I ripped the dagger she had given me from my belt as I ran towards him. This would be my only chance to take him down or he would likely kill us both.

Our bodies collided but I didn't cry out as our bodies went rolling. Eryx didn't care if I absorbed the blow of our bodies hitting the ground, he didn't try angling himself away as we rolled. All the breath whooshed out of me as he landed on top of me, hitting me square in the chest.

My fists beat at his chest, one of them coming into contact with his cheek. "You're a coward!" I shouted as I knocked his head to the side.

He let out a chuckle as he angled his head back towards me.

Then, his fingers undid the lock around my neck and he chuckled cruelly. "Fight me all you want, Alethea. You won't hurt me."

I ground my teeth as I felt my powers surge to the surface. Letting out a shout, my flames erupted from all around, from *me*. My skin, my bones and my soul became flames. I let it consume everything around me. I heard Eryx's startled cry before he stumbled off of me as the flames licked at his skin.

I pushed myself to my feet, the flames parting for me.

"I already told you once," I felt the fire dancing in my eyes as he gaped at me. "You don't know me anymore."

I threw my hand out and he narrowly avoided getting hit by the stream of flames. He rolled across the ground and shoved to his feet. His shadows leached out around him, trying to protect him from the flames as they consumed everything around me.

A gust of wind blew him back and as I glanced over at Lira, she was standing her ground with a ward around her to keep out the flames. He tumbled backwards and landed on his back with a 'whoosh'. Slowly, I made my way towards him. The flames parted for me, I raised my hands on either side of me as I approached above him. His shadows were being killed off by the fire, sizzling out as my fire took control of them.

His eyes were wide as he stared back up at me in disbelief. Those cider eyes that I had once cherished reflected the flames that flickered around me. He shoved himself up on his elbows, watching and waiting as I slowly knelt before him.

"I told you I would kill you," I breathed calmly.

I knew we needed to flee, I knew we needed to move quickly, but I also wanted to relish in this. This man had taken so much from me and so many others. This man had lied and cheated for his own selfish gain, and I wanted vengeance. Not only for myself, but for every other person he had hurt.

He lunged towards me, his body colliding with mine but as he did, his body impaled on the knife I held. He couldn't see it, I had glamoured it when Lira had distracted him.

He gulped as his eyes widened. His head slowly dropped as he gazed at the hilt of the blade protruding from his chest.

"Alethea," he breathed. His voice took on a hint of despair and a hint of disbelief.

I had told him he didn't know me anymore. I would do anything to get my mate back.

"Let's go, girl," Lira hissed as I stepped away from him.

His eyes followed me as his mouth fell open on a gasp. Blood trickled out of the corner of his mouth as I receded another step, then his eyes went vacant as I took another.

I wanted to remain there, frozen, staring at his body. Just to remind myself it was real. He had been the first love of my life. He had rescued me when I had been imprisoned. He had given me a home, food, and security. But now as I gazed down on him, my chest felt vacant of any feelings.

"Let's go, girl," Lira hissed as she gripped my elbow and pulled me back a step. "He will be found, and once he's found we will be executed."

I nodded as I stumbled back a step, away from his still form. As I moved back, his eyes didn't follow me like they had always done.

Turning towards Lira, I felt a numbness settle over my limbs as I followed behind her. She led me quickly through the halls. We ducked into the kitchens and she pushed aside a tall cabinet and then pressed on a brick. The stone scraped heinously as the door opened and it revealed a long, dark hallway. There were torches along the wall that began lighting themselves as she stepped into the tunnel.

I hurried after Lira as she stepped fully into the tunnel. Eryx and I had adventured down there once, although it had been under different circumstances.

I didn't ask her if she knew where she was going, I just crouched behind her. I kept alert the entire way. I expected guards to flood the tunnels once they discovered Eryx's dead body.

I kept a hand planted on the wall, tracing our way until we came to a break in the tunnel. There were two that headed in different directions, but Lira didn't take any time as she began down the tunnel on the right. I wanted to nag and ask if she was sure where she was going, but I knew better. She wouldn't steer me wrong.

After what seemed like an eternity, we came upon a wooden door. Lira twisted the metal handle and it opened effortlessly, opening up into a cobblestone walkway. She stepped out into the moonlight that reflected off of her grey hair. She didn't release my hand as she stepped aside, allowing me out before she closed the door. She waved her hand over it, sealing it closed in case Eryx's men used it to come after us.

"We're in the city now, we just need to make it out to the forest. That's where he'll be waiting for us."

I nodded as she slipped her arm through mine and we began walking. The cobblestone walkway led between a set of carts that were empty, as the owner wasn't there to sell their goods. Majority of the market was empty, besides the occasional straggler. There were lanterns hanging from them all, illuminating our path as we moved further into the town. We reached the portion of shops and taverns, which meant there were more people.

I gasped lightly as I saw two men, in golden armor, laugh loudly. Lira's fingers bit into my arm as she pulled me into the shadows with her as two guards trotted down the street. They each appeared to be off duty as they each held large glasses of liquor.

"Keep your head down," Lira whispered as she tucked into my side further.

She didn't bother hiding her face, as she was a servant, not many would recognize her face. But they would recognize mine instantly.

I could hear my heart hammering in my ear. She kept her arm slipped through mine as we continued down the street. The loud laugh of the guards followed us, but when I cast a quick glance over my shoulder, they were in the same place. They didn't even glance at us.

We turned another corner and I knew that we didn't have much further to go before we hit the woods. I bit down on my tongue as a large figure emerged from an alley. My fingers tightened around my blade and I drew it as the figure dropped their hood back.

"Cadmus," I breathed as blonde hair revealed itself.

I huffed a sigh of relief as Lira released me and I threw my arms around his shoulders. His heavy arms wrapped around my middle, hugging me back fiercely.

"Thank you for coming for us," I said as I pulled away.

"I'm just glad to see you both are alive and safe. When Eryx realizes you're gone, he'll be hunting us."

My mouth fell open as I stared back at Cadmus. He hadn't heard yet.

"Cadmus," I breathed as I readied myself for whatever his reaction may be. "I killed him. Eryx is dead."

His mouth fell open, but no words came out. He closed his mouth again, his brows slammed down and then he shook his head before meeting my gaze.

"He got what he deserved." He spoke the words firmly, but I could see the sadness that loomed behind his gaze. He visibly swallowed, pushing past whatever grief he may have felt. His expression evened out and he cleared his throat. "We need to keep moving."

I wanted to tell him that I was sorry, but he and I both knew I wasn't. Eryx had slowly transformed into the very thing he promised to protect me from, and I had warned him. He had a habit of not believing me.

We all froze as the sound of horns began blowing. My head snapped towards the sky as a dragon's roar sounded, then a second, and then a third.

"Let's go," Cadmus hissed as he gripped my arm and led us through the dark. We kept our heads down, refusing to make eye contact with anyone we passed.

"Run to the tree line," Cadmus commanded, and Lira and I both obeyed.

I reached for her hand, clutching it between mine as we ran to the trees. I slowed down, making sure I didn't leave her. She was one of the last few people in this wretched world I cared about, and I would not lose her.

As we reached the trees, there were two horses waiting. Cadmus rushed around them, untying their reins from the branches above them.

I whipped my head back as more dragons bellowed and more horns sounded.

"Let's go!" Cadmus growled as he gripped my hips and lifted me up onto the horse.

I gripped the reins as the horse began bouncing from foot to foot, ready to flee.

Cadmus lifted Lira onto the steed, and then mounted behind her as he lifted the reins.

"Go!" Cadmus shouted from behind me.

I slapped the reins, urging the steed to go faster as the sound of dragon's swooping through the air sounded from above us. Their roars shook the ground beneath us and I crouched over the horses neck as I gripped the reins even tighter. I willed the trees to swallow us as the fear pumped through my veins. I knew I also needed to keep my emotions low, the fear could make my powers uncontrollable.

We continued riding, away from the horns, away from the dragons, and into the woods until they swallowed us whole.

***

My ass ached from how long it took us to get to Mykill's kingdom. I nearly groaned in relief as the spires of his castle came into view.

Felix was waiting for us at the entrance. We slowed, the horse trotting to a stop before the double doors. There was an array of guards standing at attention, waiting for us, Felix was among them. I pulled to a stop entirely.

"Alethea," Felix bowed his head as he turned towards me. "Happy to see you're alive."

I nodded at him as I dismounted. "Any word on Mykill and where they might've taken him?"

Felix's gaze dropped, and he shook his head. "No, not yet."

"We need to keep searching, we need to find him."

"We will do everything we can to bring him home," Felix promised as he nodded. "I swear it on my life."

I nodded and brushed past him. I should have felt happy that I was free, that Lira was free and none of us had been harmed. But I couldn't feel anything other than the anxiety that was clinging to me like a second skin. I shoved open the doors and began my run down the hall. I needed to be somewhere that reminded me of him, I *needed him* after being with Eryx. I wasn't sure how long Eryx had kept me, but it had felt like an eternity.

None of the guards cut me off. They all cast me sympathetic stares as I ran past them. My chest heaved as I rounded the final corner and shoved open his bedroom door.

My steps faltered as his scent assaulted me. His bed was perfectly done and there wasn't a book out of place on his bookshelves flanking either side of his bed. The cloud gray walls seemed to close in around me as I turned in a full circle as if he would melt out of a wall. But I could feel he wasn't here. The space in my soul that now belonged to him could feel the span of miles between us. Wherever he was, he wasn't anywhere near me and that thought alone caused my heart to shatter in my chest.

My mate was in the hands of the enemy, *my friend* was in the hands of the enemy. And God's only knew what they were doing to him.

I could *feel* him in my chest now that I could feel my powers. But feeling him wasn't the same as him being here with me.

I collapsed to my knees and placed my palms flat on the floor as I willed my breathing to slow down. He had always been the one to tell me to calm down. But now that he was gone, I didn't want to calm down. My anger would be what led me to him and would help me burn down anyone who stood in between us.

Chapter 15

Alethea

There wasn't a hint of Mykill the next three weeks. Lira tried to teach me how to track him but I couldn't pinpoint his location. She suggested that it was probably shielded so that I couldn't find him.

I had set the dining room table on fire at the words.

My body needed him back here safely. She said that if I could feel him then it meant he was alive. She said that I would feel if he died, but the longer we were apart, the more I doubted myself. What if I couldn't feel him properly? I wasn't born fae so what if I didn't recognize the gaping bond. But then I remembered that even when I was human I recognized the feeling when mine and Eryx's bond had been broken.

My lungs heaved from excursion as I ducked below Felix's blade. I sliced upwards with my sword and Felix jumped back, barely missing it.

"Good," Cadmus praised from the edge of the mat. "You're getting faster."

I raised my blade, arching it down in a deadly swift strike. Felix barely jumped out of the way as he countered, our swords clashed again.

We had practiced night and day, longer than I had ever practiced. It was a welcome reprieve. The longer I thought of us not finding Mykill, the more weary I grew.

I knew I looked terrible. I had barely slept. I had tried sleeping in my bedroom, his bedroom, his reading room, but nowhere I slept brought me peace. I was always exhausted and training only made it worse.

"Good," Cadmus said again as I spun and ducked. "Quicker, quicker." He snapped his fingers.

I did as he said. I let myself become one with the movements, turning it into a dance. With a step, a duck and a spin. I repeated the steps, avoiding Felix's blade. Cadmus praised me from the sidelines, they normally traded off who trained me every day.

After we finished training, we all retired to our own selves. I walked down the hall to my room so I could bathe and change. Thankfully, Lira wasn't in there when I arrived and I locked my door so that if she did come by, she'd know I wanted to be alone.

I stripped as I made my way over to the steaming tub. I had mixed in a heady amount of healing salts and herbs to help with the constant ache of my body, but somehow, they never made it better.

Sliding into the water, I let out a groan as the heated water greeted me. I sunk into the tub until I was covered entirely up to my neck. I closed my burning eyes, willing for a few minutes of sleep.

When I finally opened my eyes, the water was cold and the bubbles from the salt had all but evaporated.

Dragging myself from the water, I dried quickly and dressed in a pair of leggings and a flowy tunic. I slipped on my knee high boots and braided my hair in a single braid that draped over my shoulder.

Turning once in the mirror, I grimaced at the bags beneath my eyes that seemed to grow by the day. My body itself looked stronger, leaner, but my face looked tired, and older.

Frowning, I spun away and made my way out of my room as I headed for the Cliffside. My throat burned for a drink. The taverns hadn't turned me away since Mykill had been taken. They knew I'd probably burn them down if they had.

Running down the stairs, I didn't even ask a pedestrian to fly me down. I wanted to feel the burn in my thighs, and the heavy beat of my heart. It was the only thing that reminded me I was alive when everything else I felt was fear and crippling anxiety.

I finally reached my favorite tavern called Cider's. Loud music played from inside and laughter roared, echoing down the walkway.

I stilled before the door as I caught a glimpse of a familiar cider eyes. But the figure was too small to be Eryx. The figure stepped out of the shadows.

Red lips were curled into a cruel smirk. "Alethea," she greeted as she stepped fully into the light. "It's been a long time since I've seen you."

"Freya," I breathed as I stepped away from her. "What are you doing here?"

My hand flew to my waist where I normally kept my dagger stowed, but I had left it in its sheath that rested upon my bed.

She shrugged as she began circling me. "No particular reason, mainly just to finish what I started."

I hadn't noticed that she had intended to get me with my back towards the water.

Remain on alert at all times, Mykill's words drifted over me.

Without notice, she dove forward towards me.

She shoved at my shoulders and my back hit the railing. She advanced on me before I could move out of the way. She slammed into me and the wooden railing behind me snapped with the combination of our weights. I gasped as I fell freely through the air. She drove her fist down into my nose and I felt blood burst across my cheek. It splattered across her face and I gripped her shoulders as I shoved her off of me. I brought my knees up, shoving space between us and kicked her as hard as I could.

She wailed as she free fell beside me, but out of reach. Her arms flailed and the last thing I saw was her red lips shouting before my back hit the water.

Bone chilling cold swallowed me whole, and refused to spit me out. I kicked my legs as I tried to make out my up from my down. The water was too dark for me to make out. My arms and legs flailed as I kicked, moving myself sluggishly through the murky water.

I gasped as my head broke the surface. My hair was plastered to the side of my face and the cold air felt like it was pricking my skin. My lungs heaved as I pulled myself through the water. I searched the edges of the water, looking for a way out of the water.

The waves beat at the sides of the cliff, and the Coves were still too far for people to see us. No one had been around us either, so no one would know we were down here.

My arms pumped to keep my head above the water.

I shrieked as fingers wrapped around my ankle and I was pulled below the surface. Water filled my lungs as I thrashed, grasping handfuls of water as I tried to pull myself up. I spun around and grasped Freya's face between my hands as I tried shoving her away from me. She slashed at me as I shoved away from her, and that's when I saw the blade in her hand.

I kicked my foot out and managed to kick her in the wrist. She screamed, bubbles rose up around her as she did, and the knife floated away from her. I kicked, floating towards it as I grabbed it. I palmed it and spun back towards her as I felt her reach for me.

Turning towards her, I drove the knife down and she screamed again as it embedded in her shoulder. I planted my boot in her stomach and shoved away from her as I swam towards the surface again.

Gasping as my head broke the water, I searched around me for anywhere that I could pull myself up onto.

My gaze narrowed on a cluster of rocks closer to the cliffside, and I began pumping my arms. I desperately needed to get atop that rock because I knew if given the chance, Freya would drown me.

Reaching out for the rock, my fingers bit into its jagged edges. My arms shook as I pulled myself up onto it. I blew out a breath as I pushed my hair away from my face.

Dropping my head towards the sky, I breathed a sigh of relief as I saw a pair of wings, then another and another. I cupped my hands around my mouth, ready to call for their help, when I noticed a familiar silver head. Squinting up at the figure, relief spread through me as I spotted Felix.

"Freya is in the water!" I shouted and Felix froze, straightening as he searched the water.

His gaze narrowed on something and then he pointed somewhere among the waves. He shouted something to the two men who accompanied him and they swept down. I heard an infuriated shriek and then the two men were taking to the sky with Freya in between them. Each of them held one of her wrists, and her legs flailed as they took to the sky.

Felix dropped onto the rock beside me and knelt as he scooped me up. My hands shivered as I slipped my arms around his neck and huddled into him, desperate for the body heat.

"We'll get you warmed up," he assured me as he rubbed my arm as he took to the sky.

I dropped my forehead onto his shoulder as I let the anxiety leech out of me. My hands shook partly from the cold, but mainly from the adrenaline.

I had come close to death, *again.*

If Felix hadn't showed up, I wasn't sure what would have happened.

Cadmus was waiting for us as Felix landed. Freya was on her knees with her hands bound behind her back and the two guards stood on either side of her, ready to pounce if she moved.

"How did you get here?" Cadmus asked and his head snapped up as Felix landed with me. "Are you okay?"

I nodded as I slipped out of Felix's arms and waved him off. "I'm fine." I brushed past him and marched towards Freya, who smiled cruelly up at me.

No one stopped me as I cocked my fist back and slammed it into her cheek. Then as she raised her head back towards me, I did it again. She sputtered as she landed on her back, and then rolled onto her side. She spit out a mouthful of blood before one of Felix's men gripped her by the arm and placed her back on her knees.

"That's for both times you've tried to kill me," I growled.

Freya laughed. "I've tried to kill you three times."

I growled again and then drove my knee into her stomach. She doubled over in pain as she whooshed out a breath.

"Thank you for reminding me," I growled and then spun away.

I marched past Cadmus to head back to my room to change.

"Take her to the dungeons," Cadmus said from behind me.

I heard her shout something at him in protest, and then Felix snapped at her. I headed towards my room quickly as all the questions tumbled around inside of me.

Why had she come all this way just to kill me? Why had she wanted to kill me in the first place? Was she still working for the High Priest?

I changed quickly into a warm pair of fleece leggings and a long sleeve. Then I slipped my boots back on and pulled a shawl over my shoulders. I slipped back out of my room, but wasn't surprised to find Cadmus and Felix waiting for me.

"I'm going down to question her, and I was sure you'd like to come join me," Cadmus spoke as he pushed off the wall from beside Felix.

I nodded and followed silently behind them as they led me down a familiar hall. Felix pushed open a large wooden door that opened to a thin winding spiral staircase. We followed it all the way down. I kept a hand on the side of the wall as we descended.

I had never been down to Mykill's dungeons before. I expected them to look something like Kirin's, but much to my surprise they were the cleanest I'd seen. The floors, wall and ceiling were all carved from a light beige stone, with black bars over every one of the enclosures.

"There's no doors," I frowned as I examined one of the enclosures.

Felix nodded. "Only me, and a couple men have the ability to move prisoners in and out of their cells. It's to help protect against people freeing themselves."

There were only four prisoners that I could see. Each of their beady eyes followed me as we passed. One man in particular who had to be near seven feet tall, with a long, thin body, sat on the edge of his stone bench. He ran his gangly fingers through his beard that was overgrown past his chest. He mumbled to himself as he followed our movements, but what shocked me more was that his eyes were a bright yellow, with black slits in them, much like a snake.

I shivered as I looked away from him.

Cadmus stopped before one of the last enclosures and crossed his arms over his chest.

"Cadmus," Freya greeted. "Back to see me already?" she cooed.

Cadmus merely glared, before I stepped in front of him. Her eyes slid over to me, watching me as I blocked Cadmus.

He didn't stop me as I stepped closed to her enclosure. I wanted to be the one to question her, although I should have asked Felix or Cadmus before we came down.

"Why did you betray us?" I asked.

Freya laughed and her head slowly turned towards me. "It honestly had nothing to do with you, and everything to do with my brother. Your death would have been an added bonus." She paused momentarily as her eyes took on a far off expression. "I thought it would be the perfect payback for him to lose his lover, much like I had lost mine."

My nose scrunched as my glare deepened. "You mean to tell me you came all the way here to kill me for no reason?" I demanded, and then shook my head. "No, I don't buy it."

Freya glanced away, her lips thinning as she quieted. That only caused my anger to soar. She had almost killed me three times over, the least she could do was answer my questions.

I outstretched my hand, letting an ember roar to life and then I tossed it at her through the bars. She squealed as it landed on her arm, and she scuttled backwards until her back hit the wall. But even after she managed to scrape it from her skin, it merely jumped back.

"You mean to tell me you came out here to kill me when I mean nothing to your brother anymore? Surely, you had to know he was already dead! My death would be pointless!"

She shrieked again as another flew from my hand and landed on her chest. She dropped her head back as it sizzled into her flesh and screamed.

"You had a home! A family that loved you! A brother that loved you!" I shouted.

"You have no idea what it's like!" she snapped. "I wasn't only the second born, but I was also female! That meant I would be married off to whomever paid the highest price."

"Eryx always said that your father was a kind man." I frowned as I processed her words and let the embers die.

She scoffed, anger radiating off of her body. "To him! He was the heir! My father fawned over him! I always came second and I didn't always get the side of my father Eryx did. I got the side who would slap my hands if I moved too fast or would chide me for speaking out of turn. He didn't treat me like a daughter, he treated me like a pet. The father Eryx knew was much different than mine." She turned her head, her eyes dropping to the floor. "I assume you've heard the truth of my engagement with your mate?"

I nodded, waiting for her to continue.

"The man I had been having an affair with was a guard from our kingdom. It wasn't a mating bond, but it was the closest I'd ever felt to one. He was kind to me and I loved him with everything inside of me," she laughed cruelly. "But when my father found out, he had been furious."

Her eyes went vacant as if she was recalling the events. "He forbade me from ever seeing him again, and had him thrown out in the streets. He had dedicated his life to protecting my family and my father threw him out like he was a lost woods animal!" Her frown deepened. "So I snuck him into the castle one night. It hadn't been hard to find the shadow blade my father had hidden. I knew once he was dead, then we could be together. I knew my father would find us if we ran away together, it was the only option."

"He killed your father?" I gasped. "Why did you not try discussing it more with your father?"

"He wouldn't allow it! He didn't care if it would have made me happier! Sure, you and Eryx could have married now that he was King, but my father would not have allowed it." Her eyes went vacant again. "So Killian killed him."

In the shadows, I saw the glistening of tears filling her eyes.

"Then he was executed six months later."

I cocked my head to the side. "For what?"

She shook her head. "Eryx executed him for a crime he didn't even commit. It was when he was first crowned and he was power hungry." First, a single tear rolled down her cheek, then a second and a third, until I lost count entirely.

I wanted to tell her that he was still guilty, even if he was killed for a crime he hadn't committed. But I knew she wouldn't take to it.

"Why come kill me even after Eryx and I are no longer together?" I decided to ask instead.

"I promised the High Priest I would."

My eyes narrowed in on her. "What do you know of the High Priest? Were you aware of his attack after you stole the eye?"

She nodded. "I was the one who told them we were going to search for the eye. He wanted it but agreed to take you when I told him he couldn't have it."

"Who has the eye now?"

"The barren," she said as she adjusted herself and grimaced.

"You gave it to them?" I snapped.

She shook her head. "No, they stole it from me."

"What do you know of Eryx partnering with the Barren?"

"I know nothing about it." She frowned at the words. "Although, I do have to say that it's quite surprising."

"What about the thing that haunted my dreams? I assume Eryx told you?"

She simply nodded again. "He did. My guess is the Black Mage. He's vengeful and far more powerful than people give him credit for."

"What do you know of the prophecy that concerned Eryx and I?" I questioned.

She shook her head. "I don't know anything about it."

I wanted to call her a liar, but she seemed truthful enough.

"Now if you're done berating me with questions, I'd like to get some rest now." She turned away and rested her shoulder against the wall.

I stepped away as I watched her adjust herself, and then lay down across the stone bench. Cadmus grabbed my elbow and steered me around and out of the dungeons. Once we reached the top of the winding stairs and locked the door behind us, he turned towards me.

"She has to be put to death," Cadmus said.

"What?" I nearly shrieked. "Why?"

"By law, she must be executed," Felix explained softly.

"But why?" I demanded. "She's told us nothing but the truth!"

"She's a liability, Alethea," Cadmus interjected. "If she somehow manages to get free, who's to say she won't try killing you for a third time?"

I bit down on my tongue because I knew he was right. Even though she did share the truth with us, there was nothing stopping her from killing me if she was to get free. She was a woman set on vengeance and would kill anyone merely associated with the people she wanted vengeance on so badly.

"I can't blame her," I whispered. "She was hurt badly by someone who was supposed to love her."

Cadmus' face softened as he puffed out a breath. "I know. But that doesn't make it okay for her to kill people off of a vendetta she has against her father and Eryx. You were nothing but kind to her."

I only nodded. I wanted so badly to disagree with him and tell him he was wrong. But I knew he wasn't.

"When?" was all I asked.

"Tomorrow at dawn," Felix answered. I nodded in response and stepped away from them. "Very well, I will meet you in the morning. Good night."

They both bowed their heads to me and I turned. I changed bedrooms every night. I would spend tonight in Mykill's room. Every night I prayed that I would get a semblance of rest, and every night I had ended up disappointed.

I pushed open the door and breathed in deep as his scent overtook me. It was the only piece of him I had until he was returned safely to me.

Heading over to his dresser, I pulled out one of his tunics and changed into it before I slid into bed. I wrapped the black comforter around me and inhaled. But the longer he was gone, the more his scent began to disappear. I could barely smell it now.

I clutched handfuls of it in my fist as I choked on a sob. I buried my face in the pillow and cried out as more grief took over me.

I had never thought I would have missed him so much. Blame it on the mating bond, but I also missed my friend. I missed our banter, the touches, the quick glances, I missed all of it. I wanted someone to sit with me and read in harmonious silence, or sit with me in the gardens as I stared up at the sky consumed by my thoughts. Even without the mating bond, he had filled a hole in my chest I hadn't known needed filling.

***

I had met Cadmus in the gardens in the morning. Then, he had led me to an area of the castle I wasn't familiar with. It had been beneath the dungeons, and had been a tunnel that led over to a small courtyard far in the castle with a small brick scaffold and enough standing space for about two dozen people. Behind and above the scaffold was a thin walkway where Cadmus said Freya would be led before coming down the set of stairs. There was a small block of wood with an indent where I knew she'd be led.

I stood beside Cadmus with my hands crossed in front of me as I waited. Cadmus had told me I hadn't needed to attend her execution. I couldn't imagine myself not.

Freya emerged from the set of double doors. Her wrists were shackled behind her back, and a steel collar that resembled the one Eryx had put on mine neck, rested on hers. She was escorted forward by two guards. She looked like she hadn't gotten a lick of rest, and part of me wondered if she had been familiar with Mykill's kingdoms practices and knew she would be put to death.

I had forgotten how old she was, but I knew it had to be far older than I, or any other human. Part of me wondered if it had been on purpose. She had lost her sole reason to live. She never loved someone again, and had felt betrayed by her family.

Sometimes immortality felt like a curse. It could be a beautiful thing if you had a beautiful life, but if you felt alone, I couldn't imagine living for centuries.

Part of me wondered if that had been why she had attacked me.

Her eyes met mine but there wasn't an ounce of anger in them. I offered her a wobbly smile and clutched my hands tighter before me. I wanted to interject and beg Felix to leave her.

I knew what Mykill would have done if he had been present. But I knew I held no authority over Felix and his men. I hadn't been anything other than Mykill's unwanted mate when we had first left Linterfame.

Cadmus slid an arm around my shoulders and I welcomed the friendly embrace. Freya's eyes swung to him and I saw a yearning there as her eyes bounced between us.

My heart clenched. She had only wanted a friend.

I watched as she was led before the stump and pushed onto her knees. The courtyard was so quiet I could hear every one of her breaths.

A tear slid down my cheek and I swung my head away as the axe swung down. I heard the sickening crunch of bone and the squelch of blood. I covered my mouth with my hand. I couldn't look as I heard her body slump to the ground.

My hand shook as I choked on a cry and turned fully into Cadmus' shoulder. He tightened his arm around my shoulder and then whispered words of comfort, but I heard none.

I couldn't help but grieve the loss of friendship we had, even if it had been faked. I couldn't help but mourn the broken woman that had revealed herself to me. She had been broken by her family and the expectations of them. She had wanted the life I'd been blessed to have.

"Come on, Alethea," Cadmus said softly as he began to steer me back towards the castle.

Chapter 16

Alethea

I sat on one of the plush armchairs in Mykill's study. I had finally forced myself to sit down and read a book. It had been one of my favorite hobbies but it had been hard for me to immerse myself in one when all I could think of was Mykill.

I flipped through the pages. The story was normally one I would love but I couldn't bring myself to focus. Mykill and I had spent a lot of our time reading together.

A knock sounded on the door and cut through the silence. Normally, I would have felt annoyed, but now I welcomed the distraction.

"Come in," I called.

The door creaked open and Felix stuck his head in the door. "Alethea," he bowed his head after he stepped fully into the room. "We've been summoned to Emerald mountain."

I frowned. "What for?" I asked as I snapped my book closed and placed it on the end table.

"War has broken out among them. The brothers' disagreement resulted in the kingdom trying to split."

My mouth fell open and I gasped. "What?"

"Valum has taken his brothers and their families prisoner. We've been contacted by a few men in their guard to aid them in rescuing them," Felix explained.

"When do we leave?" I asked as I stood to my feet.

Felix hesitated, and I could see the internal war waging as he tried deciding what Mykill would have wanted. I thought about reminding him that I had come along when the barren had attacked the human lands, but in the end I hadn't needed to.

Felix nodded. "I'm assembling my men now, I suggest you go get changed."

I nodded and brushed past him as I took off at a brisk walk towards my room. As I pushed open the door to my room, Lira was perched on the vanity as she sorted through what looked like a bowl of pins. She had dismissed my ladies maids, and refused to relax about the castle. She claimed that she would grow bored and throw herself out a window. She was such a dramatic one.

"I need leathers," I said to her as I strode by her and began stripping from my dress.

She didn't say a word as she moved to the wardrobe and pulled out a set of my leathers. They were the leathers Mykill had given me that were fashioned with dragon scales across the stomach. You couldn't tell, as the black scales blended in perfectly with the black of the leathers. I took them from her and dressed quickly as she began grabbing my sheaths and daggers that had all but taken residency on my night table. Lira had resisted chiding me, mainly because she knew I wouldn't pick them up, and I used them every day so it wasn't like they were just there collecting dust. She outheld the ones for my thighs and I stepped into them and grabbed my daggers and sheathed them. There was a sheath containing a dagger on each of my forearms, each of my thighs and then two swords crossed behind my back in sheaths.

I turned as she began braiding my hair into a crown atop my head to keep it from my face.

"You look like a warrior," she commented as I turned towards her as she finished.

I stared down at her and offered a small smile. "Only because of you."

She shook her head as she placed her hands on my shoulders. "No, girl, you look like a warrior because you have strength running through your veins and written across your face. I believe you will bring him home."

I sucked in a breath as she stepped away. Tears pricked at the corners of my eyes as the walls around me seemed to grow closer to me.

"I believe in you," Lira said, halting the thoughts that threatened to drown me.

It wasn't very often that I heard those words.

For far too long I had let myself believe that I wasn't strong enough to care for myself, much less someone else. I had let that thought consume me until it was all I believed.

Now I knew it to be false.

"Thank you, Lira," I said as I nodded my head towards her.

She nodded towards me and then shooed me out of the room.

I found Cadmus and Felix waiting for me with a group of at least fifty men behind them.

"Ready?" Cadmus asked.

"Ready." I nodded and then stepped up to Felix as he slipped his arms around me.

We took to the skies, the ascent taking my breath away. I clutched Felix's neck as I squeezed my eyes closed.

"Not a fan of the skies?" he laughed.

"No," I grumbled as I tightened my hold before releasing him. "I feel like my stomach is going to fall right out of me."

He laughed again.

"Did flying not scare you when you first started flying?"

He shook his head. "I was flying before I even remembered flying. It's as easy as walking."

I chuckled. "I couldn't imagine having a toddler with wings."

He laughed. "Me neither."

"I take it then you don't want kids?"

He shook his head. "No, my job is too dangerous."

I cocked my head to the side and frowned. "Then why wouldn't you quit?"

"Because my loyalty is to Mykill, " he vowed. "I know you don't know me well, but he took me in when I was a teenager. I owe my life to him. Having a family would take away from that."

"I'm sure Mykill wouldn't want that from you. He wouldn't want you to put him over having a life and family of your own."

His brows furrowed slightly and his lips pinched. "I'm sure you're right," he finally said. "But I couldn't imagine anything else."

"Maybe someday," I said, letting it drop.

"Maybe someday," he echoed his agreement.

We flew in silence the rest of the way. I watched the skies as the sun slowly drifted across it. Birds flew by us, not even sparing us a second glance as they continued their journey. I almost asked Felix how much longer it would be until I saw the spires of the elven kingdom peaking above a hill.

My mouth gaped as we crested the hill at the scene before us. The great city that had once glittered like it was covered in jewels was now cloaked in a shadow of gray. Shouts drifted up from the streets along with the sounds of swords crashing together.

We dropped, finding a clearer street to land. I jumped out of Felix's arms, ready for action and turned as Cadmus and Felix stood side by side.

"We will move in quickly," Cadmus said as he adjusted his fingerless glove. "We move in quietly and seamlessly. We fight off anyone who attacks us, but we need to get out unseen. These women are part of the Royal Court."

"Are there children?" one of the female warriors asked.

Felix nodded. "Yes, there will be two women and six children."

My mouth threatened to drop open. He had kidnapped his two sister in laws and then nieces and nephews?

My stomach felt like it was about to roil as disgust filled me.

"Let's move, Alethea, you're with us," Cadmus called, and I fell in line behind him.

We entered the castle quickly the same way we had when we had come here last. Bodies littered the halls and frantic maids ran about the halls crying. Cadmus tried to direct them to our men waiting outside.

"We received word that they're being kept in a dungeon below the castle," Cadmus said over his shoulder. "I believe it's this way."

"You don't know where it is?" I whispered as I stepped closer to him.

"They gave me a verbal a map, I'm going to follow it as best I can."

I nodded as we continued down another hall. The further into the castle we moved, the smaller and less traveled the halls seemed. As we entered another hall, we came face to face with a dozen or so elves. They swung towards us and immediately charged.

I unsheathed two knives as I prepared for their attack. I dove forward as a man with a short blade came at me. I crossed my two long daggers in an 'x' as his blade arched down towards me. I raised my leg, my booted foot landing on his chest, before I shoved him backwards.

He growled as he tried to keep his foothold as he stumbled back a few steps. He pulled a dagger from a sheath around his thigh as he threw it at me. I stepped to the left, narrowly avoiding the flying dagger.

The sound of clashing swords sounded all around me as we fought off the elven guards. Someone cried out beside me, but I couldn't risk looking as the elven man charged me again. I threw my hand out and a wave of flames flew forward. The elven man screamed as it wrapped around his body, coating his clothing and skin. His scream intensified as I crushed my fist and his neck snapped.

He fell to the ground in a heap as I stood over him. My chest heaved as I stared down at his still form as the flames sputtered out.

"Alethea, duck!" Cadmus commanded and I obeyed.

I lowered onto one knee and felt the air above me rustle as a knife hurled through the air. It embedded in the wall above me as I raised back to my feet. I spun and pulled a blade from my belt and let it fly towards the assailant.

Pride filled me as it embedded in the side of his neck. He let out a gurgled cry as blood spilled over the sides of the blade and coated his neck and shoulder. He dropped to his knees, then face first to the ground.

I turned towards Cadmus as he stepped over a dead body.

"Surrender or be killed," Felix growled as he held his dagger to one of the elven man's throats.

The man glared up at him with violet colored eyes. "Kill me then."

Felix didn't hesitate. He dragged the blade across the elves' throat. Blood spilled over the blade and dripped from the corners of his mouth and then his body slumped forward.

"He was the last one," Felix said as he wiped the blood from his dagger on his leathers. "Let's keep moving."

We followed closely behind him as we ducked into what seemed like a servants tunnel.

"In here," Felix hissed sharply.

We ducked through the narrow tunnel. Dust kicked up around us, meaning that no one had been down here recently. Squinting my eyes, I leaned in around him as bars came into view. I gasped as I took in the sight of the two women clutching the kids to them the best they could. The first woman's head snapped up and she began shoving the children behind her.

"Leave us be!" she protested, her voice shook with fear.

"It's okay," I said softly as I held up my hands. "We're here to help you."

"It's Alethea Divine," the other woman gasped.

"My husband?" she asked. "Is he-?" she cut herself off, not able to speak the words into existence.

"He's alive," I assured her. "We will rescue him too. For now, we need to get you all to safety. So please follow us, and please listen to our every command. Our only duty is to get you out alive."

The women nodded and began speaking to their children in a tongue I didn't recognize. I hadn't even been aware that the elves could communicate in a different language.

Felix took the keys and undid the lock. The heavy metal door creaked as it opened. One of the mothers stood, two of her children clutched her hands. She silenced their cries and released their hands as she knelt to lift one of the toddlers into her arms. Once the toddler was secured in her grip, she reached back down to grasp the hands of the two smaller children. The second mother followed suit as Felix led the first mother out. Then, the second mother followed. They tried their best to hush the children as we began down the tunnel.

I kept my blade drawn, all of us did. We would risk our lives to get them to safety. Valdom was as disgusting as Eryx to involve women and children. Killing an innocent soul was beyond treacherous.

Cadmus spoke softly to the women as they continued down the halls. We emerged from the servants tunnel and began down the hall where we had come, when the sound of elves shouting at us sounded.

I turned as a man ran at me.

"Go!" I shouted as I ducked below the man's spinning blade.

I heard Cadmus' booming voice as he commanded the women to keep moving. The sound of their children crying drifted towards me, urging me to move faster. If I died, then I was one less person protecting them. If I died, my friends would be in danger and I couldn't have that on my soul.

I spun, my sword clanging with his. I grunted as the impact shook my arms, an ache building in my muscles. I was thankful for Cadmus, Felix and Mykill, for never taking it easy on me when they trained me. Otherwise, I would have been thrown off by the man's strength.

I drove my heel into the ground behind me and slashed, my sword arching towards his stomach. He deflected and my blade bounced harmlessly off of his.

"You're a weak bitch!" The elf spewed.

I didn't dignify a response and dove forward. I had killed barren before, but the barren were something different entirely. They didn't have souls, but *elves*, they were no different than I. Fae, elf, human, we were all one in the same but with different abilities and lifespans.

Steeling my courage, I drove my blade up and it slid into his chest. His mouth dropped open and his sword slipped from his hands. It clanged off the ground and I ripped my sword from his chest.

I turned as one of our men swung his leg in a wide arch and brought his man down. I dove forward and drove my blade into his chest as well.

"Thank you," he gasped as he stood to his feet, and his chest heaved.

I nodded as I glanced down the empty hall before us. "Let's go."

I kept my sword outstretched before me as we began jogging down the hall to catch up with the others.

Thankfully, they had made it all the way back to the entrance safely with both of the women and their children.

"Alethea!" Cadmus gasped as I came into view. "Thank Gods you're alright."

"I'm fine," I assured him and went to look around him. "The wives?"

"They're safe, the other group rescued their husbands."

I watched as the doors opened and the brothers were led forward.

"Helene," the brother I recognized as Broncrias gasped as he surged forward.

The second brother, Heliar, called for his wife, Via, and then fell to his knees to embrace their four children. My heart clenched at the sight.

My attention snagged as two of our men dragged the third brother, Valdom, between them. His wrists were bound behind his back, and there was a gash across his chest that bled through his tunic. His lip was split and there was a bruise forming beneath his eye.

"What are you doing?" Valdom spit as he fought between the two men flanking him. "You won't be able to kill me! I am the ruler!"

One of the brothers, Broncrias, turned towards his brother. His eyes narrowed and his jaw set in a straight line as he turned from his wife. He kept an arm across her waist, shielding her from his gaze. Their two children clutched to her legs behind him.

"You will be tried as a war criminal," Broncrias said as he gazed unsympathetically at his brother. "Not only did you kidnap my wife, but you harmed and betrayed our guests. You broke the pact between us, which means you're no longer ruler, we are."

"You can't do this!" he shouted as he was yanked to his feet.

His screams echoed down the halls as the guards dragged him backwards towards the dungeons.

"Thank you," Heliar spoke as they both faced us. "We are indebted to you."

"Alethea," one of the wives, Helene called, drawing my attention. Turning towards her, I offered her a small smile. "Thank you for rescuing us, and saving our husbands."

"It wasn't me, it was them." I waved a hand to the men around us, waiting to head back home. But I grabbed her hand. "Let us know if there's anything you need from us," I said as I squeezed her hand. "Just send word and we will come."

"Thank you, Lady Alethea." She bowed her head and her eyes glistened with unshed tears. "You truly are as kind as they say."

I only nodded.

Felix ordered his men to line up as we assessed the casualties. Six of our men would stay due to their injuries and would return later in the week. Two of our men had perished, and I knew Mykill would take their deaths hard since he hadn't been here to try and prevent it.

The flight home was tiring. I knew my body was tired, but Felix's must have been double as tired considering he had to carry me the entire way home.

Once we made it home, I quickly bathed and started down the hall towards Mykill's room. Today had been a victory, but now I knew the weight he felt whenever one of his own died, one of *our* own.

Pushing open his bedroom door, I paused at the threshold. It had taken us too long to accept what had been between us, but part of me knew that I had needed the time. Not only to heal from Eryx, but to also grow more confident in myself. Eryx had stunted me, and it had made me fear getting into another relationship.

But as I sat in his bed, beneath the covers, I couldn't help but chide myself for waiting so long to accept it.

Chapter 17

Alethea

After waking up, I changed quickly and headed to breakfast. Most mornings I ate alone because I woke earlier than others. But I had become well acquainted with the kitchen staff as I requested them to dine with me on more than one occasion.

Petunia, the cook, was seated across from me as she stirred her porridge. She had gasped as if it was a crime when I had first asked her to eat with me. Then I informed her that I wasn't royalty, and that seemed to appease her.

"How long have you worked for Mykill?" I asked as I took a large spoonful and brought it to my lips.

"For about ten years, My Lady," she answered.

I had tried convincing her not to call me that, but she had refused.

"Were you born here?"

She shook her head.

"May I ask how you migrated here?"

She frowned at first, then cleared her throat and raised her gaze to meet mine.

"He saved me and my family," she whispered with a slight tremor to her voice. I glanced at her wingless back, then back at her wrinkled face. "My mother and father were refugees during the war. He took us in, gave us jobs, paid us way more than he needed to and gave us a roof over our heads. He's been kinder to us then anybody else has."

I offered her a small wobbly smile. "He's a good man."

"That he is, My Lady," she agreed and then turned her attention back to her porridge.

I allowed her to eat in silence for the remainder of our time together. I didn't need words to fill the space between us, I just wanted the company.

My head perked up as I heard her chair screech off the floors. "It's been a pleasure, My Lady." She bowed her head as she rose.

"Thank you for joining me." I smiled back at her and she nodded towards me once more before disappearing back into the kitchen.

I sighed to myself as I turned my attention back towards my bowl. My porridge was nearly gone and I dropped my spoon and brushed off my hands before standing. Exiting the dining room, I headed towards my chambers to change.

I changed quickly into leathers and headed towards the training grounds.

Cadmus and Felix had said they didn't have the availability to practice with me, so I decided to practice archery.

I spent hours practicing, sinking arrows one after the other into the bullseye, although some were further to it than I would have liked.

The day thankfully had passed quickly and I was now wandering the halls as I headed outside to the gardens. I hummed softly to myself as I walked through the hall.

The only sound beside my humming was the sound of my slippers scraping off the floor.

A panicked looking Cadmus appeared from around the corner, cutting me off. I frowned as my steps halted. "Cadmus? What's wrong?"

"They're coming!" Cadmus said as he brushed past me.

"What do you mean they're coming?" I demanded as I followed after him. "Who's coming?"

"The Barren!" he exclaimed as he spun towards me. His eyes were wide with fear and his chest heaved slightly. "The Barren, mages, all of them. We're vastly outnumbered."

My mouth fell open and then I shook my head as Cadmus turned away again.

"I need to find Felix."

"I'm coming with you." I fisted my hands as I clutched the tie of my robe and followed quickly after him.

I had never been to Felix's room, but Cadmus led me right to it. He pounded his fist on the door until an exhausted Felix opened the door. He was in sleep pants and no shirt, and I immediately averted my eyes.

"The barren are coming for us," Cadmus breathed.

Felix's eyes widened in shock as he answered Cadmus.

But his response drowned out as I noticed the small form lying in his bed, and I fought a smile. The woman kept the sheet clutched tightly to her chest as she gazed at us.

"I'll join you in a few minutes." He closed the door to dress and I turned towards Cadmus.

"What do we do?" I asked, and then followed after him as he began back down the hall.

"I'm going to tell our men to send messengers to the other kingdoms of the Inner Kingdom. I will request troops from them all, under the Treaty, they will have no other choice."

I nodded as he quickened his pace into a jog, and I followed after. We headed to the guards gathering place, and found a good portion of them there. The message would spread to all of Mykill's men quickly.

The men were all lounging around three long tables flanked with benches on either side. There were trays of food spread out across it, and tall taper candles to illuminate the space. Their laughter roared as they all cheered with tall pints in their hands.

"Attention!" Cadmus called and clapped his hands.

The chatter died down, and the guards all turned their attention towards him. Some set their pints down and stood, saluting Cadmus as they did. Although it wasn't necessary considering most of them were off duty.

"Send men to the surrounding kingdoms," Cadmus exclaimed. "The barren are coming for us. They will be at our doorsteps before the sun rises."

Gasps broke out among the rank, and they all glanced at one another in shock.

"Get ready for an attack. Make sure every unit is fully stocked. Ready the catapults, send men to the edges of the mountain to watch."

The men all rose to their feet as one and offered him a salute before Cadmus dismissed them. We stepped to the side as the men began filing out of the room.

My hands shook as I thought of the barren coming here and destroying the haven of peace that I now called home.

"Let's go to the King's study," Cadmus said as he turned towards me and gripped my elbow.

We weaved through the lines of men that were moving through the halls. They moved as one, not a single man out of step as they all made their way to their units. Mykill's men were trained well.

I saw Felix's silver head of hair weave through the crowd. He stopped and addressed a few men before I saw him disappear into the crowd.

Cadmus pushed open the door to Mykill's study and stepped aside, letting me in first. He closed the door behind him and turned towards me.

"Just get some rest, Alethea, you will need your strength."

I shook my head and couldn't keep the wobble from my voice. "No, I don't think I can. What of Mykill?"

Cadmus' gaze turned sympathetic and his shoulders relaxed. "You would know if he was dead."

He had said that before. But I knew the words rang true. I could still feel him, even if distantly. I nodded as my breathing kicked up. I stumbled back a step and the back of my knees hit the couch.

Cadmus was right, I was exhausted.

His heavy hand landed on my shoulder. "Just get some rest, sleep here. I'll still be here."

My throat clenched as tears burned the back of my eyes. I nodded as I met Cadmus' gaze. "Thank you."

Cadmus offered me a small smile and then reached over me to grab the blanket resting across the back of the sofa. My eyes burned as he motioned for me to lay back. He draped the blanket over me and I nestled down beneath it with my hands tucked beneath my cheek.

"Thank you for being my friend," I muttered as my eyes drooped.

Icy eyes haunted my dreams. Blood coated every part of him. I was screaming, screaming for him to be okay, screaming for someone to help me. But no matter how loudly I screamed, he slipped away over and over again.

"Alethea," Cadmus' voice broke through the haze of sleep. "Alethea, it's time."

I jolted awake, throwing myself up. The blanket crumpled to the floor in a heap as I shoved off the couch. I rubbed at my eyes as the adrenaline surged through me.

It was time for battle.

"I had Lira bring you leathers to change into," he said as he rose to his full height. "They're on his desk."

"Thank you," I mumbled as I pushed myself to my feet and rubbed the bleariness from my eyes.

"Hopefully you got some good rest."

I nodded once, and then my breath hitched as my fear slammed into my chest.

"What if he's not with them?" my voice quivered as I placed my palms to my cheeks.

Cadmus' face fell in sympathy again and I should've been tired of that look. Everyone had given it to me since Mykill had been taken.

I felt my bottom lip tremble as the tears surged forward. Cadmus stepped towards me, embracing me as the tears slid down my cheeks.

"If he's not with them, then Felix and I will set out to retrieve him ourselves, even if it means our death."

"Mykill wouldn't want you to do that," I quipped.

"I would do it for you," Cadmus responded and dropped his arms as he stepped back. "You're one of my dearest friends, and your happiness is important to me."

My mouth fell open as I stared up at him. The man who had been the General of my first love. The man who had helped rescue me. But this man had turned into a close friend. He encouraged me, taught me, treated me like I was his equal and had been there for me more than anyone since Mykill had been taken.

I swiped at the tears beneath my eyes and offered him a wobbly smile. "You mean more to me than you know Cadmus."

He offered me a smile, showing all of his teeth, which was rare. "Why don't you change and meet us in the courtyard."

I nodded and he stepped out of the room and closed the door behind him. I picked up the leathers that were draped across the second armchair. All of my sheaths and weapons were placed neatly on Mykill's desk, carefully not to disturb his belongings.

I changed quickly. My hands trembled as I dressed and assembled and buckled all the sheaths around my thighs, arms and back. Then, I sheathed all of my weapons. I had a sheath with a dagger around each thigh, then around each forearm, and then one crossed across my back for two swords.

I braided my hair, and then tied it in a twist at the base of my neck. I breathed out a deep breath.

This was different. This was war.

Everything before this had been battles. Battles with small armies, and we had won every one. But this was war.

War meant mass casualties for both sides. War meant that there was a greater chance that I wouldn't be coming home. War meant that I might never see Mykill again. War meant that blood would stain my hands and skin.

I breathed out again as I tried to calm my nerves. All of my training had led up to this. Mykill, Cadmus and Felix had wanted to make sure I was ready for when this day came, and I couldn't let them down.

I checked each one of my sheaths one last time before I opened the door. I began down the hall as I pushed back the anxious thoughts that wanted to take root in my mind.

Chapter 18

Alethea

Cadmus was waiting for me before the doors that led out to the courtyard.

"You look like a warrior," he said as way of greeting me.

I wanted to ask him if warriors hearts clenched as tightly as mine did, or if they had fear coursing through their veins?

"Thank you," I laughed with little amusement as I stopped before him. "Who came?" I asked as I adjusted the buckle across my chest again, nervously, as I followed behind Cadmus.

"Everyone." He waved and the double doors glided open.

My steps faltered as I took in the mass now surrounding Mykill's castle. Men and women alike, all dressed in battle armor. Some winged, some not. Some were armed with various weapons while others only a sword.

The army extended farther than I could see.

"Is this enough?" I gasped as I glanced over at Cadmus.

"It will have to be," he answered as he turned his attention to Felix.

"We should start moving," Felix said as he propped his hands on his hips.

"What shall I do?" I turned back to Cadmus.

I could see his brain churning as he stared back at me. Part of me felt like he would ask me to stay, but there was no one who could stop me from going after Mykill. I would abandon them all to save my mate, even if it meant giving up my life.

"Let me at least use my bow and arrow," I said before Cadmus could come up with an answer. "Let me at least do something."

"You can join the firing squad. They will be perched up in the mountains. Amira!" Felix called.

A beautiful woman with white wings turned towards us. Her hair too was white and her eyes a startling shade of blue. Her golden skin glowed, such in contrast to the lightness of the rest of her features.

"Take Alethea with you. Protect her with your life." Felix's voice was firm, leaving no room for negotiation.

"It's an honor," she responded and waited for me to join her.

I glanced once more at Cadmus, who gave me a curt nod, before turning back towards Amira and following her to her group of winged men and women.

"I assume you know how to use that?" she said as we marched down the line of people.

I nodded. "Not as well as you're able to I'm assuming, but well enough."

"As long as you can aim, and hit your target 80% of the time, you'll do just fine."

She continued marching until she reached her group of soldiers. They all had bows and arrows concealed in a sheath at their backs. Each of them turned towards me, taking me in.

"It's an honor, Alethea Divine." One of the men bowed his head, the others followed.

"The honor is mine," I deflected. I didn't deserve their honor.

Felix and Cadmus shouted their commands as the soldiers all lined up. I fell in line with Amira's men, keeping my bow and arrow sheathed at my back like the others.

"Alethea, you will fly with Roe." Amira waved to the tall man beside me.

He bowed his head, but didn't speak as he turned towards me. Roe slid an arm beneath my knees and another beneath my shoulders and took off into the air. I could feel the tenseness in his arms and in the way he avoided curling his fingers around me. Like he thought Mykill would jump out of the clouds and pummel him for touching me.

The bastard probably would.

We didn't fly for long, we merely flew over the trees that surrounded the castle and to the large fields behind it. I watched the hills and felt my heart drop into the pit of my stomach. On the horizon I could see barren, thousands of them. I couldn't hear them yet, but I knew I'd be able to soon.

Roe dropped, descending towards the mountains that skirted the field. Amira's men all followed, dropping to their feets as they set up position.

"Spread out!" Amira called.

Roed placed me on my feet, and I took up my position beside him.

"Get in position!" she commanded.

I followed beside Roe as everyone lined up on the edge of the mountain and notched their arrows.

I watched the horizon as we waited. The barren hadn't crested it yet, but we would hit them with everything we had once they did.

My arms didn't grow weary as I waited. An anxious energy buzzed beneath the surface of my skin. My powers danced beneath my fingertips, wanting to reveal themselves and devour anything in their path. My breathing was quick, but even.

My eyes remained as focused as a hawk's on the horizon.

At first, all I saw were the tips of spears. Then I saw the crowns that rested atop their heads.

Elves.

They were the elves that had sided with Valdom. They had either been banished after we imprisoned Valdom, or they had left of their own choice.

They marched forward in their white armor that glittered like diamonds beneath the sunlight, giving them the appearance of Gods.

Their army was massive, at least double the size of ours. Thankfully, the barren weren't gifted with powers, and as far as I knew, they weren't well trained. They were brutes that would tear through flesh and bone, but there was no strategy beneath them, at least not much.

Another line of men appeared.

The army of mages.

Each mage was mounted on a black horse and instead of spears, they held wooden staffs in their right hands. They each wore dark blue robes over their armor and their hood was drawn over their head.

"Ready your arrows!" Amira commanded as she marched up and down the line of archers.

I pulled an arrow back, readying it.

"Fire!" she shouted, her voice rising above the wind.

Releasing our arrows, they soared through the air as one. They arched over the front line of the Barren and rained down upon them. Roars broke out among them but they held their front line.

"Ready!" she shouted and we all pulled another bow from our sheathes. "Aim! Fire!" we released them as one again.

I watched as the line of arrows arched down towards the mass of barren. Screams broke out among them, and they fought to break through their defense line, but then I heard another roar, commanding them to remain in position. We were counting on their chaos, we needed them to break their ranks so we could get the upper hand. I hadn't asked Cadmus how many troops we had, but from the looks of the amount of men we had, it wasn't anywhere close.

"Ready? Aim!" Amira's shout rose above the wind again. I notched another arrow, waiting for her signal when an idea crossed my mind.

Glancing at the tip of my arrow, I willed fire to consume it. As it did, the fire grew down the line, engulfing every tip in flames.

"Good work," Amira smiled behind me. "Fire!" We released our arrows together, and then notched another. As the arrows hit their targets, flames broke out among their ranks. The sound of their pain filled shrieks was like music to my ears.

That was what we needed.

Their front line broke, barren breaking free of it as they charged us. I felt my heart hammering in my chest as I watched our front line of defense. They remained frozen, waiting for the barren to slam into them.

My gaze fell on the men shouting behind our swarm of troops. There were a dozen catapults lined behind our army. Someone shouted something and a large winged beast materialized out of the air. It's red feathers glinted in the morning light. He was at least half the size of a dragon, but his large talons were both wrapped around boulders. He swooped down and dropped the boulders on top of the catapults. The commanding officers commanded something and I watched as the men readied the catapults.

Another shout, and it swung back.

I watched as the boulders hurled through the air. Some barren froze and stared up at the sky with open mouths. The line of mages intercepted the first ones. They outstretched their hands and flashes of purple lit up the skies and the boulders exploded. But more immediately followed.

The next boulders crashed into the sea of barren. There was a series of screams and shrieks that broke out among them. They tried scattering as the boulders slammed into the ground, crushing barren beneath their weight. The barren scattered around them, and I could see the mages shouting back at them, commanding them.

"Ready!" Amira shouted as I watched as our men readied the catapults again.

I turned my attention back towards the barren army and pulled the bow taunt. I breathed out a breath as I focused on them. My body blended in with the bow, making itself a part of me.

"Fire!"

As one, we released our arrows as they soared through the sky towards the barren army. Half a dozen boulders followed behind our volley of arrows.

"Again!" Amira commanded as the arrows hit, then the boulders fell immediately after.

We all pulled our bows taunt and released up on her command, one after the other.

After we had released another two dozen arrows, the barren were closing in on our army. My heart hammered in my ears as I watched the line of mages break down the middle and fan out. The barren broke free, resembling water as it broke free of a dam. My heart lurched into my throat as I watched them surge forward. They ran forward with their arms extended, and mouths open on snarls, much like the animals they were.

Just as the barren reached our front line they rammed into the shields. I could hear the rake of their nails as they tried to shred unsuccessfully through them.

"Hold!" I heard the command rise above the shrieks.

"Ready!" Amira shouted behind us. "Aim for the barren at the front line! Our goal is to take out as many as we can before they break our line of defense!"

I aimed at one of the barren who repeatedly threw its body at a shield. Drool leaked from its cheeks, it dripped over its bottom lip that jutted out and pooled onto his chest.

"Fire!"

I released my arrow and watched as it embedded itself in the chest of its target. We followed her command as we did the same thing repeatedly.

Dozens and dozens of barren lay at the feet of our soldiers.

My eyes flicked up as another large figure breached the top of the hill.

"The Barren King," I gasped as my eyes honed in on him. He rode on the back of a large tiger, who's stripes glittered beneath the sunlight.

"Our new target is the Barren King," Amira shouted behind me. "Take aim!"

Our bows grew taunt simultaneously.

"FIRE!" Amira shouted.

We all took aim at the Barren King and released our arrows. He didn't notice, didn't turn towards us as a volley of arrows embedded in his back. He spun, clawing at them as fire broke out across his back. The flames consumed the robes hanging from his shoulders. The Barren King dropped his head back on a roar and as he spun towards us, the second volley of arrows embedded in his front.

Pure chaos ensued.

The Barren King's body went down as the flames swallowed him entirely.

We continued our assault of arrows, taking down as many barren as we could. Our sheaths magically refilled themselves. My arms quivered, but I would do this until my body dropped from exhaustion.

Our men held their defensive line as we pelted the barren with arrows. We had dropped at least hundreds of them, but more poured over the hill, replacing one with three.

Everything seemed to move in slow motion as a barren ducked beneath one of the shields and raked his claws across one of our soldiers legs. He cried out as he stumbled back and then three barren pounced on him. I heard his screams as they ripped into his flesh.

They had broken our line.

I gasped, choking on air as the barren broke through our front line.

"Hold your positions!" a voice shouted, but the stream of barren continued pouring in, breaking our men into two groups.

"Focus!" Amira shouted. "We cannot let this hinder us. Ready, aim, fire!"

We did as we were told. Soon enough. more bodies littered the battle ground, many of them barren. But the longer my eyes scoured the grounds, the more I noticed the bodies of fae and elves alike littering the ground. My heart twinged. This was different from the attack in Grithel, these men had gone into the fight, knowing very well they could lose their lives, and some of them had.

Scanning my eyes across the ground below me, I searched for a pair of black wings larger than the rest, but came up empty. I didn't feel anything particularly different in regards to his location. All I could feel was the presence of him.

My eyes found Cadmus as he slashed his dagger, cutting open the throat of a barren. It gripped at it's throat as the blood poured over it's hands, and then it crumbled to the ground in a heap. My gaze narrowed on a barren who's body turned towards Cadmus, then honed in on him.

My gaze bounced to Cadmus, but he was distracted as he fought another barren off.

My breath quickened as I watched the single barren tear through the crowd, heading straight for Cadmus. I waited for him to turn, to defend himself, but the other two barren before him were keeping him fully occupied.

"Cadmus!" I shouted, though I knew he was too far for him to hear me.

The Barren hit his back at full speed, sending him flying into the dirt. His clawed hands shredded down his back and Cadmus screamed.

Sheathing my bow and arrow, I broke from my position and ran down the line of men.

"Alethea!" Amira shouted but I continued running.

Running towards the edge of the cliffs, I prayed to every God I could think of, praying and hoping that what I was about to do wasn't completely mental. As I reached the edge of the cliffs, I threw my arms out and jumped.

I let my body become flames, willing me to spread across the ground and down the side of the mountain. My vision blurred as I felt my body moving. Amira's shouts died out as I flew across the ground. The very air I breathed was pure fire, replenishing me as I landed on my feet.

"Cadmus!" I shouted as I unsheathed my sword.

I spun, driving it into the chest of the nearest barren. It squealed as the blade ripped through its chest and stomach. I kicked it back as its body limped and ripped my sword from its body.

"Alethea, what are you doing?" Cadmus demanded. I could hear the pain lining his voice as he spun towards the barren that had attacked him. I tried to ignore the missing clumps of skin from his back and leathers as he spun towards the barren. He raised his leg, his boot landing square in the barren's chest.

"You were about to die!" I snapped as I swung around towards another barren that barrelled towards me.

I imagined that we were practicing, that we were joining in on that dance of swishes, jabs, ducks, and spins as we had done before.

Barren swarmed all around, their teeth gnashed and saliva dripped from their chins. Half of them were in shredded clothing.

Cadmus and I kept our backs flat as we fought in a circle. We took down barren after barren, the pile around us growing. My arms grew heavy as they continued their attack.

I screeched as a pair of razor sharp claws raked down my arm. It ripped open my leathers, exposing my skin to the cold air. Spinning towards the barren, I let my blade fly until it hit bone. The barren didn't get out another squeal before it's head fell from its shoulders and rolled towards my feet.

Lowering my sword, my breath heaved as I let my body rest for a moment. I raised my head, my eyes clashed with Cadmus. His mouth was open on a gasp and his wide eyes moved down to the head now resting at my feet.

My arms shook with the effort to keep my blade up. I had exhausted nearly all of my powers, and needed to recharge before I could use them to the same capacity. Cadmus was trying to work his way through the crowd to the edge of the battle so I could rest. My body was beginning to shake from exhaustion, and I knew if I didn't rest, I'd collapsed.

I agreed once I rested, I'd rejoin the archers at the top of the cliffs above us.

I froze as a familiar face emerged from the mass of bodies. A face that haunted my nightmares up until my mating bond with Mykill had been completed.

The High Priest.

He laughed as he slowly began circling me.

"Alethea," he cooed as a sinister smile pulled at his lips. "My, I see immortality suits you."

"You did this to me," I growled.

"I did this to you?" He laughed as he shook his head. "No, I *gave* this to you. You were a rotting hunk of flesh before I gave you immortality."

"Why did you do it?"

He shrugged his shoulders. "Boredom. Curiosity. I had countless reasons."

"You killed my entire family."

"Well, your mother, yes. Your father's death is on your head. Your sister," he paused as he twirled the glittering blade sword in his hand. "Well, she played me. She died helping you flee, so I would say her death is on your head too. But even your mother's death was the result of you fleeing, so I'd say her death is your fault too."

I gritted my teeth as I tightened my grip on the hilt of my sword. "You took everything from me!" I spat. "Everything!"

Flames sputtered across the ground, catching at the ends of his cloak. The High Priest spun, trying to extinguish the flames. I dove forward as he spun back towards me, and as he did, I drove my blade through his gut. His mouth fell open on a gasp as he leaned into me. I caught him with an arm across his shoulders as he slowly sunk forward. His knees hit the ground as I pulled out my blade and leaned into his ear.

"I told you I'd kill you," I breathed as I sheathed my sword with one hand and pulled my dagger from my belt.

He choked again as I dug the dagger into the side of his neck. I ripped it out as he gurgled on his own blood that spilled from his lips, and stood. I stared down at his slowly dying body. I was fed up with so many underestimating me.

"I must say," an unfamiliar cold face said from behind me. "I didn't expect you to show such strength."

I whipped towards the voice, my skin turning to ice as I took him in.

I could feel the death that clung to his skin as he circled me. His skin was ghastly white and constantly shifted. If I stared too long, I could see faces that looked like they were trying to break free from the confines of his skin. Ghostly faces twisted in agony before the face disappeared.

My eyes slid up his cloaked form.

My blood had raised him, it was linked to him, so I recognized him right away even though I had never met him.

The Black Mage.

"I killed your lackey," I pointed the tip of my sword towards the High Priest.

"He was power hungry," The Black Mage shrugged. "I would have killed him myself eventually."

"Alethea" Cadmus interrupted behind me.

The Black Mage's eyes slid behind me, narrowing in on Cadmus.

"General," the Black Mage greeted. "Or should I say *former* General?"

Cadmus moved in front of me, blocking the Black Mage's view of me. But this wasn't a time where I would be careless. I knew the Black Mage was here to kill me, kill us all.

"My, you two seem to be quite close. Was King Eryx aware of that when you two were living in his castle?"

I gritted my teeth as my hands fisted. "Eryx is dead, his opinion no longer matters to me."

The Black Mage laughed. "I expected that. I could see the anger festering inside of you the longer you remained with him. I just wish I could've been there to see the look on his face when your powers consumed him."

Cadmus outstretched his arm before me as the Black Mage stepped closer.

It was like the barren around us knew we were off limits. We weren't theirs to kill, we were his.

The thought should have been unnerving, should have had me cowering and begging for mercy. But I would do no such thing. His words stirred something in me, something that had remained hidden for far too long. The part of me that longed for justice. This man was responsible for hundreds of deaths. He was a murder that relished in other's pain, and I would rather relish in his, becoming the monster he was, to protect those I loved.

"Don't move towards her," Cadmus growled.

The Black Mage laughed as he cocked his head to the side. "And what are you going to do about it? Even your powers combined are no match for mine."

Cadmus dove forward, throwing his hand out and a blade went flying towards hhe Black Mage's head. He flung his wrist and the blade went flying straight back towards Cadmus. I cried out as the blade embedded in his shoulder.

Cadmus grunted as he stumbled back a step and gripped the wound.

"You can't defeat me," the Black Mage laughed as he threw his hand towards us.

Cadmus' arms went around my waist as he swung me away from the stream of shadows that erupted from his palm. The Black Mage's laugh followed. My skin felt like it turned to ice as the shadows tried licking at my skin.

"Run, Alethea, run!" Cadmus shouted and then his arms fell away from around me.

I whipped my head towards him only to find shadows had crawled up and curled around both of his legs. Cadmus clawed at the ground as the shadows began pulling him backwards towards what I could only describe as what looked like a black pit in the mud. Part of me knew that if he was dragged into there, he would remain the Black Mages prisoner for eternity.

"Cadmus!" I screamed as the shadows continued to drag him backwards.

I threw my hand out, forming a whip out of flames that wrapped around Cadmus' wrist and dropped my body back as I pulled. I used my other hand and lobbed balls of fire at the shadows. As the flames made contact with them, they hissed and the shadows fizzled away.

The Black Mage tsked as his shadows dispersed entirely. "That was sneaky." He opened his mouth to speak again but froze as a smile spread across his lips. "Another player has joined the match," the Black Mage laughed.

My steps halted as pure, godly power wove through the battle ground. I could feel him as the ground trembled beneath his footsteps. I felt the air shift, electrifying. Turning, I first saw the tip of pitch black wings towering over the heads of people in battle.

"Alethea," Cadmus said and his hand wrapped around my elbow.

"Mykill," I gasped as the battle before me seemed to part.

No one dared cross his path as his wings extended on either side of him.

He was pristine, unscathed and God-like. There wasn't a speck of blood on him and not a single bruise.

His icy eyes clashed with mine and it felt like that ice sucked all the air from my lungs. I ripped my arm from Cadmus' grip and my feet were moving before I could stop them. I needed to touch him, to confirm that he was in fact alive and breathing, even if I could still feel him through the mating bond. My legs and arms pumped to push myself faster as I made my way towards him.

As I neared him, I opened my arms but was met with a rounding kick to my side. I gasped as I fell backward into the mud. All the air rushed from my lungs as pain wound it's way up my spine.

"Mykill, what are you doing?" I gasped as I cradled my side. I pushed up on one arm and glanced up at him.

His eyes darkened as he towered over me. His leg swung towards me and I used the agility that he had taught me to roll away. His deep laugh followed as I stumbled to my feet and swung back towards him.

"Mykill." My voice broke on the plea as he turned to face me.

There wasn't an ounce of recognition in his gaze as he cocked his head to the side and laughed again. "Is that my name?"

Goosebumps erupted across my skin at the deep timbre of his voice. But that voice held so much violence, a promise of death and I knew that he wouldn't hesitate to kill me.

"What are you doing?" I breathed in disbelief as I fell back another step as he stepped towards me again. "No, don't come near me." I outstretched a hand towards him.

"Oh but that's not what you wanted a minute ago," he teased, but there was no humor in his voice.

"What did they do to you?" I gaped. "You would never hurt me. I'm your mate!"

"You don't mean anything to me," he responded.

He moved quicker than I could track. His fingers wrapped around my throat, lifting my feet off the ground and his other fist flew into my already bruised rib cage. I wheezed out a breath as he threw me back again. I rolled a couple times before hitting what I could only guess was a body. I shoved myself up as he began prowling towards me.

As I shoved to my feet, I pulled my bow out, along with a single arrow.

"Mykill, stop!" I commanded as I notched the arrow and aimed straight at his heart.

His steps faltered and a small smirk pulled at his lips. His arms were suspended on either side of him, like he was trying to balance and he shifted all of his weight to his front foot.

"What are you doing?" I heaved and ignored the tremor working its way from my battered ribcage.

"What I was told," he simply said as he outstretched his hand.

I didn't have time to respond as a stroke of lightning flashed across the sky and then wrapped around my wrist. My mouth fell open in protest but before I could speak, my bow was ripped from my hands. It cluttered across the mud away from me, leaving me entirely defenseless.

My head snapped back up to take him in and I could see the predatory smile pulling at his lips.

"Would you like to try something else?" He raised an eyebrow at me and then smiled cruelly. "So that I can just as easily disarm you?"

My hands fisted at my sides. I knew he was goading me, even if he didn't recognize me, there was a part of him that could see the way his arrogant attitude grated on me.

He dove forward, his arms wrapping around my body as we both sailed towards the ground. He didn't care to shield my body from taking the blow as we hit the ground. I cried out as I clutched to the front of his leathers. I rolled onto my back and he slowly rose above me.

"Please don't do this," I pleaded.

He didn't even look at me as he reared his leg back. His boot landed a blow, crunching bone, to my ribcage again and I went flying back. All the breath whooshed out of my lungs as my back hit the ground. Mud erupted all around me and my eyes closed as my head snapped back onto the ground. Pain flared up and down my limbs as I tried to force one breath after the other.

I thought he would have been there to help us. To help us defeat the barren, the Black Mage, and help put an end to this war.

"Mykill, please," I begged as I scurried backwards on my elbows. "Please, don't do this. I don't know what he's done to you but he's in your head."

Mykill's lips turned up in a sinister smile as he advanced on me. He spun his blade between his fingers and as quick as lightning, he flung his blade forward. I cried out as it embedded into the side of my thigh. He unsheathed his sword as I clutched my leg with shaking hands.

"Mykill, please stop!" I screamed and yanked the blade from my leg. I wrapped my fingers around the hilt and grunted as he shoved me down with his boot.

I didn't have time to react as he drove his sword into my shoulder. My back arched and I screamed as it broke through bone out onto the other side, embedding into the ground beneath me.

"You're weak," he spit and laughed as he released the sword and circled my body.

The world around me seemed to swim, moving in slow motion as realization crashed over me.

This was what he meant when he said that a mating bond left no room for selfishness. If I were being selfish, I would fight him until he killed me because I knew there was no way I could overpower him. If I were being selfish, I would hold onto that hope anyway until he smeared me into the mud beneath his boots. If I were being selfish, more mothers would have to weep over the bodies of their babies, father's would hold the bodies of their wives and children they couldn't protect. If I were being selfish, I would have given us more time.

Fated to love, fated to fall.

I wrapped my fingers around the blade still strapped to my side he had somehow overlooked. Tears burned my eyes as he lowered himself to his knees and knelt over me. He gripped my face and smiled, the smile equally haunting and equally beautiful.

I looked into his eyes one last time and my heart panged at the darkness of them. But that was what gave me the courage to do what needed to be done.

"I love you so much," I breathed and then using every ounce of strength in my body, I slid the blade into his chest.

His eyes bulged as the hilt hit bone and I released it. His mouth fell open as he pushed off of me. He tried to stand but fell to his knees beside me. He stared at the protruding blade and then back at me. I could see the realization set across his face of what he'd done as the darkness faded from his eyes.

"Alethea," he gasped before his body fell to the ground beside me.

His cold hand found mine, our fingers intertwined.

"Alethea," he rasped again.

Please, I prayed, *if you take him, take me.*

The tears slid down either side of my face as my eyes grew heavier.

"I'm so sorry," I sobbed as I laid there. If he was going to die, then death would have to take me too.

"Mykill? Alethea?" a voice above us gasped and then I felt hands skim down my arms. "Oh my gods. Help him, I've got her."

I forced my eyes open and managed to open them in slits as I stared up at Felix.

"Alethea," Felix spoke as he slid a hand around the back of my neck and lifted it lightly. "I need to take the blade out."

I wanted to tell him it was too late for me, I could feel my life being pulled away by something otherworldly.

"He's alright," someone said and then I felt freezing hands grasp my face.

"Alethea," Mykill begged as he placed his trembling lips to mine. "Alethea, my love, I am so sorry. Please just hold on."

"The prophecy," I breathed. "It wasn't talking about me and Eryx. It meant you and I." My vision blurred as my head fell to the side.

"Shhh, it's okay love," Mykill whispered as he gripped my cheeks and pressed another kiss to my lips. "Please, keep your eyes open. We're going to get you to a healer, I just need you to hold on."

"I can't," I breathed as my head slumped to the side.

"No, love, Alethea!" he cried but his voice sounded so far away. "Alethea! Alethea!"

I knew as the cold leached over me, cold so different from Mykill's cold, that I wouldn't be rejuvenated. Unlike Mykill's touch, this cold would pull me down and under until I crossed the veil.

Mykill

"Alethea!" I called frantically as I grasped her face in between stained hands.

Red marred her cheeks where my blood soaked hands touched them.

Where *her* blood touched them.

Her eyes drifted closed and I could tell by the heavy fall of her chest, that it was her last. I gripped onto her shoulders as I tried to push any semblance of life into her that I could.

"Please, no, no, no," I begged as I felt my bottom lip tremble. "I'm so sorry, I'm so sorry," I repeated the words over and over again, just hoping they'd somehow reach her.

I had killed her.

Shock radiated through my limbs as I fell back, resting on my heels.

I had killed her.

I had been terrified the Black Mage, or the High Priest, or even the barren would kill her. But in the end it had been me.

Me.

Her lover, her mate.

She had become my undoing, and in turn I had become hers.

"No," Cadmus gasped as he slid an arm beneath her shoulders and pulled her up into his lap. "No, you will not die! Do you hear me?"

I wanted to tell him it was too late as I stared at his grief filled face. She was gone. Alethea was gone.

My shining mate was gone, now duller than the night sky.

The war continued raging on around us as if the world hadn't just lost the only semblance of light it had.

My hands shook as I fisted them in my lap, my powers roared beneath my skin, needing to lash out at something. I dropped my head back as a roar tore from my throat. It ripped through me, shredding through everything it came in contact with as the ball of power left me in a mighty whoosh.

There was no reason for the war to continue if we lost her. There was no reason for life to continue if we had lost her. My mate who had lost so much, and in the end sacrificed herself.

She knew what she was doing.
She knew.
I had once told her that a mating bond didn't leave room for selfishness and I could see that thought replaying in her tear stricken eyes as she buried her dagger into my chest.

I rubbed absently at where I knew the scar would be as I felt tears surge forward. Cadmus rocked slightly with her body as he muttered prayers to the Gods.

"Gods, Alethea," I breathed as I reached for her. Cadmus released her immediately as I lifted her against my chest. "I'm so sorry," I breathed into her neck as I tucked her against my chest.

I felt a sob break out of me as I tightened my grip on her.

"I'm so sorry!" I cried as I burrowed my face into her skin, if only to breathe her scent one last time before it drifted away with her.

My strong Alethea. One of the strongest women I had ever met in my life, who was full of so much spunk, so much laughter, so much mystery but also so much brokenness. This broken girl had in turn broken me.

Chapter 19

Alethea

Mykill's frantic gaze was the last thing I saw.

I smiled softly as the words, *I love you, I love you, I love you*, settled over me until his love burned through me. It settled over me like a warm blanket, comforting as the coldness pulled me deeper. So deep I couldn't hear him anymore. I couldn't feel anything. I didn't feel sad that I wouldn't get to spend the rest of my fae years with Mykill. I didn't remember the names of the ones we lost on the battlefield.

A breath expelled out of me and my body felt like it was floating, drifting in an endless river of nothing but air. The air wrapped around me, pulling me to its destination.

I must have crossed the veil.

Brief images danced across my mind. Images of rushed kisses and secret affairs. Two faces that were so familiar but lives that were so different but the images confirmed my suspicions. The face was pale as a sheet with pitch black hair and eyes colder than a glacier. The human man smiled back at me, so warm but so wrong. This man looked identical to Mykill but the spirit within him was so different. Not the man I had come to love, but the man *she* had come to love.

The woman looked exactly like me with ruby red eyes and strawberry blonde hair. But she carried herself with power, grace. When she stepped, the ground trembled, waiting to obey her every command.

I watched as their lives unfolded before them. I watched as she gave up her powers, ripping out a piece of herself to be with the man she loved, the memories engulfed me until I was her.

I hunched over as the fist around my heart tightened.

"There are consequences for such actions," a deep voice boomed around me.

"I don't care!" I cried out as I dropped my head back.

"Please, my love, please stop this!" Stephian begged.

"I want to be with you!" I exclaimed. "I don't want immortality if I can't have you!"

"These actions cannot be undone," the deep voice boomed again.

"Just take them! Take my powers!" I said and no sooner than the words left my lips, did that fist tighten entirely.

My body hunched over as I wheezed out a breath. Stephian caught me as I fell forward, my hands clawed at my chest as I fought for my next breath.

I was dying, I was sure of it.

My chest burned with lack of air. I felt my heart begin to beat, something it had never done before. I felt the blood in my veins begin to flow, warming my skin, keeping me alive.

Mortality was so painful, each breath I breathed grew weaker and weaker until I would one day not breathe again. My limbs ached with the heaviness of themselves. The glow of my skin had died, leaving me pale and plain.

I lifted my head to find his blue eyes fixated on me. There were wide with fear.

"I'm okay, my love," I said as I reached up to cup the side of his face.

"You scared me," he breathed and I felt my heart crumble at the sight of tears that rushed to his eyes. Then his eyes scanned over me, surely making sure I was unharmed. "Your glow is gone."

I nodded as I rose up onto my knees. "I am no longer immortal."

He nodded slowly as his eyes fixed themselves once again on my face. "You're so beautiful."

I felt my lips stretch into a small smile as his arms fell around my waist. His love crashed into me as his body enveloped me. I dropped my head onto his shoulder and sighed. I would never have to face a day without him. We would one day die together, and face death together.

I couldn't think of a greater joy.

I gasped as I was ripped from her memory. I still felt the faint hands of his arms around me, but to me it felt wrong. It felt familiar, but still so wrong. The man she loved, although an ancestor to Mykill, was not the man I loved.

"Well done, Alethea," A feminine voice echoed around me, *my* voice echoed around me. "You have saved your lover, and in turn saved yourself."

I wanted to frown, or ask what she meant, but my lips wouldn't work. It felt like I was being pulled through a pool of sludge. Everything around me moved slowly, my thoughts, her voice even. I didn't know where I would be pulled out of this pool of sludge, but I hoped it was somewhere I could at least see my family.

I felt the sludge slink away as it felt like I was placed down on my feet. The space around me was clear, but also endless. As I spun, I froze at the sight of the small cottage before me. I glanced around it, but there was nothing around it. There wasn't green grass, there wasn't a chicken coop, a garden, nothing that made it the home I had grown up in beside the familiar look of it.

But something inside called to me. I slowly took a tentative step forward. But as I did, I was almost thrown forward. The space around me blurred and as it cleared, I was standing inside the cottage facing the door, the inside of the door.

"Alethea," a soft, unfamiliar voice spoke from behind me.

I swung towards the voice, and outstretched my hand ready to protect myself. "Who are you?"

There was a man and woman standing side by side. He was at least two heads taller than her, with a broad build, and she was the total opposite. She was thin and dainty, the epitome of femininity with her long golden hair and soft brown doe eyes.

Something in me called to her even though I had never seen her before. I cocked my head to the side as I stepped towards her.

"Who are you?" I whispered.

She cocked her head to the side too, matching my movement as a slow smile spread across her face. "I think you know who we are."

My mouth fell open in shock. The longer I stared at the two of them, the more I could see the resemblance. My small nose, light skin and hair, I had the same hazel eyes as the tall man.

"Mother? Father?" I breathed as tears rushed my eyes.

It couldn't be.

Her smile grew as tears pricked the corners of her eyes too. She nodded.

My feet moved before I could even think another thing. I ran forward and threw my arms around both of their middles as I pulled them to me. She laughed softly, followed by his deep chuckle as their arms circled me.

Something inside me shattered at their touch. The touch I had craved since I had first learned of them. I could feel them, smell them as the tears flowed freely over my cheeks.

"We're so glad to have met you finally as an adult," Mother whispered as her hand stroked my hair.

I pulled away and shook my head.

"I'm so sorry," I choked. "I didn't want you to die for me! I didn't want any of you to die for me!"

"We died protecting you," she whispered as her hands cupped my face. "And we wouldn't have had it any other way."

"But you didn't get to see me grow up, you didn't get to experience my life with me!"

She cocked her head to the side and stroked her thumbs across my cheeks. "We were always watching."

I nodded as she wiped the tears away from my cheeks. Her touch warmed something in my chest in a way nothing had before. Her touch was relaxing.

"We love you," Father spoke as he ran a hand down the back of my hair. "We will always love you, and we will always watch over you."

"There's someone else who wanted to see you." Mother waved a hand behind me and I felt my back stiffen before I slowly turned back towards the door.

There was a thin, tall body standing in the door frame. Her lips were spread into a wide smile, showing her teeth, and her blonde hair was pulled up into a braid that was draped over her shoulder. My eyes scanned her body, searching for the blood that had marred her body from the last time I had seen her.

She was moving towards me before I could finish.

"Laney!" I cried as her body slammed into mine.

Her long arms embraced me, and I felt the tears come full force as I tightened mine around her.

"Oh sister," she breathed into my hair. "I'm so sorry I couldn't be with you."

"It's not your fault, I'm just sorry I couldn't protect you."

"Alethea," another voice called.

The mother and father who had raised me.

My mouth fell open on a sob as I pulled away from Laney.

I tried to form words as I stared at their pristine forms as they stepped up beside us. But all I could do was flubber before I felt another part of me break. More tears fell as they stepped forward and embraced us.

"We missed you, biscuit," Father whispered.

I cried harder in response to his nickname.

"You've got to go back," Mother said as she pulled away and placed her hands on my shoulders.

I shook my head. "But what if I don't want to?"

Mother smiled at me and chuckled. "Your mate is waiting for you."

Mykill.

His face filtered into my mind, familiarity settling over my bones as I pictured his chiseled face. Blue eyes as cold as a glacier, skin that was always smooth and cold to the touch.

My heart clenched, I missed him so much.

I nodded as I stepped away from Mother. She stepped aside, letting me pass and I paused as I placed a hand on the door frame.

I glanced back at the five of them and smiled. They were together, and waiting for me whenever I crossed into death. It was a serene feeling, although death seemed like a scary thing, I knew they would be waiting for me with open arms one day.

Stepping through the door, I felt a tug in my chest, and as I closed it, I let out a gasp.

Pushing my eyes open, I groaned as I turned my head to the side. It felt like pokers were stabbing behind both eyes and my stomach was a raging inferno of hunger.

"Alethea," Mykill's voice gasped and I felt cold hands on my cheeks. "Love, take it slowly."

"Mykill?" I grumbled. "Are you, you?"

Cold hands landed on my arms as I continued trying to push myself up. "You should move slowly, you were gravely injured."

"What happened?" I grumbled again. I swallowed trying to wet my parched mouth and throat. I shoved his hands away as I sat up fully, ignoring the lightheadedness.

"Alethea, I am so, so sorry. Please forgive me," he begged as he dropped to his knees and bowed his head. "I understand if you never want to see me again but please know that I am so, so sorry."

"Mykill," I said as I tightened my grip on the bed on either side of me. "Please, look at me."

He remained frozen for a moment but as he slowly raised his head, I inhaled. His eyes were full of unshed tears and were bloodshot. "Alethea-"

"Just come up here," I begged as my voice broke. "I just need you."

I barely finished the words as he rose to his knees and wrapped his arms around me. I ignored the pain shooting through my aching body as he tightened his arms around me. I didn't care about it, I didn't care about anything but being here with him.

"It wasn't your fault," I whispered into his shirt. "There's nothing to forgive."

I needed him to hear the words, I needed him to believe them because they were the truest words I'd ever spoken. There was nothing to forgive.

His arms tightened around me and it sounded like he tried to say my name, but it came out a strangled cry.

And my beautiful, strong mate wept.

I kept my arms tightened around his neck as his fingers curled into me. He held me like I would disappear if he let go. Every sob he let out was like a knife to the chest. So I held him, comforting him, letting him know that I was alive and well.

"Mykill," I breathed as I cupped his jaw, tilting his head back. There was no wall in his eyes this time, his eyes communicated the despair he'd felt about how he had hurt me. They communicated the grief and guilt that was eating away at him. "Kiss me."

He was moving before the words fully left my lips.

He rose up, sealing the space between our lips as he pushed me backwards. My hands cupped his face and my thumbs brushed the tears away from his cheeks.

I wrapped my arms around his neck as I pulled his chest flush to mine. I didn't want any space between us.

There wasn't space for anything else, just us and our love wrapping around us, filling us until we could feel nothing else. His lips found mine as I arched off the bed, pressing myself further into him.

"Please," I begged as my knees tightened around his hips.

He groaned into my mouth as his hands traced down the outside of my thighs and then calves as he rose up on his knees. His eyes pierced into my soul, latching onto me in a grip so tight it made my chest constrict. His hands fell on my hips as he lowered himself back on top of me and sealed our bodies together. One of his hands delved into my hair as the other squeezed my hip. We became one in a single thrust and I arched into him as he claimed my mouth as his own once again.

My thoughts blurred together until there was a single coherent thought, and it was him. He was where I started and where I ended and everywhere in between. His love filled every broken crack in my broken soul. His love breathed life into my battered lungs. He completed me in ways no one else had.

His name slipped from my lips as I shattered in his embrace, and he followed shortly after.

We remained tangled together for quite some time before he rolled off of me and settled on the bed beside me. Even then, we remained quiet as our thoughts consumed us both. We had been so lucky to make it out alive, especially when so many others hadn't. So many had risked their lives, so many would have to bury their family members, and the thought alone took a piece of my heart I knew I wasn't going to get back.

Turning my head towards him, I took in his neutral expression. The wall was back as his eyes followed along the length of my body.

"Can you drop the wall?" I whispered as my fingers danced along his cheek.

He stared at me, his breath coming out in quick pants before I saw it. I saw that glacier between us come tumbling down until it lay in scattered shards around him. I could see every emotion across his face. I could see the guilt that continued eating him up, I could see the wonder written across his face as he stared at me and every other emotion, the pain, the fear, all of it.

I offered him a small smile as his hand rested on my hip, giving me a knowing squeeze.

"The prophecy meant *we* were supposed to fall. That was the only way it could be fulfilled. One of us had to die, but by the prophecy being fulfilled, I was given new life," I finally spoke. "I saw *them*, our ancestors, I saw their lives, and their love. It was beautiful."

Mykill only nodded as he trailed his finger down my cheek. I smiled and closed my eyes as it trailed down my neck and chest before he rested his palm on my stomach.

"I want to take a bath," I grumbled as I pushed up off of the bed and headed towards the washroom.

"I'll join you."

I laughed as he came up behind me, his arms encircling my waist as we stumbled forward together.

Chapter 20

Mykill

I kept my arms around her waist as I carried her into the bathroom. We stumbled around like love sick newlyweds, but I didn't care how ridiculous that made me feel. I would rather have a lifetime of feeling ridiculous compared to a lifetime of never seeing her again.

I dropped my arms from around her as I moved towards the bath but then I stilled as she froze in front of the mirror. Her lips parted as a small gasp slipped from them.

"It scarred," she breathed.

I didn't need her to explain.

I stepped up behind her, my eyes falling on the scar that had taken up permanent residency on her shoulder. The scar *I* had given her.

"I did everything I could think of but Lira said there was nothing else that could be done." My throat clenched at the thought of seeing the scar on her shoulder.

Not only would it be a forever reminder to me, but to her, that I hurt her. I was so close to killing her. If she hadn't stabbed me, I would have ripped her heart from her chest. When I had looked down at her, there wasn't an ounce of familiarity, all she had been was a face I had been ordered to kill.

Her eyes slid over to me, and then shock and confusion flitted across her pretty face.

She turned towards me, eyes wide as they fell on my bare chest. "What happened?" she demanded.

She raised her hand, placing the tips of her fingers at the edge of the raised skin across my chest.

"Forever a reminder of my imprisonment," I said quietly as she ran the tip of her finger over it.

Her mouth fell open as she gasped for words. Tears glistened in her eyes, slicing my chest open as the words tumbled out of her. "Mykill, I'm so sorry. I-"

I lifted my arms and wrapped my fingers around her wrists as I pulled them away. "My love, you have nothing to apologize for."

Her lips parted again and her gaze dropped back to the scar. But the tears didn't recede, they only grew until they slipped down her cheeks silently. I slid my arms around her shoulders and pulled her into me. I felt her hands cover her face as her voice choked on a cry.

"Please don't cry for me," I breathed as I tightened my arms around her.

"I can't help it," she whispered into my chest.

Gods, I thought. *How had I gotten blessed with such a compassionate soul?* She had been the balance I needed, the splash of color for my otherwise gray life.

She was the sun in my darkest night, the light that lit up every corner of darkness in my soul. She was the emotions I had refused to feel, and the laughter that had evaded me the majority of my life.

When her tears subsided, I coaxed her over to the bath.

Grasping her hands, I lowered her into the back and followed behind her. My bath was much larger than the one at Emerald Mountain. The tub was deep enough to swallow both of us whole. She laid back on my chest for a few peaceful moments and I let my fingers brush through the strands of hair that rested on her arms.

After we sat there, in our blissful silence for some time, I nudged her slightly. She shifted forward and brought her knees to her chest. I grabbed one of the bottles of shampoo that rested on the lip and squirted some of the creamy liquid into my palm.

"The Black Mage escaped. No one has seen or heard from him," I explained slowly as I worked the soap into her locks.

"What are we going to do?" she asked, panic rose up in her voice. "If he's out there, he will come for us again."

"I've got men out here searching, we will find him," I tried to assure her.

The Black Mage was the last thing I wanted her to worry about. I had dozens of my men scouring the surrounding kingdoms, slipping into villages to see if there was even a whisper of him. I knew there probably wouldn't be, he was probably hiding somewhere the Barren had supplied him.

I summoned water to rise up on either side of her shoulders and then gently worked its way through her hair as it washed out the soap. Suds danced atop the surface of the water as it did until there wasn't a sud left in her hair.

She let out a sigh as she reclined fully against my chest, and I dropped an arm around her waist.

The silence spanned between us, but neither of us spoke as we basked in the presence of each other. I couldn't get the image of her broken and bleeding out in my arms from my mind. Whenever I blinked, it flashed behind my lids. The feel of her warm blood that coated my hands and the sound of her shallow breaths.

I hadn't told her that her heart had stopped and she had stopped breathing. She had died in my arms, and it would be something I would never forget. For the several minutes I thought she was dead had been the worst in my miserable existence. If her heart hadn't started beating, I would've slit my own throat. She had died because I had killed her. Her body had been broken because of me. I was the one who drove that sword through her shoulder that secured her to the ground. I was the one who had driven the blade into her thigh. Every drop of blood of hers that had been spilt had been because of me.

"I killed Eryx," she breathed, interrupting my thoughts.

I stiffened behind her, stroking my thumb across her forearm. "Lira told me," I finally said.

"I wasn't even sad," she laughed bitterly. "We went through hell together but in the end it was me against him. Everything we went through together for it to end like that. The Fates must enjoy their little games."

"I'm sorry," I whispered and then placed a light kiss to her bare shoulder.

She was silent for a few moments before she spoke again. "I'm not. He made me his prisoner, and took you from me. In the end, he deserved what he got."

She dropped her head to the side as I kissed her bare shoulder again. My lips moved up her shoulder and I smiled as I felt her shiver against me.

My hand landed on the inside of her thigh, slowly moving towards the center of her legs. I felt her body stiffen partially, as she inhaled sharply. Her chest rose and fell quickly as I let the tips of my fingers skate up the inside of her thigh. I hooked my feet on the insides of her ankles, angling her legs open as my fingers continued their ascent.

She let out a breathy moan as her head fell back on my shoulder, and I claimed her mouth with a kiss before she made another sound. Her palms rested on my arm that remained secured around her waist, securing her to me. Her fingers curled into my skin as the tips of my fingers met the bundle of nerves between her legs. She yelped against my mouth, and I swallowed it with a growl. I tightened my arm around her waist, pulling her impossibly closer until there wasn't a breath between us.

She tried pulling her legs closed, but I wouldn't oblige, keeping them captive.

"Mykill," she gasped as she tugged against me again.

I flicked a finger and the stopper unplugged and began letting the water drain from the tub. I kept an arm secured around her waist as I lifted to my feet and stepped out of the tub. I grabbed the towel draped on the chair beside it and began drying us both down. Her eyes were hooded and her cheeks were flushed as she watched beneath her lashes.

After I dried us, I stepped up to her again and she dropped her head back. I smiled as I cupped the side of her face and kissed her again. She breathed in content as I did and I slid an arm around her waist, sealing her to me and then lifted her. Her legs wrapped around my waist as I began carrying her into the bedroom.

Her fingers slid up the back of my neck and tangled in the hair at the nape of my neck as I reached the end of the bed.

Laying her back on the bed, her strawberry blonde hair fanned out in wet waves around her head. She began moving backwards towards the headboard, waiting for me to join her.

I took my time as I crawled up her body. My lips skimmed over every inch of her as I marked it. My tongue swirled against her skin, tasting every bit of her before I finally settled above her.

She gazed up at me with hooded eyes as her legs tightened around my hips. My thumb stroked her cheek as I pecked her lips softly with mine as I slid into her.

Her back arched off the bed, and I slid an arm around her, needing to feel her silky skin. I pulled her further into me as her lips parted on a gasp.

She whimpered my name which was nearly my undoing as I let her consume me.

Alethea

"I'm starving," I said as I finished lacing up the bust of my blouse.

Mykill outstretched a hand to me as I dropped my hands. He tugged me after him as we made our way out into the halls. My stomach roared for the millionth time and I grumbled as he barked out a loud laugh.

He waved a hand and the door opened and my feet froze. I had forgotten that the table was still charred.

"Did you have fun in here without me?" Mykill asked as he glanced back at me.

My cheeks heated and then as I glanced at the table as tears flooded my eyes again. I recalled the hopelessness I had felt. The mere thought of him being in their hands again was enough to nearly drive me to my knees.

"I did that when I couldn't track you through the mating bond." My voice was so quiet I wasn't sure he heard me.

"I'm here love and I promise you I'm not going anywhere," his voice was tender as he turned towards me and gripped my cheeks.

I only nodded as my chest picked up. He was here, he was standing in front of me, he was touching me but I couldn't get the fear that had etched itself into my very bones to go away. Just the thought of him being taken nearly sent me into a spiral as his thumbs stroked my cheeks.

"I was so scared I'd never see you again," I finally sobbed.

No sooner than the words left my lips did Mykill wrap his arms around me. He pulled me into him as I buried my face in his chest. The tears came harder the more he consoled me. My fingers curled into his chest as his hands stroked down my hair.

"I'm here, my love," he whispered and then pressed a kiss to the top of my head.

I pulled away as I wiped beneath my eyes. "I know, I just feel like I can't breathe when I think about it."

"No matter what they would have done to me, I would have found a way to crawl my way back to you. Even if the very ground claimed me, at least I would be the soul beneath your feet."

My mouth fell open as I stared up at his face. He leaned towards me and placed a kiss to my forehead.

"Let's get you some food," he whispered before turning back towards the entrance to the dining room.

Mykill's steps faltered and I grumbled as I crashed into his back.

"What are you doing?" I mumbled as I went to move around him but his arm shot out, blocking my path.

"Alethea, run." His voice was so low, it sent chills cascading across my skin.

Fear spiked in the back of my throat as I gripped his arm. I poked my head out from behind his folded wing and my heart plummeted into my stomach.

"You didn't think you'd be seeing me so soon, did you?" The Black Mage chuckled as he waved a hand.

My head snapped to the side as the three sets of doors surrounding us all slapped closed, sealing us off from the world beyond. I felt the sliver of wards down my spine, locking us in entirely.

I glanced over at Mykill as I felt my heart lurch into my throat. He didn't look at me as he kept his gaze pinned on the Black Mage.

My hands shook slightly as fear leetched its way into my body.

"What do you want?" Mykill asked slowly.

His voice sent shivers down my spine. I had only heard him speak in such a tone a few times, and it had only been when I had been in danger.

"I want to see you dead," the Black Mage said before he threw a hand towards us.

Mykill shouted as the purple ball of crackling energy soared through the air towards us. I outstretched my hands in front of me, throwing up a ward and watched as it fizzled out around it.

I could feel the shock radiating from Mykill, but he had been away for a while and wasn't aware of the things I had learned to do.

The Black Mage's beady eyes settled on me and I felt the tremble of Mykill's powers as they flared in response.

"Come on, *King*," the Black Mage taunted as he extended his arms on either side of him.

Mykill threw out his hand, a bolt of lightning flew from his hand and arched straight towards the Black Mage's chest. The Black Mage laughed as he deflected the bolt and then threw his hand out.

I gasped as my body went flying backwards, spinning through the air before I crashed into the wall. Pain flared across my ribcage as I crashed to the floor. My cheek bounced off the marble, making my head spin as I slowly pushed myself up on my hands and knees.

I raised my head as Mykill crawled towards me. His wings were tucked in behind him.

"Alethea, run," he whispered as his hand covered mine.

"I'm not going to leave you," I panted as I raised my head to meet his gaze.

"He's going to kill us. He'll kill *you*." Mykill's voice broke on the word.

I could hear the Black Mage's footsteps getting closer to us but I tightened my hold on Mykill's hand. I glanced up at him as my breath labored in my ears.

"I'm assuming neither of you can sense the babe in her belly?" the Black Mage's voice floated over to us.

My head snapped in his direction to see the cruel smile curled across his mouth. My hand fluttered to cover my stomach in disbelief as I frowned.

I couldn't be pregnant, I had been taking a tonic since I had been taken to Eryx's kingdom.

But I hadn't been.

I hadn't taken it since I had fled here with Mykill, there hadn't been a reason for it.

Shock froze my limbs as I stared at Mykill. His head slowly turned back towards me and his eyes were as wide as saucers. His icy eyes were filled with so much fear that it rolled off of him in waves.

"*Run,*" he breathed and then a wall of ice formed between us.

"What?" I gasped as I rose to my knees and stared back at Mykill's distorted body on the other side of the ice that was only growing thicker. The ice slowly pushed me backwards. "No! Mykill!" I shouted as I rose to my feet and pounded my fist to the ice.

"Run!" he shouted.

His voice sounded distorted due to the glass, and his eyes were wide and full with a heady mix of terror and determination.

My heart dropped into my stomach. He knew he couldn't take him on alone. The Black Mage was going to kill him.

I needed to help him. My hands shook as I pounded them against the ice, but he didn't turn back to me.

His wings flared on either side of him as he drew the Black Mage's attention back to him.

That bastard. That *bastard.*

I shrieked in outrage as I slammed them against the ice one more time before.

I didn't know how to help him.

Pushing to my feet, I turned and began running down the hall in search of someone, anyone. But as my bare feet slapped off the floor, I didn't find a single soul. Everyone was gone.

I ran towards the door that led to the cliffside. There had to be people outside the castle. I gripped the handle and began to turn it and cursed in outrage as it remained firm. Gripping the handle, I threw my body into it but it didn't budge.

My breath echoed heavily around me as I let go of the handle and tried to figure out what to do. I couldn't just let my mate die. He was the father of our unborn child!

Tears pricked at the corners of my eyes as my hands began to shake. Hopelessness settled over me like a lead blanket, crushing my chest and stealing my breath away. My knees shook, forcing me to lower to the ground. I flattened my palms on the floor as I tried to get my haggard breathing under control.

He had told me he had stashed a shadow blade in his quarters.

The thought slammed into me, demanding my focus. My head snapped up and I shoved myself hastily to my feet. My feet flew across the floor as I ran towards his bedroom.

I waved my hand as his room came into sight and his door pounded open. I barreled into the room and immediately began ripping through his belongings. I yanked out every drawer of his dresser and turned them upside down, dumping the contents at my feet. I shifted through the clothing but did not come upon a shadow blade. I had never seen one but it sounded ominous enough that I would be able to recognize it when I saw it.

I pulled out every drawer in his entire room, and still turned up empty. Then I began yanking the books off of the bookshelves by fours and let them fall to my feet.

Normally I was one to care about the condition of books. I never wanted a drink too close to them, or their spine to get too cracked, but I could burn them now for all I cared.

I shrieked in outrage as I stepped away from the still full bookshelves. There was no way I'd be able to find it in time to save him.

My shoulder sagged as my breath continued to heave.

The scrolls. The scrolls could tell me!

My breath pounded in my ears as I barreled down the hall towards my bedroom. I kicked open the door and yanked open the top drawer of my nightstand. The scrolls were stowed away in a fake bottom that I all but ripped out, giving myself several splinters as I did it.

I ripped open the scrolls as I tried to keep the tremble from my hands.

"Where is the shadow blade?" I screamed at it.

The map flared to life at my voice. Gold letters inked themselves on the parchment.

My eyes widened and I nodded as I began running back towards Mykill's room. I kept the scrolls tucked beneath my arm as I barreled back down the halls.

The door slapped off the wall as I threw it open with a wave of my hand.

Waving my hand, his mattress went flying off the bed, revealing what looked like a compartment in the wood. Running up towards the bed, I crawled across the wood and gripped the small handle that jutted out from the wooden door. As I touched the handle I felt a power wrap around my wrist and slid up my arm. I shivered as the invisible band turned icy, burning the cold into my skin. I shrieked as I scratched at my skin, wanting it off of me but as I tried wrenching my hand away the power only tightened its hold.

Breathing out, I dropped my head back and revealed the bond to the entity. As I bared open my soul, the powers paused their descent. I showed it the piece of my soul that was Mykill, that belonged to him.

The powers paused, and then I felt them retreat. At first nothing happened as I stared down at the compartment. Anxiety latched itself around my heart, squeezing it until it felt like it was going to fly out of my throat. Then, slowly the wooden door opened.

Shadows poured out over the edges as I gaped down at it. It wasn't straight like a normal blade, it was jagged almost like a lightning bolt. The blade itself glowed silver and shadows poured out around it in tendrils. The black handle was fashioned wide with intricate designs engraved into it.

I reached for it, my breath freezing in my chest as I did. Ice descended down my veins as I took it in hand.

I smiled in triumph as I shot to my feet.

I wrapped my fingers around the hilt of the blade as I ran out of his room and down the hall. The shadows leaked off the blade and wrapped around my wrist. Fear pumped my limbs to move faster. There were still no guards in sight, which meant we didn't have anyone coming to save us.

I decided to try and enter the dining room through the kitchen staff's entrance. I knew Mykill would be blocking my entrance from the way he had shoved me out.

Silently I shoved open the door and the scene before me caused me to stop dead in my tracks. Mykill was on his hands and knees and the Black Mage was stalking towards him. Mykill's back bowed at an unnatural angle and he bellowed. The Black Mage laughed as he circled around him.

"Once I kill you, I will cut your wings from your body and nail them above your throne as I take it for myself. Then I will take your mate and child for my own."

Mykill's hands curled into the marble beneath his hands and then he swung towards him. He outstretched his hand and a bolt of lightning shot from it, but the Black Mage anticipated that. He absorbed the lightning and as he did, it cackled around him, as if it became part of him. Electricity danced across his fingers as he twiddled them.

"Fascinating," he breathed before looking back down at Mykill. "Imagine me taking your mate as my own. *Every. Single. Night,*" the Black Mage laughed at the words.

"*Please,*" Mykill begged as he slumped to the ground as his chest heaved. "Please don't touch her. I'll do anything."

"I know you will." The Black Mage's icy laugh danced across the space as Mykill rolled onto his side. "Maybe I'll keep you alive. That will ensure that she'll do what I say, because I'm sure she'll do anything for you too."

Finally collecting the courage to move, I palmed the hilt of the shadow blade and charged. Mykill let out another bellow as the Black Mage shot a bolt of lightning straight towards his heart. His back arched off the ground, and a fine sheen of sweat coated his skin.

The Black Mage noticed me too late as I launched myself onto his back. I secured my legs around his waist and an arm around his neck. He swung around in an attempt to throw me off and lightning erupted across the room. I bit my tongue at his thrashing and groaned as I tasted my own blood. Keeping an arm secured around his neck, I tightened my grip on the blade and raised it above my head. My breath hammered in my ears as I brought the blade down and slid it into the Black Mage's chest. His body stiffened and he let out a breathless cry right before his body collapsed. As he hit the floor, I launched off of his back and rolled as I hit the floor. I tumbled forward once and landed on my feet, popping back up.

I glanced once at his convulsing body and fisted my hands, ready for an attack. His back bowed off the floor and his mouth fell open on a silent cry.

I turned towards Mykill who was turned over on his side.

"I told you to run," Mykill gasped as I dropped to my knees before him. "The baby-"

"We don't have a life without you," I breathed as he slid an arm around my back, and we both turned our attention to the Black Mage.

The shadows arched above him as one, and then a moment later they all swept towards his heart. I watched in shock as the color drained from his skin, turning it gray. Then, the shadows slipped into his mouth, nose and ears and I watched as his veins turned black. The shadows were taking every part of him. They left nothing behind besides the husk of his body. There was no blood, nothing to show that he had been alive merely minutes ago.

The doors crashed open and a pale looking Felix stumbled into the room with an army of guards at their backs.

"We were all knocked out by some sort of spell. Are you two alright?" Felix asked a set of guards to step past him to retrieve the body lying beside us.

"Help him up," I answered as I rose to my feet.

Felix and another guard surged forward. They stooped down and each slipped an arm around Mykill's shoulders and lifted him. Mykill groaned as they helped steady him on his feet.

"Take him to the healer," I commanded frantically.

My head was spinning but I managed to remain upright.

"Alethea, you're bleeding," Felix pointed out as he began carrying Mykill whose head had slumped forward entirely as he tried to regain the strength to stand.

I wiped at the blood dripping from my nose. "I'm alright." As I said the words my body swayed and I felt Mykill's powers rumble through the room.

"Alethea," he groaned and shoved off of Felix and the guard.

My knees buckled as I swayed again, but as I did, his arms caught me.

"We need to get both of you to the healer," Felix said and then I heard him near me.

"Don't touch her," he growled.

I would chide him for being rude to Felix later.

But for now, I let him hold me as he carried me to his healer.

Chapter 21

Mykill

"Tell me he's okay, please tell me he's okay," Alethea repeated over and over again as she paced back and forth. At one point, smoke had drifted from her heels from her emotions stirring her powers, but thankfully we had noticed before she caught flame.

"Love," I said as I reached a hand towards her. "I'm alright, please just sit down."

Fredira, my healer, said Alethea had almost fainted due to lack of food. Now that she was with child, she would have to make sure she ate more regularly so it didn't take too much of a toll on her body.

"He'll be alright, My Lady," Fredira assured her for the millionth time.

I was near to the point where I was going to use magic to pin her down to a chair. I didn't want her working herself up and fainting again.

Fredira stitched up the cut across my shoulder and then lobbed a dark green ointment on it, saying it would heal within a few days. That didn't help Alethea calm down.

I rose as I slid my shirt back on.

"Please sit down," Fredia motioned for Alethea to sit down once again and she shook her head.

"Are you sure he's alright?" she asked as her wide eyes slid over to me.

"Sit down, Alethea," I commanded.

My voice didn't leave much room for her to argue. But that didn't stop her from leveling a glare worthy of the God of wrath at me before she stalked by. She sat down on the table I had just resided on. I watched as Fredira ran her hand over Alethea's body. She nodded in satisfaction and then leaned over her table as she grabbed a small bowl.

"You'll be alright, just a few cuts," Fredira said as she lobbed on a thick layer of the ointment on the gash across Alethea's cuts.

"What about the baby?" Alethea asked as her hand fell to her still flat stomach.

"She's fine," Fredira answered.

My mouth fell open the same time Alethea's did. Her eyes shot to me, wide in what I could only read as shock.

I had remembered her telling me that she had thought that being a mother would constrain her. But I'd give up my throne to make sure that didn't happen. I would do anything to make sure she wasn't tied down to just being a mother.

Tears flooded her eyes and I stood to my feet.

"Can you give us a moment?" I asked Fredira without looking at her.

I didn't look as she left the room silently, sealing the door closed behind her.

I stepped up to her as I reached up to cup her face.

"We're having a girl," she breathed. "We're having a *girl*!" she repeated.

I nodded as I stared down at her. Of course joy filled my chest, but I was more concerned on how she was feeling.

"I'm sorry," she breathed. "I had been taking a tonic, but once Eryx and I-"

"You don't need to explain yourself," I said as I stroked my thumb across her bottom lip. "I'm happy, truly, but is this something you want?" Her mouth fell open, but her words fell short. She lowered her face as her brain reeled. I surprisingly didn't detect an ounce of regret in her, only shock.

"You know, I always thought I didn't. But when the Black Mage brought up our child, our *daughter*, I've never felt so protective of something in my life. I would die for her and I've just barely learned of her." Tears glistened in her eyes again. "I feel like this is a gift from the Gods."

I placed my palm on her stomach, taking in the life beneath it. Warmth spread through my chest as I leaned into her.

"I don't deserve to walk by your side in this lifetime or the next, but I'm honored to do so," I whispered as I leaned in closer to her, if only to breathe her in like it was the last time I would do so.

"I love you," she breathed as she pushed up a little straighter. Her breath danced along my cheeks as she leaned into me.

"I love you," I answered before I kissed her.

Alethea

Lira adjusted the folds of the dress that fell around my ankles. I had been standing in front of this godforsaken mirror for what felt like hours. The dress was a deep cream, Lira said it radiated power while also purity. Exactly what people yearned for in a leader.

No, not just any leader, a Queen.

I wanted to tell Lira to go get Mykill. I felt the nervous sweats about to set in.

I frowned as I turned towards the door as it opened. Mykill was wearing black trousers with a matching black shirt and jacket. There was a cream sash across his chest, to match my gown, and he donned a silver crown.

"What are you doing in here?" I frowned at him as I turned towards him.

I ignored Lira as she squealed in outrage.

"I felt you calling," Mykill said as he ran a hand through the curls resting over my right shoulder. He traced the tip of his finger across the exposed skin of my shoulder and the corner of his lip tipped up as I shivered.

I swatted his hand away and frowned. "Stop touching!" I hissed.

He smiled as he dropped his hand to my slightly bulging stomach. It hadn't been announced to the kingdom yet that I was pregnant. We had purposely chosen a flowy gown for my coronation as we hadn't decided when we would tell them.

"You look beautiful," he whispered as he leaned into me and placed a soft kiss to my lips.

"Thank you," I whispered back as I placed my hands on his shoulders.

"Are you nervous?" I nodded and he let out a soft chuckle. "It will be over before you know it."

I nodded in response and then leaned into him as I laid my head on his chest. I could feel the concern flittering over him, but his arms settled around me and then he pulled me further into him.

"You'll do great, love," he whispered as his fingers stroked the skin exposed at my back.

But it wasn't nervousness making me lean into him, it was the gratitude I felt as tears pricked my eyes. I couldn't have dreamed I would be where I was now.

I pulled away, willing the tears back and nodded at him.

He placed his hands on either side of my face as he cupped my jaw. "I believe in you," he whispered.

The words would have broken me if it had been two months prior, but now they made me feel empowered.

With his love, I knew I could do anything. He would encourage me in all, support me in everything, and stand by my side through whatever life weathered our way.

As I walked the halls, I couldn't help but remember everything that had happened over the months leading up to this very moment. Every death that sometimes felt like it still permeated the air.

I had personally checked up on the little girl who had been left an orphan when Eryx and the barren attacked Grithel. She had been adopted by a young couple and was thriving. The last time I had seen her, her blonde hair was braided in two long braids and she had been chasing a winged boy around her age with a wooden sword. Mischief gleamed in her eyes as she did so. I couldn't help but laugh.

As I turned the last corner towards the throne room, Felix stood waiting for me. Cadmus held the handle of one door, and another guard held the handle of the other door.

Felix outstretched his arm to me and I smiled as I slid my arm into his. As Mykill's General, he was to escort me.

"You've got this," Felix smiled as he patted the top of my gloved hand.

"Thank you," I laughed nervously.

Cadmus smiled at me as he opened the doors and then stepped aside.

Mykill stood at the end of the aisle before his throne. There was a marble pedestal at least half his height that rested beside him. The room was full of men and women, some with wings and others without. The construction of the village for those without wings had finished two months ago and they were settling in well. We had also improved the stairwells down to the Cove so that they could easily access them.

Hundreds of candles floated around the room, illuminating the space.

Mykill offered me a small smile as I stopped before the stairs that led up to the dais.

Not long ago, we had thought we would die in this room. But now as we stood in it, we were not only victorious, but we were *happy*. For the first time in my life, I felt happy. I felt freeing joy. I had lost everything, and the thought still hurt and I still grieved both of the families I had lost, but Mykill had become *everything*. He was the very air my lungs yearned for.

"Alethea," he bowed his head as I stopped before him as I climbed the last step.

I bowed my head in response but said nothing, as he had instructed me.

His eyes met mine and they glimmered beneath the candlelight. Unlike so many times before, there wasn't that icy wall in them. I could read all of the emotions that swirled in the ocean of his eyes - love, respect, peace.

"Alethea, you have sacrificed blood and sweat for this kingdom. You have defended its people fiercely and loyalty. The people have chosen you as their Queen." He raised an eyebrow at me and I fought the tremor that wanted to work it's way through my hands. "Will you accept their call?"

I swallowed heavily as I nodded. "I will."

I could see the corners of his mouth fighting back a grin as he continued.

"Will you govern your people with grace, dignity, wisdom and respect?"

"I will," I answered.

"Do you promise to uphold all laws with knowledge, power and mercy?"

"I promise," I echoed.

Mykill let his lips pull into a tight smile as he stared down at me and then turned to pick up the crown that rested on a fluffy white pillow on the pedestal beside him.

"Then it is my honor to bestow this crown on you." I stepped towards him and bowed my head like he had instructed me. I felt the heavy weight of the crown settle on my hair before I rose and faced him.

Mykill smiled as he placed a fisted hand over his heart. He ducked his head and slowly lowered to one knee.

"All hail, Alethea Divine," he said, his voice booming through the throne room.

"All hail, Alethea Divine!" The room echoed.

I folded my hands in front of me and turned towards the room. I smiled at every one of them and then bowed my head as I kneeled.

Chapter 22

Alethea dropped her head back as she bellowed. Pain clenched across the bottom of her stomach and she blew out a breath as she slowly rocked forward and then slowly rocked backwards. Her fingers curled into the sheets beneath her palms as sweat slicked down her neck and back.

Mykill's hand stroked down her braid and then he gently massaged her back.

"I can't do this," Alethea cried as she dropped her head in defeat, her arms ready to give out beneath her.

Mykill dipped his shoulder beneath her and held her up. Her body trembled as the contraction subsided and she slumped into him.

"I can't do this," she cried again, her voice breaking.

"You can," Mykill said as he stroked a hand down her hair again and then his fingers wrapped around the back of her neck. "You can do anything."

Alethea's warm breath warmed his chilled neck as she breathed heavily. She kept her eyes closed, savoring her mates strength, drawing it into herself as she prepared for the next contraction.

"Alethea, when this next contraction comes I need you to push, okay?" Lira said as she stroked her back.

Alethea nodded against his shoulder but didn't speak.

"Push!" Lira commanded and Alethea gripped Mykill's shoulders as she did. She dropped her head back as she let out a battle cry and then beared down.

Mykill held her up by her elbows as her face scrunched in determination but also pain. Her body shook with the effort and then relaxed. Alethea huffed out a breath and then a wail followed. Her ruby eyes glittered beneath the candlelight as her eyes flew open. Tears filled her eyes as she collapsed into Mykill entirely.

"She's okay," Lira cheered as she took the babe and bundled her in a small blanket. "She's beautiful!"

"You did it," Mykill breathed as he stroked his hand down her back as Alethea sobbed in relief. "You're so, so strong. You did it, love."

***

The babe's maroon wings were tucked into her back as she snuggled down into Alethea's chest.

"She's beautiful," Mykill whispered as he kissed the top of Alethea's head and stroked his thumb across her arm.

Alethea dropped her head back and smiled. Mykill's chest nearly imploded at the sight. She looked exhausted but she was the most beautiful creature he'd ever seen.

"What do you want to name her?" Mykill asked.

Alethea's nose scrunched as she stared down at their daughter for several long minutes before she answered, "Lana."

His lips stretched into a smile. "That's beautiful."

Alethea turned her attention to her mate and smiled up at him before glancing back down at Lana.

Alethea had never wanted to be a mother. She had always thought it would have restricted her too much, binding her to a life of sleeplessness and slaving away. But as she stared down at the little body bundled in her arms, she knew she had been wrong. This little life was a part of her and her mate.

"This is the perfect way for us to begin our life together," Alethea whispered as she wiped one of the tears that slid down her cheek.

Mykill's arm around her shoulders tightened as he stared down at his mate and daughter. Never once had he thought he would be gifted a life with a mate and a child.

Gratitude filled his chest. The lives that were lost would live on through this new life bundled against his mates chest. His daughter was being born into a world that was once again deemed safe with a mate who would do anything to protect their daughter; And he would do anything to protect them.

Chapter 23

Thank you to every one of my readers who gave my silly fantasy book a chance! This series means so much to me and I hope it did a work in you too!

I'm not going to lie, if I had my way, Alethea's story would have ended very differently, but they say characters write themselves and it couldn't be more true. The direction I had intended for her story took a turn I didn't expect, much like mine had. A piece of her and her story reflects much of my own and I couldn't help but relate to her.

I know the pregnancy trope isn't for some people, but there are those of us out there who do love it, myself included. I couldn't think of a better way to end their story. Being a mother sounded terrifying to me, but I can say first hand that my daughter saved my life. She brought me much joy in a season of hardship and heartbreak.

I'm so thankful for you and for this series! Closing out this series is one of the saddest things I've done but I can't wait for this next chapter and new projects! Follow along either on Instagram or TikTok @authortrinitymatthews for updates on new projects!

Printed in Great Britain
by Amazon